MW00653982

BRUTAL SILENCE

To: Edna,

BRUTAL SILENCE

MARGARET DARDESS

All best wishes,

Margaret Dardess

March 3, 2018

 Mason Point
Press

Copyright © 2017 by Margaret Dardess

All rights reserved. This book or any portion thereof may not be reproduced or used in any manner whatsoever without the express written permission of the publisher except for the use of brief quotations in a book review or scholarly journal.

First Printing: 2017

ISBN 978-168418831-4

Library of Congress Control Number: 2017900190

Mason Point Press
www.brutalsilence.com

Ordering Information:
Special discounts are available on quantity purchases by corporations, associations, educators, and others. For details, contact the publisher at the above listed web address.

U.S. trade bookstores and wholesalers:
Please contact
booksales@margaretdardess.com

Bulk copies are available via Ingram Spark and Published on Amazon Create Space.
10 9 8 7 6 5 4 3 2 1

Cover design by Alyssa Stepien
Interior design by SP Rankin

Printed in the United States of America

*To all those who work heroically to
combat human trafficking.
Proceeds from this book will go
to benefit their efforts.*

CHAPTER ONE

Alex felt eyes boring into the back of her head. She was used to men staring at her, but this was different. She shifted in her seat. The hotel concierge had warned her not to travel outside of Mexico City alone, but today was the last day of vacation and her girlfriend, Kelly, was stuck in their hotel room with Montezuma's revenge. Alex had learned about the beautiful holy city of Teotihuacán back in college, and it had taken hold of her imagination in the way that some people felt about Machu Picchu. She was determined to see it in person before her trip was over. Surely she couldn't get into trouble on a public bus.

She looked behind her. A stocky, bull-shouldered man stood at the back of the bus, looking directly at her. Another man was beside him, taller, dark-skinned with a six-inch puckered scar dissecting the left side of his face.

The back of her neck prickled. She shrank into her seat and focused on the scenery, ignoring the men. An old mission, a farmer's market, the small houses of a sprawling barrio flashed by the window. She tried to memorize the scenery. In two days she'd be back to the hectic pace of her clinic in North Carolina with only fond thoughts of the warm sunshine and burnished gold of the Mexican landscape.

The bus slowed. Its brakes squealed. The tires ground in the dirt and the doors slowly opened. Alex strained to see why they'd stopped.

The people around her exchanged glances, shifting in their seats. When she tried to make eye contact, they looked away. No one stood up. The engine idled. Alex squirmed in her seat.

Something moved behind her. As she turned, she caught the full force of the stocky man's body, smashing into her, then yanking her up into the aisle.

She screamed, pulse racing, panic rising. She reached up and dug her fingers into the soft flesh into the man's eyes as hard as she could. He howled and grabbed her wrists, pushing her backward.

Scar-face grasped her from behind, wrapping his arms around her, crushing her against him. She choked on the strong mix of sweat and cologne. Her adrenalin surged. She kicked back, connecting with his legs, tearing at the skin on his arms.

The stocky man came at her and punched her in the stomach, knocking the wind out of her. She tried to breathe. Panic squeezed her like a fist.

She felt herself lifted by the arms and dragged down the aisle. She called out for help, reaching out to grab the seats as she passed, her fingers sliding across the slippery surfaces, unable to hold onto the plastic upholstery.

"Help. *¡Auxilio! Soy americana. Turista. Por favor, ayúdenme!*"

The other passengers stared straight ahead, rigid in their seats.

She grasped the ankles of a woman passenger and hung on. The woman kicked until Alex lost her grip.

The men dragged her to the steps. Her head pulled along the floor until she thought her brain would explode. She clutched at the door frame. Hot spears of pain shot up her arms. She let go and fell forward, cracking her forehead on the edge of the door.

The stocky man picked her up like a rag doll, flung her over his shoulder, carried her down the steps, and threw her onto the dirt. She flung out her hands instinctively as she landed, flinching as gravel ground into her hands and knees.

The engine roared, the wheels turned, and the bus moved away, leaving her alone with her captors. She struggled to her feet. Her head pounded. Her heart thudded against her rib cage.

"Who are you? What do you want?"

Scar-face gave a mocking laugh.

"Is it money? You have my purse."

The stocky man smashed his fist into her temple, and the world swam around her.

———

She didn't know where she was or how long she'd been there. All she knew was that she was hot and sore, and the floor beneath her was hard. Fluorescent lights flickered above, dim, but still strong enough to hurt her eyes. Her head throbbed. Her hands felt sticky and wet with blood that oozed from the cuts and gouges on her palms. Her knees were bloody too. She grimaced as she stretched her stiff legs. Where was she?

She breathed in air that was heavy with the stench of sweat and dirt. Unwashed bodies. She looked up, her heart racing. More than a dozen women crowded around her, murmuring to each other. Faces seemed to swim close, then recede. She strained to sit up. Her stomach muscles screamed in pain. She sank back onto the grit-covered cement.

"Lie still," a young woman said in a whisper. "You have a big bump on your head."

The woman, little more than a girl, spoke in Spanish with an accent that Alex could barely understand, despite her years of supposed fluency.

"My name is Cristina."

Alex looked around, trying to make sense of her surroundings. Dust motes danced in the sunlight that seeped around the door and through seams in the metal walls. She managed a feeble smile. "I'm Alex. Where am I?"

"You are in a bad place."

A chill gripped her. She looked around the warehouse, shivering despite the brutal heat. She had to get out of here. She sat up, rolled over onto her hands, and cried out. White spots flashed across her eyes, merging into a single light. When she woke again, she was still on the floor, and only the girl, Cristina, was beside her.

Cristina's fingers touched the streak of white that swirled from Alex's forehead through her straight, chestnut hair.

"You are pretty, like someone in the movies. Are you famous?"

"I'm just a tourist. I run a health care clinic in a place called Dalton in North Carolina. *El Norte.*"

The girl gave Alex a skeptical look, then helped her stand and take a few tentative steps.

"Who are all these women?" Alex asked. "How did they get here?"

"Bad men brought us all one by one from many places. I came here two days ago. They keep us here. Give us little food. They take women away. Some come back. Others do not."

A wave of nausea washed over her. Her sweat-soaked blouse was cold against her skin. She tried to control her panic, taking big gulps of air. No one knew where she was. Kelly was most likely still asleep back in the hotel and wouldn't miss her for hours, and the bus driver and passengers would be either too afraid to call the police or wouldn't even care. She was on her own. She tested her legs, taking small steps, then, feeling stronger, began to look around the warehouse for a way to escape.

"We have to get out of here, Cristina."

"Those who try to escape die. The men shot two women yesterday."

Alex looked at the other women. Many seemed very young, still teenagers or in their early twenties. Some appeared dazed. Others were curled on the floor, asleep. Only Cristina was paying attention to her and trying to communicate.

"It will be worse if we stay here."

She had to get ahold of her rising terror. The men who had brought her here could come back at any minute. She didn't dare try the front entrance. She limped to a side wall and began feeling along the corrugated metal for any weaknesses. The metal was solid, and the seams were tight. She continued pressing. Nothing. She moved to the back and tested the wall there. It held. She worked her way across the entire expanse to the other side of the warehouse before she found a rusty place where rainwater had dripped from a hole in the roof. She poked at the rust. Her finger went clear through to the outside.

She turned to Cristina, who had been following her through the warehouse.

"If we can break through here, we can get away. Help me find something to smash the metal."

"We can't. The bad men will hurt us."

"It's our only chance. Hurry, before they come back."

Cristina followed with hesitant steps as Alex searched through empty bins and cardboard boxes until she found a broken-handled shovel under a pile of old rags.

"This is exactly what we need."

Alex had grasped the shovel and swung it over her head, ready to smash the wall, when the front door to the warehouse began to roll open. She dropped the shovel and pushed Cristina back into the shadows.

The door opened, and the two men from the bus came in and stopped, their eyes traveling over the women.

"You." The stocky man pointed to a plump woman in a red blouse. "And you," he said to a slightly built young woman beside her.

The men seized the two trembling women. The plump woman cried out and tried to hit the stocky man; he slammed his fist in her face, knocking her to the floor. The slight woman shrank back, tears streaming down her cheeks. The men grabbed both of them and shoved them through the open door. It closed behind them. A motor turned over, and the truck drove away.

One woman started to sob. Others joined in.

Alex seized the broken shovel and ran to the rusted-out corner, propelled by rage and fear. She smashed the shovel against the rusty metal wall with all her strength over and over, sweat pouring off her until at last she'd ripped a hole in the metal large enough to crawl through.

She called to the women. "Come on. We can get out this way. Hurry before the men come back."

They looked at her. No one moved.

"They'll kill us," a woman called back.

"Please. We have to save ourselves. We'll die if we stay here."

The women turned away. A few covered their ears.

Exasperated, Alex turned to Cristina. "You'll come, won't you?'

Cristina's brown eyes widened. Her face was white, her hands shaking.

"Trust me. We'll be gone before they come back."

Cristina took a deep breath and nodded.

Alex climbed through the jagged opening, taking care not to cut herself, and turned to help Cristina. They emerged onto an area littered with broken glass and plastic containers and stood together, squinting in the bright sunlight. The putrid smell of rotting garbage made Alex gag. She put an arm around Cristina's shaking shoulders and led her around to the front of the building. She looked around. Neither of the men was in sight. She could hear the sounds of the highway in the distance.

"We're going to be okay, Cristina. We'll keep low until we reach the highway. Someone will help us. See that pile of rocks? It must be about halfway. We'll run to the rocks and hide. As soon as we're sure no one's coming, we'll go the rest of the way to the road."

Even as she said it, her stomach lurched. None of the marathons she'd run had been as daunting as the expanse of land between here and the road. She took Cristina's hand and led her through the rubble to a rough patch of dirt.

"Come on, Cristina. This is our only chance."

She started to run with Cristina close behind. Tall, spiky grass tore at their legs. When they reached the rock pile, they stopped. So far so good. She turned back and looked at the warehouse. A worn picture of a beer bottle and the logo for a brewery covered much of the front. Once they were safe she'd get the police and come back for the others. She tugged at Cristina's arm and started again, crossing open flatland, closing the remaining sixty yards or so to the road.

They were halfway there when she heard the squeal of brakes ahead. A rickety truck slowed and turned into the warehouse driveway. Alex felt her throat closing. She pulled Cristina down into the tall grass and turned to look at the truck. She could just make out four figures, two in the cab and another two in the back.

Cristina knelt and closed her eyes. *"Dios te salve, María."*

The truck stopped, the men climbed out and went inside.

Alex helped Cristina to her feet. "Come on. It's not far to the road. We can make it."

Cristina's knees folded. Her body shook. "They're going to kill us."

"Not if we run."

Alex took off as fast as her battered body would let her, dragging Cristina with her. When they were within twenty yards of the road, she heard a man yell.

Four men were racing towards them from the warehouse.

"*Dios mío, no puedo,*" Cristina said, freezing.

"We're so close, Cristina." Alex grasped the girl's wrist.

Cristina didn't move.

The men were coming fast.

A bullet whistled past their heads, then a second and a third.

Cristina cried out and fell forward.

Alex bent down and slipped a hand under the girl's arm, struggling to support her body.

The men kept coming. A bullet whooshed by Alex's ear.

Cristina slipped from Alex's grasp and slumped to the ground, blood staining her blouse and the ground beneath her.

The men were almost on them.

Alex tried to lift Cristina, staggering under her weight. She couldn't carry her. She had to get help. She took off, zigzagging away from the gunshots, toward the road, stopping only when she reached the highway. She looked back. Cristina was trying to crawl away. One of the men raised an arm and hit Cristina with his fist over and over.

The two men from the bus were coming for her.

She raced across the busy highway, choking on exhaust fumes, barely able to see through her tears. The roar of the traffic was deafening. Horns blared. A speeding car swerved to miss her, tires screeching. Her heart pounded. She waved her arms and prayed that someone would stop.

An ancient truck rattled to a stop beside her. From the truck bed workmen hooted at her. The passenger door swung open. The driver leered. "*¿Hola,* pretty lady. Looking for business?"

A bullet pinged off the metal door frame. She leapt onto the running board, jumped into the truck, slammed the door shut, and flattened herself against the seat.

The driver looked at her wide-eyed. A second bullet hit the window above her head. Glass showered the front seat.

"Go. They're trying to kill me."

The driver's foot hit the gas. Gravel spun. The truck jumped forward and merged into fast-moving traffic. Alex leaned forward and looked in the rearview mirror. The two men were standing at the edge of the highway. The stocky man was talking on a cell phone. Scar-face stared after the truck. She ducked down as if the man could see her through the back window, and tried to stop shaking.

CHAPTER TWO

Emilio Vargas's men said that when his left eyelid twitched, people died. It was twitching now.

"*¡Idiotas!* You left them alone?" You lost two women yesterday and two more today. That's time and money gone."

Vargas's men stood in a circle around him. All of them were sweating. He could smell their fear. Cuchillo was the only one who dared to step forward. Never as clever as Vargas, Cuchillo was stockier and a lot stronger, and had been Vargas's devoted supporter from the time they had been boys in Los Perdidos. No one in the schoolyard made fun of Vargas for being puny when Cuchillo was there. Diego stood behind Cuchillo. A jagged scar cut across the left side of the man's face, pulling the side of his mouth into a permanent sneer. The others had joined Vargas over the years as his business grew. They knew they'd be rich if they stuck with him, dead if they didn't.

Cuchillo cleared his throat. "The *gringa*'s the one that got away."

Vargas's eyes narrowed. He felt blood rush to his head. "The Harrington *puta* got away? You idiots. We watched her for days before we could get to her."

"She ran so fast we couldn't catch her. We dumped the *puta* who escaped with her behind the warehouse and moved the others," Diego said.

9

"So we have three dead women in two days, one escaped *gringa*, and a warehouse we cannot use again. Get out. You will pay for what you have cost me."

The men filed out without a sound. Vargas stood alone at the window, looking out at the arid Tenancingo landscape. Heat exploded through his body. He hated to lose. He had come from nothing. He'd fought his way up, skinned men alive who crossed him, women too when they tried to run away. His name evoked terror, and he liked that. He was important and rich beyond his dreams. He owned a luxurious villa in Tenancingo and a condo by the sea. He wore Italian suits and custom-made monogrammed shirts. A stylist cut his hair with a razor and manicured his nails.

He knew he wasn't handsome. His skin was pock-marked, his eyes were too close together, his shoulders too narrow, but since he'd had money, the women loved him. His agents bought winning quarter horses for him. His newest and best acquisition, Lucky Dan, was running in the Texas Classic Futurity that weekend. The horse had been sired by champions and would win millions. Emilio Vargas, the poor boy from the barrio, would stand in the winners' circle of one of the most important races in the world.

How could a stupid girl like that get away from a powerful man like him? He would get Alex Harrington. She wasn't going to run away from him again.

CHAPTER THREE

Alex leaned back in her chair. She was looking forward to an evening alone at home after a long week. A sharp, insistent tapping on the glass made her jump, scattering papers across the floor. A round brown face appeared at the French doors.

She grabbed the skeleton key from the desk and raced to the door. "Carmela?"

"Miss Alex. Please."

She could see panic in Carmela's face. The old key stuck in the lock. She jiggled it until the tumbler fell into place. The door swung open, and the office cleaner staggered into the office, carrying the limp body of a young woman.

"I know her. It's Mariana," Alex said.

Carmela lost her grip. The woman slid to the floor before Alex could grab her. "Gladys, come quick," she called.

"What is it?" Gladys's ample frame emerged from the clinic. "My God, Carmela, what happened?"

With the precise movement that came from years of nursing, Gladys soon had one arm around the woman's waist. "She's unconscious. Let's get her into the clinic."

"We need to get her to the hospital."

"No, no hospital, no police. I promise her you help. No police," Carmela said.

They put the woman on a table in the clinic. Large brown eyes flickered open, radiating pain and panic.

Alex grasped the young woman's limp hand. "She needs a doctor, Carmela. She's got a gash on her forehead. She's bleeding."

"Her pressure's very low," Gladys said, reaching for the phone on the clinic wall and dialing nine-one-one.

Carmela stood beside the table, twisting her skirt into a knot. Tears streamed down her soft cheeks.

The overhead light illuminated a chain with a tiny gold cross encircling Mariana's neck. Bruises covered her arms and legs, some fresh, purple, others faded to a yellow-green. Blood covered the front of her low-cut blouse.

Alex brushed a strand of brown hair away from the pale face and frowned.

"Carmela brought Mariana in last week with an infection. The doctors said she had a heart condition too and wanted her to see a specialist. She didn't keep the appointment I made for her." She turned to Carmela. "Do you know who did this to her?"

Carmela shook her head, backing away from the table. "*Dios mío.*"

"She's going to need stitches, a lot of them, and I think there's internal bleeding too," Gladys said. "At least the hospital's close."

It felt like hours before she heard the sirens in the distance, growing louder. Alex ran to the lobby, pulled the front door open, and waited for the ambulance.

When the medics arrived, she motioned toward the clinic. "The patient's in there."

Three paramedics rushed past.

Before Alex could close the door, a rail-thin police officer with gray sideburns came into the lobby.

She shut the door. "This way," she said, leading the officer into the clinic. "We have a young woman who's badly hurt. She's clearly been beaten and who knows what else."

"I'm Officer Craven. Your name, ma'am?"

"Alex Harrington. I'm the director here."

Craven's craggy face leaned closer to her. She could tell from the officer's raised eyebrow that he didn't think she was old enough to direct anything. She was used to that by now and forced a smile.

"This is the Center for Child and Family Health, and I've been in charge for the past year."

The officer pulled out a pad and pencil and nodded toward the table. "Who's that?"

"Her name is Mariana. She's a patient. We were closed for the night. Gladys, she's the chief nurse, and I were the only ones still here when Carmela brought her in."

She walked toward the table with Craven.

"Who's Carmela?"

"Carmela Flores. She's the center's cleaner."

Craven wrote the name down on his pad. "Where is Ms. Flores now?"

Alex nodded toward Carmela who was cowering against the wall at the far side of the examining room.

The officer looked at Carmela, then at the woman on the table, frowning. "You get this kind of thing often?"

"Sometimes we get trauma patients. We mostly care for women and children. We provide general health care like well-baby check-ups, cholesterol screening, Pap smears."

The doorbell rang. "I'll get that," Alex said.

Alex reached the lobby just as the front door flew open. A lanky, red-haired man in jeans and a loose-fitting jacket pushed past her and looked around the room and the clinic beyond.

"Jeez, Murray, you here?" Craven yelled from the clinic. "That scanner must be attached to you."

The man waved to Craven and looked at Alex. "Hi, I'm from the *Dalton Herald*."

Alex was about to answer when one of the paramedics shouted, "I'm losing pulse here."

She raced back to the clinic.

Mariana's face had taken on a bluish tinge. The paramedic applied paddles, and the body jumped in response to the electric charge. The line on the portable monitor didn't move. The beep was steady. The woman's long hair coiled beneath her head, golden brown like Cristina's.

Alex closed her eyes and thought of Cristina, lying in the dirt, bleeding. Alex had returned with the police hours later to find her body discarded with the garbage behind the warehouse. The men were gone, along with the rest of the women.

She forced herself to focus on the table. Fluorescent lights buzzed overhead. The paramedic applied the paddles again, then again. Alex said a silent prayer, willing Mariana to live. The monitor squealed. The line on the electrocardiogram began to bounce on the screen, showing a weak but steady heart rate.

Alex let out a breath she hadn't known she was holding.

Craven looked around the room. "I don't see Ms. Flores. Where'd she go?"

"She was right here a minute ago," Gladys said.

"Would you look outside please, Gladys? She can't go far on foot," Alex said.

Craven looked at the woman on the table, glanced at his notepad, and then looked back up at Alex. "Where is Carmela Flores from?"

"Mexico originally, but she's here legally, if that's what you're asking. She has a green card."

Craven tapped his book. "How long has she worked here?"

"Carmela's been at the center since it was founded ten years ago."

"What time did she leave here?"

"Around five o'clock as usual today, about an hour before this happened. She lives in the Rag Town area and ordinarily takes the bus."

"No way she went home and then brought that woman back here from Rag Town on a bus," Craven said. "She must've got her from somewhere around here."

"We're a free clinic. Carmela often brings women here. The Hispanic women especially trust her."

"You got an address and a last name for Mariana?"

"I'll look, but often they don't tell us much about who they are or where they live. We don't insist."

Gladys came back inside, breathing hard. "No sign of Carmela."

"She's stable enough to move," the lead paramedic said.

Alex watched the paramedics ease Mariana off the table. She followed them out of the clinic and into the lobby. Gladys watched with her as the paramedics carried the gurney out the front door.

Craven flipped open a cell phone and called in a report. When he was done, he closed the phone and looked at Alex. "I need Ms. Flores's address too."

Alex went into her office and found an address for Carmela, but nothing for Mariana. She walked Craven to the front door. The officer promised that someone would be back with her the next day.

Gladys leaned against the lobby wall. "Look at this place. We have some work to do."

"We'll get it done," Alex said.

She went back to her office. A pain knifed across her shoulders. It had only been an hour since Carmela's face had appeared at the French doors, but it felt more like ten. She bent down to pick up the papers she'd dropped earlier when a voice came from the direction of the French doors.

"You're Alexandra Harrington?"

She started and turned to see the tall man she'd met earlier in the lobby. "How long have you been standing there?"

The man held out his hand. "Sorry. Didn't mean to scare you. Name's Murray, Mike Murray. I'd just like to ask you a few questions."

At over six feet, the reporter's height would have made him intimidating if it weren't for the shock of red hair that fell across his freckled face and for his crooked smile. She took his extended hand without thinking, pulling it back seconds later when she realized he was holding it a little too long.

"It's okay. I'm just a bit jumpy these days. You're a reporter?"

Murray grinned and reached in his jacket pocket for a pen and a notebook. "I heard about your nine-one-one call on the police scanner, and thought I'd check it out. What can you tell me about the woman who just left in the ambulance?"

"Time to go, buddy. We don't need publicity," Gladys said, coming into Alex's office and taking hold of the reporter's coat sleeve.

Alex suppressed a smile as Gladys shoved the man into the lobby and out the front door.

Murray's voice came through the door. "I'll catch you later, Ms. Harrington."

Gladys's expression relaxed for the first time that night. "Come on. Let's get out of here. We've had enough."

Alex led the way through the messy examining room toward the back of the building and opened the door. The humid August air was heavy with the scent of honeysuckle. The screech of the cicadas was deafening. Maybe it was the dense cloud cover that made the night so much darker than usual. She looked around the parking lot before stepping outside. Since returning from Mexico City six months ago she was edgy, always on guard.

She crossed the lot to her car and followed Gladys's SUV down the rutted gravel drive. Shadows seemed to move under the twisted limbs of the old oaks across the street. She tensed, gripping the wheel, and turned toward home.

CHAPTER FOUR

Alex was still tired when she woke up. Last night she'd crawled into bed, craving sleep, but as often happened since she'd returned from Mexico, sleep wouldn't come. One o'clock, two, three, the hours rolled by. When at last she had fallen asleep, Mariana's face had appeared in a dream followed by Cristina's and then the faces of the other women in the warehouse.

Sunshine streamed through her bedroom window. Seconds passed before she was awake enough to understand that she was home in her own apartment. The street outside was quiet.

She glanced at the clock. Nine-thirty. Her feet hit the floor. Gladys would be here any minute. She scooped up her robe from the back of a chair and headed for the bathroom. A quick look in the mirror made her flinch. Her hair was a tangled mess. Red rims and dark circles made her eyes look greener than ever. She stepped into the shower, letting water as hot as she could stand wash over her back and shoulders, lathering on twice as much gel as usual. Steamy air filled her lungs while the knots in her muscles loosened one by one.

Ten minutes later she felt human again. She pulled her still damp hair into a ponytail and wrapped an oversized towel around her dripping body. Her cell was ringing when she came out of the bathroom. The display read, "Harrington." She groaned and answered. "Hello, Mother. Can I call you right back? I just got out of the shower."

She hung up before her mother could answer, scrambled into a bra and bikini briefs, pulled a striped sundress over her head, then retrieved her mobile phone from the bedside table, and raced to the kitchen. She hit speed dial, steeling herself for her mother's habitual caustic comments.

"It's about time," Renee Harrington said when they reconnected. "What's this about a battered woman at the center? I had to read about it in the *Dalton Herald*. Why didn't you call? I am still a director on your board."

Alex could picture the creases that always formed between her mother's deep blue eyes when the woman was displeased. She hadn't for a moment considered phoning her last night when she got home. No apology, she knew, would stave off the onslaught. She put the cell on the counter, reached for the canister of coffee beans and the grinder, and slipped a paper filter into the holder. She hit the green button.

Her mother never seemed to believe the phone would carry her words unless she shouted. "Don't grind your coffee while I'm talking to you. It says here in the paper that the police are seeking Carmela Flores as a material witness. What does Carmela have to do with this?"

Alex held the cell away from her ear. She walked to the front door and opened it. The morning paper lay on the mat.

"Alex? Are you still there?"

She went back to the kitchen. "I'm here, Mother, reading now. A reporter was at the center last night. It's all here in his column, even Carmela's disappearance. What do you think could have scared her enough to make her run away?"

"Carmela's been with us as long as Gladys, almost since we opened. In all the years that I ran the center, she was never a problem. Now this."

"Carmela must know something. Whoever beat Mariana is still out there. We have to find out who did this so they won't do it to anyone else."

"You stay out of it. Let the police handle it. It's not your affair."

"It is my affair. I left Cristina to die. I'm not going to abandon Mariana. I think they could both be victims of human trafficking."

"Really, Alex. Why would you think that?"

"Mariana is from Mexico, and the way she was dressed, she could be a prostitute."

"Carmela should know better than to bring a prostitute to the center. You're there to help mothers and children, respectable poor people, not criminals."

"When I came back here after college to take over the center, you and the other board members assured me that it was a refuge for all women, no matter who they were."

"We didn't mean prostitutes. You have to think of the reputation of the center. We have to keep this quiet somehow."

Alex splashed hot coffee into her favorite mug, took a big gulp, and felt it burn all the way down.

"The donors are the least of our problems. What does Daddy have to say?"

"He's out of town on business again, so I doubt he's heard. I haven't talked to him since he left last Sunday, but he promised he'd be back in time for the party at the club tonight. All the donors will be there. You had better be there too, to show that everything's under control."

"I have other plans."

"No you don't. You haven't had a social life since you came back from Mexico City. All you do is work. I ran into Kelly at the hairdresser yesterday. She said she hadn't seen you in weeks. Your friends miss you. They're going to think there's something wrong with you. Why don't you call them? You won't be young forever. I know that well enough."

"Working helps."

"Really, Alex, I do understand that you had a bad experience in Mexico, but you must put it behind you. You barely wear makeup any more, and that white streak in your hair is getting stronger. I do wish you'd dye it to match the rest of your pretty hair."

"What time is the party?"

"It starts at six. Travis Bingham will be there. Such a dear boy. He's sweet on you, though I'm sure I don't understand why, the way you treat him. You're not getting any younger. Please wear something nice." The phone went dead.

She groaned. Her mother was not an easy woman to say no to. No doubt her mother's next call would be to Travis's mother to tell her that Alex was going to be there that night. Travis came from a good family. The Binghams were on the same social level as the Harringtons. She could swear her parents had picked Travis out for her when the two were in kindergarten, and Travis seemed only too happy to oblige. He'd followed her around the playground and everywhere else all through grade school and high school. Once, at a party when they'd been in junior high, the lights went out and Travis had held her and kissed her. She'd kicked him in the shin so hard that he still had a scar. He delighted in annoying her by pulling up his pant leg to show anyone who would look what a tiger she could be.

She didn't want to see Travis tonight, but actually, her mother was right; she hadn't been interested in dating anybody at all since coming home from Mexico. The therapist her mother had insisted she see said it was normal not to want any kind of relationship for a while after what she'd been through. There was time enough for that when she was ready. In the meantime she had her work and a whole pile of good books.

The doorbell rang several times. It had to be Gladys. She ran to the door and looked through the peephole. A distorted image of the red-haired reporter from the night before looked back at her. The bell rang three more times.

She pulled the door open. "Enough."

"Hi there. Remember me? Mike Murray? From the *Herald*."

The reporter pushed his way into the living room, still wearing the same shirt he'd had on the night before, more rumpled now. Ginger-colored stubble covered his chin.

"Well, don't stand on ceremony. Come right on in," she said, following him into the living room.

"Thanks. Got any more of that?" He nodded toward Alex's mug.

"How did you find me?"

"I aspire to be an investigative reporter. Finding you was easy. I want to know about that woman last night. Where did she come from? How'd she get to Dalton?"

Murray looked around the large sunny living room, stopping at the brass plaque on the coffee table that read "North Carolina 1500 Meter Race, Best in Class."

"You're a runner? That's pretty cool."

"Track was high school. I still jog and work out."

Murray picked up a book from the coffee table and thumbed through the pictures. "Wow, self-defense too?"

"I started self-defense classes six months ago after I got back from vacation." Her heart beat faster at the memory. She looked away.

Mike gave her a quizzical look, as if he could read more in her face than she was willing to tell him.

"Want to tell me about it?"

"No thanks. I'm fine."

She changed the subject. "I just read your story. My mother was very upset by it."

"I don't know why. There wasn't enough there to bother anybody. I'm working on a follow-up. What can you tell me about your patient? I know she's from Mexico, and I'm guessing she's a hooker."

"That's offensive. You must know that I can't talk about our patients."

"Any idea why Carmela Flores ran?"

"You would have to ask her."

"I will when I find her. Help me do that. We'll find her faster working together."

"Why would I want to help you?"

The doorbell rang again, and a muffled voice announced the Dalton police. She went to the door with Murray close on her heels. He really was being annoying. She pulled the door open and looked into the face of a very elegant African-American woman. At five-eight Alex didn't feel short, but this woman seemed to tower over her at least two inches above six feet.

"I'm Detective White with the Dalton P.D."

"Hello, Keisha. I heard you caught this one," Murray said.

White looked over Alex's shoulder at the reporter. "You got up early. I'm here to talk with Ms. Harrington, alone."

"Never went to bed. Please let me stay. It'll be a better story for the police if I know what's going on. I'm going to find out anyway."

"Not from me you won't. You'll get your information from the media liaison officer like everyone else."

White looked at Alex. "Ma'am, is there somewhere we can talk, without him?"

"We can talk in the living room. Mr. Murphy is just leaving."

"Murray. It's Murray. I can take a hint, even one as subtle as that. See you later, Alex. I'll take a rain check on the coffee."

She closed the door behind him with a snap and led the detective inside. "Coffee's a little strong, but it's fresh."

White followed her into the galley kitchen. "Thanks, I could use some. I got called out on this case early this morning."

"Is there an update on Mariana?"

"She died at the hospital."

Alex's hand trembled. Scalding coffee splashed the front of her tank top. She wet a dish towel and dabbed at it. "I thought she was going to make it. What happened?"

"Doctors couldn't help her. She had internal injuries. We won't know for sure until the final autopsy results are in, but we're treating her death as a homicide. What can you tell me about her?"

"As I told the officer last night, I don't know much. She was a sweet girl, but very shy. She never talked about herself. I wanted very much to help her."

"Why was that?"

"I guess she reminded me of someone."

"Was she legal?"

"I have no idea. We take care of anyone who comes in the door, no questions asked."

"There are FBI reports of human trafficking activity in our area. I'm surprised the INS isn't all over you, the FBI, too, if you're running illegals through your clinic without reporting them."

Alex met White's stare. "We're a free clinic. We help poor people. There's nothing more to it than that."

"If you know anything that connects Mariana's death with human trafficking, you need to tell me now."

Alex felt her cheeks burn. "Believe me, the last thing I want is to help human traffickers."

"Your office's cleaning person ran away. She must know something."

"That reporter was at the center last night. He said the same thing."

"Mike Murray. I saw his story. My advice to you is stay away from all reporters and especially that guy. He's not about to do you or us any favors. Where do you think Carmela Flores would go?"

"Other than her cousin's, I really don't know.

"How well do you think Ms. Flores knew the deceased?"

Alex flinched at the word "deceased." "I saw Carmela talking with Mariana and another young woman in the garden about a week ago, so maybe they did have some connection outside the center. I meant to ask Carmela about it, but I got distracted and never did."

White put down her coffee cup and stood. "We checked out the address you gave Officer Craven last night. It's her cousin's apartment, an Elena Casas. According to the cousin, Carmela didn't come home last night."

The doorbell rang again. This time it was Gladys at the door, a baseball cap pulled low on her forehead, ready for anything as always.

White handed a card to Alex. "I have to get going. If either of you find out anything about Carmela Flores, please let me know immediately."

Alex shut the door. "Mariana died."

"I know. A friend who works at the hospital called me. Poor girl."

"Detective White made it sound like the police think there's a connection between the center and human trafficking. What was Carmela doing?"

"All I know is that something strange is going on. A guy on a motorcycle followed me home last night. Big guy, dressed in a black tee shirt. He hung around outside for a while, watching my apartment."

"You should have called the police. Why would anyone follow you?"

"I don't think it was because he was interested in fat old me."

"This is all pretty weird. The one thing I do agree with Detective White about, though, is that the sooner we find Carmela, the better."

CHAPTER FIVE

Vargas listened to the Southern drawl on the other end of the phone. His knuckles turned white. His famous eye twitched. The *gringo* he called El Caballero, the gentleman, often sent him into a rage, but this time he was close to killing the bastard.

"A woman is dead and you want to shut down the whole operation? You tell me that powerful people live in your pocket, yet you do nothing?"

He could hear the tension increase in El Caballero's voice as he spoke.

"We have to close down the operation and ship the remaining girls up north. The Dalton house is too close to the clinic where the police found Mariana. They're combing the neighborhood. They're going to find the house."

"You will not shut down the operation. Dalton is our franchise model. We hold it up to all prospects as our greatest success. There's a shipment on the way to you now."

"No. You have to stop it. It's too dangerous. You've got to divert the shipment elsewhere."

"No? You tell me, no? I have killed many people for less. You have a short memory. You do not care about your family? You know what happens when you do not do as you are told."

El Caballero's voice cracked. "*Señor*, please. I'm begging you. I'm only thinking about the business. We could lose our whole investment here. We could all go to jail."

"You grew up rich. You had cars. Cuchillo and I had to take the bus. You don't know what to do when things get hard. Now you are going to work." Vargas slammed down the phone and glared at Cuchillo. "I don't trust him. He's weak, and he's scared. That's bad."

Cuchillo was at his elbow. "When do we leave?"

"Tomorrow morning, early. Get ready. El Caballero's useful because he knows important people, but he's not reliable. I think I'm gonna have to get rid of him soon."

Vargas's cell rang. He answered. "Tell me everything."

CHAPTER SIX

Mike Murray's much-loved, red 1965 Mustang hung several car lengths behind until the SUV pulled up in front of a two-story wood frame apartment building in Rag Town. The mid-day sun penetrated a damp haze, sending the heat index to the red zone. He drove past the SUV into an empty lot next door and parked next to a pile of tires and a rusted refrigerator with its doors removed.

The two women climbed out and picked their way across loose bricks and broken glass to a rickety wooden outside staircase that led to the second-floor landing. They started climbing. Alex Harrington rang the bell while the center's nurse, Gladys something, braced the weight of a large shopping bag against the door jamb.

"*Buenos días, Señora* Casas. We are Carmela's friends," Alex called through the door in perfectly unaccented Spanish. She knocked, louder, and looked up and down the street. A curtain moved, and a young boy's face peeked out. An adult hand pulled the boy back into the room.

"*Señora*, please open the door."

Mike held still, watching. No sound came from the apartment. Alex tucked a strand of hair behind one ear. Rag Town was a high crime area, not the best part of town for someone as classy as she was. He'd like to get to know that lady a whole lot better.

The apartment door opened a crack, and a younger, thinner version of Carmela peeked out at the two women for what seemed like a long time before stepping out onto the landing. Alex said something in a low tone he couldn't make out. The woman reached out, grasped Alex's arm, and pulled her into the apartment. Gladys followed, shutting the door behind her.

Mike climbed out of his car and scanned the neighborhood, looking from the Mexican market, *Mi Tienda*, across the street, its storefront window plastered with red, yellow, and black signs, to a small unpainted house next door whose dirt yard was littered with broken bottles and crushed beer cans. Plywood covered one window of the house. The porch sagged under the weight of a threadbare couch.

The street was silent. The apartment door was still closed. Half an hour passed. Murray's mind wandered. His editor was not happy about assigning a murder story, particularly a murder in a socially well-connected non-profit, to a junior reporter who until now had covered car wrecks and school board meetings. Never big on taking orders, he had fought for it. "Who else is going to do it? You fired all the senior guys."

In the street, dust devils swirled. A greasy wrapping from Church's Fried Chicken blew across the street and wound around his foot. He was bending to pull it off when the apartment door opened. The women stepped out onto the landing. He inched closer, staying low behind a row of scraggly bushes, and crouched in the shadows beneath the outside stairs so he could hear what the women said. He could just get the gist of the cousin's rapid-fire Spanish from the rudimentary Spanish he'd picked up from the Hispanic kids he'd played with growing up in Arizona.

The top step creaked under the weight of the three women. He thought he heard Alex say something about finding a better place for Carmela to hide. She had to know where Carmela Flores was. How was he going to get her to tell him?

"You have my number, Elena. Call if you need anything."

Alex hugged her and followed Gladys down the stairs, careful to place her feet in the middle of each creaky step.

Elena watched until both women reached the bottom and then went back in the apartment, shut the door, and turned the lock with an audible click.

Gladys started toward the SUV. Alex followed.

Mike crept up behind Alex. "Is she in there?"

Alex jumped. "Damn it. Don't do that. You're following me, aren't you?"

He tried a winning smile. "Sorry. Let's try this again. What did you learn in there?"

"None of your business."

"Sure it is. You know where Carmela Flores is."

Gladys turned around and glared at Mike. "How many times do I need to tell you to get lost?"

"I'm only trying to help."

Alex climbed into the passenger side while Gladys hefted her ample frame into the driver's seat. The SUV pulled into the street, spraying him with dirt. Alex looked back at him, her face framed by the car window. Would a cool-looking chick like that ever be interested in a blue-collar kid like him? He could only hope. He watched the SUV disappear around the corner before he crossed the street in the direction of *Mi Tienda*.

CHAPTER SEVEN

Three men in gang colors emerged from the unpainted house next to *Mi Tienda* and stood on the porch watching Mike. A skinny teenager followed them. The four came down the steps to meet him.

"Hey. I'm a reporter from the *Dalton Herald*, looking for information about a woman who was killed over in the Tryon Park area. You hear about that?"

No response.

"I'm also trying to find a woman named Carmela Flores. Her cousin lives across the street." He pointed to the apartment.

The men looked at him.

"Guess not." He shrugged and walked on toward the market. When he looked back, the three had split, the two older ones going back into the unpainted house. The teen stayed on the street, watching him.

Mike continued on to *Mi Tienda* and pulled open the screen door to the store. Inside, a grizzled old man stood chatting with a middle-aged Hispanic man behind the counter, the owner most likely. All conversation stopped.

He smiled. "*Buenos dias, señores*. A woman was beaten to death last night. You know anything about it?"

"We know nothing," the owner said.

The old man shook his head.

Mike turned to three customers who were waiting by the cash register, a man in work boots carrying a hard hat, a stocky middle-aged woman in a loose, embroidered white blouse and a young woman with a baby on her hip.

"Do any of you know Carmela Flores?"

They looked at him, silent.

An old woman pushed through a curtain behind the counter and began to speak in heavily accented English. "The police come here first thing when we open this morning. They ask us questions, like you. They show us a picture of a girl who looks dead. Is bad, very bad."

"Did you recognize her?" he asked.

The old woman's eyes were moist. "There were two young girls, the one in the picture and a younger one. They come to *Mi Tienda* last week. A man was with them, many tattoos. American. The girls buy things—soap, curlers, pads. They say they are from Mexico, from the south like us."

"Ma, you talk too much. This has nothing to do with us," the owner said and turned to Mike. "Leave now. Don't come back. We don't need no trouble."

Mike picked up a box of doughnuts and laid a ten dollar bill on the counter. He bowed to the old woman, opened the door, and went out. The woman knew more than she was saying. He'd come back later.

The teen he'd seen with the gang crashed into him in the market doorway, fell backward, and landed on his butt in the dirt.

Mike gave him a hand up. He pulled a card from his coat pocket and handed it to him. "You hear anything, you call me. Okay?"

The boy took the card. "The cops were here. We tell them nothing."

A gang member he hadn't seen before came out of the unpainted house and crossed the street. Mike guessed the man had to be older than the rest, in his thirties, with tattoos on his forearm and a blue bandana around his head. More of the gang filed out of the house, all in the same colors, all a few years younger than the man who now stood in front of Mike.

Mike held the palms of his hands up and backed away. By the time he reached his car the street was empty. He turned his key in the ignition. He was starting to write his story in his head when he heard a roar.

Two Harleys came around the corner. Two men, both in black,

rode their bikes onto the sidewalk and stopped in front of the apartment. They dismounted, and stood looking up at the second floor.

He held still.

The bigger of the two, his face covered by a heavy gray-streaked beard, led the way to the outside stairs, followed by a skinnier, short biker. Boots sounded on every step. When they reached the landing, the bearded guy banged a fist on the door and yelled, "Carmela Flores."

Mike turned off his engine and got out of the car.

"We know you're in there."

The door stayed shut. The long-haired biker raised a boot and kicked. The door held.

A trickle of sweat rolled down Mike's neck. He slid out of the Mustang, pulled out his cell, and dialed nine-one-one. He talked to the dispatcher in a low voice while the biker put his shoulder to the door and rammed it. The hinges broke.

Across the street another door flew open. The gang poured out onto the porch of the painted house, the older one first, and went for the apartment stairs, clutching chains and knives.

"*Lárgate*," the leader yelled.

The bikers pulled knives, bracing themselves.

The gang raced up, shaking the stairs with each step. The leader reached the top step, threw himself at the long-haired biker, and pinned him against the wall. The biker's knife flew up into the air. The others jumped the smaller biker, pinning him against the railing.

The stairs gave a loud crack and pulled away from the building in slow motion. The landing buckled. The steps broke, each collapsing onto the one below. The men fell, yelling, bodies piling on top of each other. Mangled pieces of wood crashed to the ground.

As the dust settled, the leader got to his feet, choking, and grasped a hunk of wood, going for the long-haired biker. The smaller biker threw his knife. The other biker caught it, got to his feet, and went for the leader. The knife slashed the leader's right arm. He stepped back, blood gushing.

Two of the gang moved in with pieces of wood. The two bikers fought back to back. The gang closed in. The smaller biker went down under repeated blows. The long-haired biker broke free, picked up the other biker, and dragged him away. The gang came after them.

The bikers reached their Harleys. The long-haired biker pulled a gun from his saddlebag and held it on the gang while he mounted his bike. The other biker jumped on his bike and, stone-faced, the two kicked their bikes into gear and pulled out of Rag Town.

"Stay the fuck out of here," the gang leader yelled after them and limped past the Mustang toward the unpainted house. The rest followed.

Mike's cell rang. The display read, Dalton P.D.

"You told the dispatcher two men were attacking Carmela Flores's cousin's apartment?" Detective White said.

"Hey, Keisha. You missed the action. A Hispanic gang got into a fight with two bikers who came looking for Carmela."

"We're coming up on Rag Town now."

A fire engine rounded the corner and stopped, and an unmarked car pulled in behind. Keisha leaped out just as an ambulance arrived from the opposite direction and parked across the street.

"Over there," Mike yelled and looked up to where the top of the stairs had been.

Above, in the ruined doorway, Elena Casas held a little boy close, and beside them the stocky figure of Carmela swayed, clutching a rosary.

"Well, I'll be damned. She was there all along," White said.

The firefighter laid a ladder against the house and climbed up. With help, the women came down the ladder while a second firefighter carried the boy. The paramedics took over from there.

Within minutes all the equipment was gone. Keisha White was gone too, taking the Flores-Casas family with her. The street in front of *Mi Tienda* was empty. The market was dark, and a sign on the door said, *Cerrado*.

If not for the ruined stairs and the gaping hole on the second floor where the door had been, anyone would think nothing had happened. Mike opened his laptop and started typing.

CHAPTER EIGHT

"Alex." She heard her name coming from the steps of the Dalton Country Club. She wove through the gleaming BMWs and Mercedes toward the oak double doors where a skinny middle-aged woman in a bright pink outfit and matching shoes tottered at the top of the stairs, a drink in one hand and a cigarette in the other. "It's been ages, sugar. Your center is all over the news."

Alex reached the top step and turned her cheek to receive air kisses from Peaches Bingham.

"I just know your mama's worried about you, bless her heart. We never stop being mothers no matter how grown up our children are. Why, only yesterday you walked up these very steps on my Travis's arm, such a pretty debutante in your long white dress and gloves. I remember how happy y'all looked."

Alex remembered it differently. After weeks of arguments, her mother finally won, insisting that she, like all girls from the "best" Dalton families, come out at the annual debutante ball. The designer dresses, red roses, fancy jewelry, and the bright smiles on the faces of the well-brought-up young women had seemed to go on forever. She'd had the urge to take her clothes off and run naked through the clubhouse, laughing hysterically. She hadn't. She had done what was expected of her, and after college she came back to Dalton and a quiet life, until Mexico City.

She was trying to maneuver around Peaches when her mother

sailed through the oak doors, a multicolored silk wrap billowing behind her like a spinnaker. "Peaches, Sweetie. You absolutely must get rid of those cigarettes. You know they're bad for you."

Not a strand of ash blonde hair was out of place when Renee Harrington reached Alex's side and put one arm around her daughter's waist, guiding her toward the clubhouse. Big band music filled the ballroom. A banner hanging over the musicians read, "The Nifty Fifties." Silver balls covered with little glass mirrors bounced above the crowd, sending circles of light around the dance floor. The older crowd was dancing to "I Only Have Eyes for You."

Kelly was at the bar with a group Alex knew from high school. Alex waved, feeling guilty that she hadn't called Kelly since she got back from Mexico six months ago. She and Kelly had been inseparable all though school, but even before the horror of the kidnapping, Alex had begun to realize that they had very little in common. Kelly still cared about fashion shows and the latest gossip while Alex was increasingly serious about her work at the center. Not only that, the very sight of Kelly brought back a time she would rather forget and reminded her of Cristina's death.

"Where have you been?" her mother's voice hissed in her ear. "I've been leaving messages for you everywhere. Your father is here. Everyone is asking for you. Push your hair off your forehead and smile."

She looked around the room. "I've been with Gladys all day, Mother. We found Carmela. She's at the police station. Some thugs found out where she was hiding and went after her. Gladys is with her. I should be there, too."

"You're needed here. What can you do that Gladys can't?"

"Hey, good lookin'."

She jumped as Scott Foley draped an arm around her shoulder. She could smell the musky scent of the Harrington family lawyer's cologne and see the web of tiny veins across his nose and cheeks. His thick gray hair was combed straight back from a widow's peak.

"Tell me what all's going on at that clinic of yours."

Renee Harrington's pale blue eyes widened. "Scott dear, Alex was hoping you'd be here tonight so she could tell you all about it. Go ahead, honey."

Foley squeezed Alex closer. "Rumor is that your cleaning lady brought a woman of ill-repute to the center. I hear the cleaning lady's missing and the woman's dead."

Foley was the chair of the center's board and its attorney. Alex knew she was supposed to be agreeable. She forced a smile.

"Where did you hear that, Mr. Foley?"

"I read it on the *Dalton Herald* blog this afternoon, by a local reporter. Fascinating reading. Getting a lot of hits."

She frowned. "The police didn't want Carmela's disappearance to get out."

Foley beamed. "Ha. I knew it. The blog didn't say anything about the cleaning lady. I was just fishing, sweetheart."

She felt color rise in her face. "That's not fair."

"It's hardly a secret. You just told me," Renee said.

"I thought you could keep it in confidence, Mother."

Alex cast her eyes around the room, looking for a way to change the subject, and was relieved to see her father working his way toward them through the crowd, his silver hair glistening in the overhead lights. She gave him a quick wave. Sandy Harrington stopped several times to visit before he finally reached his daughter's side and handed her a glass of white wine.

"Harrington, you old scoundrel, when did you get back in town?" Foley said.

"Evening Scott, are you harassing my little girl?"

Foley took a sip of his martini. "I'm only trying to find out what's really going on at the center. Nothing very exciting ever happens in Dalton. Not on our side of town anyway, and your sweet little daughter knows a whole lot more than she's saying."

"The cleaning lady brought some woman to the center, and the poor woman later died. It's too bad, but there isn't any more to it than that," Renee said.

"Her name was Mariana, Mother. We can't just pretend it didn't happen," Alex said.

"Any death is tragic, darling," Sandy said, hugging her and turning to Foley. "Alex cares very deeply about the people in her clinic. That's why she's so good at what she does."

At least her father was trying to help. She tried to calm down.

"Where did you go this time, Harrington?" Foley asked, apparently deciding it was time for a change of subject.

"Mexico, and it was hot as Hades."

Alex balled her hands into fists and pretended to look at the band. The mention of Mexico made her stomach churn.

"Here's our boy, Travis." Foley stuck his hand out to a man in his late twenties, resplendent in a light blue jacket and razor-pressed yellow slacks. A yellow and blue striped bow tie rode directly above a prominent Adam's apple. A matching pocket square folded in three peaks adorned his breast pocket.

"Travis, dear, what a surprise. We were hoping you'd be here tonight, weren't we, Alex?" Renee said.

Travis shook hands all around, getting to Alex last. "Y'all wouldn't mind if I stole this pretty lady away for the next dance, would you?"

Anger swelled in her chest. Everywhere she turned somebody was pushing her in Travis's direction. He fit well into the world of dinner dances and golf tournaments that her parents had raised her for. It was a world in which she was never comfortable no matter how many White Gloves and Party Manners etiquette classes her mother made her attend. Since Mexico, it all made even less sense.

"Did you know that this young man is joining my law firm next month? Top of his law school class at Duke, three years of experience in the district attorney's office. He's a prize," Foley said.

Alex's mother put one hand in the middle of her daughter's back and propelled her toward Travis. "We are so proud of you, Travis. That's well-deserved and a real credit to all your hard work. You two run along and dance now."

Sandy motioned for her to go ahead. "The music is especially good tonight. Listen, they're playing 'Carolina on My Mind.' The next dance is mine, sweetheart."

"Are you mad at me, Alex?" Travis asked when they reached the dance floor.

"I'm mad at everyone, Mother most of all."

"I know you feel for the poor woman who died, but you need to leave it to the police."

"That's what everyone says, but I can't do that. She was our patient. There may be others like her out there. We have to help them."

Travis dropped her into a graceful twirl, then dipped her backward, holding her there a little too long before bringing her up again.

"Want to get out of here, maybe hit some clubs downtown?"

"No thanks," she said, looking around for her father.

Her father cut in at last. "He's an impressive young man, Alex. Why don't you like him?"

"Travis plays the perfect Southern gentleman, but underneath, it's all about Travis. He's always looking over your shoulder to see if someone more important is in the room. Besides, I hate bow ties."

A club steward approached them. "Excuse me, Miss Harrington. I have a phone call for you on the club phone. A woman says it's urgent."

Gladys's voice was tense. "I've got Carmela and her cousin and son in the car. The police let them go. We're heading to my place."

"I'll be there in fifteen minutes." Alex hung up and turned to her father.

"Something's come up. I have to go."

"Not on your own, you don't. I don't want you running around at night alone in some Godforsaken part of Dalton. I'm going with you."

"I'm only going to Gladys's apartment. I'll be fine."

"I'm going to tell your mother we're leaving. Wait here for me."

She watched him disappear into the crowd, then slipped through the front door toward the parking lot. She was backing out when she heard a loud bang on the trunk.

Her father yanked the passenger side door open of her old Civic and jumped in. "What do you think you're doing?"

Her hands tightened on the steering wheel. She pressed her lips together and stepped on the gas.

———

Gladys's mouth fell open. "Oh, Mr. Harrington, you came too. How nice."

Alex smiled to herself. Even Gladys wasn't immune to her

father's charms.

"Carmela is lying down in the bedroom. Her cousin took Victor for a hamburger," Gladys said.

"Did Carmela say anything to the police?"

"Nothing helpful. They let me stay with her, I think because she was so agitated. She claims she found Mariana just wandering around on the street. I don't think they believed her, and I can't say as I do either. She wouldn't say what she was doing from the time she left the center until she came back with Mariana."

"You think she'll tell us?" Alex said.

"Maybe. She's safe here. I talked her into spending the night. Her cousin and the boy, Victor, too."

The bedroom door creaked. Carmela peeked out, then backed away and closed the door.

Alex moved close to the door. "Carmela, we're so glad you're all right. Do you want to talk about it? My father's here. He may be able to help."

Carmela didn't answer.

"She'll be better after a night's sleep," Gladys said.

"You're right. We aren't going to get anywhere tonight. Let's go, Daddy."

The front door flew open. A narrow-chested boy of about nine or ten burst in, followed by his mother.

The boy stopped, breathing hard. "Our house is on fire."

Elena pushed in behind him. "*Virgen María*. It's true. We saw it on TV at the restaurant."

"Daddy, this is Mrs. Casas, Carmela's cousin, and her son."

"How do you know it's your apartment?" Gladys asked.

"The television man said there was a fire. In Rag Town. We saw *Mi Tienda* across the street," Victor said.

Gladys clicked the remote. A grainy picture of a two-story building appeared on the television screen.

"That's our apartment," Elena said.

The telephone rang. Gladys picked up and listened. "Whatever you say, Detective White." She turned to the others.

"The police are at the cousin's apartment building now. Detective

White wants Elena to go there. Maybe she can see something that will help the police."

"Carmela should come too," Elena said.

"Detective White wants Carmela to stay here so that no one will know where she is," Gladys said.

Alex opened the door. "We'll take Mrs. Casas over there now. Gladys, you stay here with Carmela. Mrs. Casas and the boy will come with us."

CHAPTER NINE

Fire trucks and emergency vehicles blocked the road in front of Elena Casas's apartment house. Water streamed into the street from the fire hoses. Mike parked a block away and made his way through the fast-gathering crowd to the old oak tree, and for the second time that day he stood in its shadows, watching and listening.

White stood a few yards away next to the fire marshal, her dark skin glowing in the orange light. Beside her a young Hispanic couple with three young children stood transfixed by the fire, clutching the few possessions they had been able to grab as they fled the building. A baby shrieked in its mother's arms. Firefighters climbed up and down ladders, pumping water through the smashed windows of Elena's apartment. Smoke poured from a hole in the roof.

Mike moved in closer, keeping to the edge of the growing crowd, hoping that Keisha wouldn't spot him and push him back. He listened, just barely able to make out what she was saying.

"No doubt it's arson," the fire marshal said as water dripped from his slick yellow suit. "It took a lot of accelerant to make this place go up that fast. Top unit's a disaster. Looks like somebody targeted that one apartment. If anybody'd been in there, they wouldn't have made it out."

"I've got officers canvassing the neighborhood, but so far nobody saw anything. Is there a chance we can get in there tonight? I'd like to bring in the forensic team."

"No way. The roof could go any minute. There won't be much left to find anyway. The building inspector likely will condemn the whole structure."

Mike spotted Alex's car pulling up beside the emergency vehicles. Elena climbed out of the back, a little boy, her son no doubt, got out behind her, and Alex drove away.

"*Madre de Dios*," Elena said over and over, clutching a rosary.

The boy ran ahead of his mother toward the fire.

The fire marshal caught him. "Not so fast, son."

Elena pulled her son close against her.

"Good evening, Mrs. Casas," Detective White said. "Do you see anyone here that you recognize, maybe the men who came to your apartment earlier today? People who start fires sometimes stay to watch them."

Elena wiped away her tears and scanned the rapidly growing crowd. She shook her head and turned back to the fire. "It's all gone. Clothes, TV, pictures of our family in Mexico. We got nothing."

Mike saw Alex coming from around the end of the line of parked cars. A tall, stately man walked behind her. So that was Alex's father. While Alex's skin had an olive tone and her eyes looked almost amber in the light of the fire, Alexander Harrington was fair-complexioned with steely gray eyes. Still, there was something that made them seem alike. Mike watched them, trying to figure it out. They were both slender and athletic-looking. Maybe that was it.

"Detective White, this is my father," Alex said.

Harrington extended his hand. "Good evening, Detective. These old buildings are tinder boxes. I'm surprised that more of them don't catch on fire."

The detective shook hands with Sandy Harrington and looked at Alex. "This is no accident. Someone set this fire, and I'm betting Carmela Flores knows more than she's saying. Did she tell you anything?"

Alex shook her head. "Not me or Gladys either. The fire makes it looks like somebody's sending her a message."

"It'll be even harder to get her to talk after this," White said.

A thunderous roar came from the apartment building. The roof buckled and then collapsed. Flames shot above the roof.

The fire marshal waved his arms. "Get back."

Red-hot sparks rained down. The crowd fell back, screaming.

The old woman from *Mi Tienda* pushed through the crowd, ran to Elena, and hugged her.

"You and the boy stay with us. We'll take care of you."

Elena hesitated, looking at Alex.

"If you would be more comfortable here, you should stay. We'll take care of Carmela," Alex said.

Tears stained Elena's cheeks. "*Gracias.* You will tell my cousin that we are okay?"

Alex hugged her. "Of course."

The old lady took Elena's arm. "Come. You and the boy must rest. There is no more you can do here."

Victor followed. The market door closed behind them.

The skinny teen from the gang stood watching the fire from the front yard of the unpainted house.

Mike crossed the street. "Hello again. What do you know about the fire? You guys didn't start it, would be my guess."

"Shit no, man. Not us. These are our people. They're from Mexico, like us."

"Any idea who did?"

"Sure. Those fuckin' bikers. Same guys you saw us beat up before. We kicked their asses. Now they come back to show us who's boss. We gonna get them for this."

The gang leader came out of the house and threw an arm around the teen's neck, jerking him toward the house. "Mañuel, how many times I got to tell you to shut the fuck up?"

He pushed the boy back into the house and slammed the door.

Mike looked back at the road. Alex and her father were walking toward the Honda. He ran after them. "Hello Alex. How's Carmela Flores doing?"

Alex glowered at him. "I suppose this will all go in the paper."

"I got to tell the story, it's my job. But if you tell me something's off the record, I won't publish it. Tell me about Carmela. I know she's not at the police station any more. Is she at your place now?"

"I'm not talking to you."

"I'm telling you we can figure this whole thing out a lot faster if we work together. The woman in *Mi Tienda* said Mariana came into the market some time before she died with another young woman. Ask Carmela what she knows about another woman. Like I said, I won't publish it, if you tell me not to."

"This guy's obviously a reporter, Alex. There's no such thing as off the record."

"Mike Murray," Mike said, holding out his hand. "I'm pleased to meet you, Mr. Harrington."

"So you're the one who's making a big deal of this story. I've read your article and your blog. It's not helpful. You're building it up as a human trafficking story. It's nothing but yellow journalism. Why would anyone in Dalton be involved in that, for God's sake? All you're doing is getting people stirred up."

"Human trafficking's big business. The police, the FBI are both looking at it. I think that's what's going on here."

"Young man, you are out of line. Alex, get in the car."

"Nice talking with you, sir. See you later, Alex," Mike said.

He walked back toward the fire, his mind filled with thoughts of Alex. He probably shouldn't have made her father mad.

CHAPTER TEN

Smoke clung to Alex's clothes. Her hair was matted and her face was covered with flecks of soot. Her favorite sandals were soaked, destined for the trash. She looked back at her parents, standing a little apart from each other on the steps of their Tudor-style mansion. Her father's face was creased with worry. Her mother was frowning in annoyance. Nothing more was going to happen tonight, she'd assured them. However tempting the prospect of a night in her old room and the promise of a steamy bath and freshly ironed sheets, she had to get back to Gladys's apartment. Someone was out there looking for Carmela, someone who would beat a woman to death and set fire to a building where families were asleep.

She turned onto the main road, her mind on the fire, and soon realized that the car behind was following her at every turn. The glare of its lights filled her rearview mirror. She couldn't make out the driver's face. When she went left, the car went with her. She drove through downtown Dalton to the freeway, speeding up, slowing down, anything to get rid of it. The car stayed right on her bumper. Who was this guy? She didn't want to lead him to Gladys's apartment and was about to call the police when the car pulled alongside. The passenger side window lowered.

"You cut me off, you bitch! Where'd you learn to drive?" The car sped away. She let her breath out. Just a jerk with a bad case of road rage. If she weren't so strung out, it would be funny.

Her thoughts returned to Carmela. The police didn't believe Carmela's story. If this was about human trafficking, could Carmela be involved? Something had made the office cleaner run when the police started asking questions. Alex had been happy when Carmela began bringing Hispanic women to the center a few months back because the women reminded her of Cristina. She'd wanted to help them. She hadn't questioned where they came from or why they were all reluctant to talk. She wished now that she'd asked Carmela more about them.

She reached Gladys's apartment and started to turn into the lot when a dark blue van careened toward her from behind the building, tires screeching. She slammed on her brakes. The van rocked up on its right wheels, missing her by inches, righted itself, and went past her out into the road.

"Damn, and I don't know how to drive?"

She started up again and pulled into the near-empty lot. Lights shone from Gladys's living room window. She scanned the few other parked cars. The lot looked safe enough. She got out of her car and walked toward the building entrance.

Something moved in the shadows. Alex jumped.

A yellow cat streaked across the lot. Growling noises and ear-splitting screams came from the bushes, followed by silence. The yellow cat emerged, head high, and stalked off toward the back of the building.

Even a cat fight could set her off these days.

A man and woman came out of the building, laughing. Another car pulled into the lot and parked. She began to relax. Everything was all right. She continued toward the apartment.

Footsteps sounded behind her. She jumped again and spun around.

Mike Murray threw his hands up. "Whoa. It's just me."

"You're doing it again. Why are you following me?"

"Sorry, I never meant to make you jump. I didn't follow you. I heard you tell Keisha White you were going to Gladys's apartment. I found her online and came straight here. I've been waiting for an hour."

Maybe it was the crooked grin, but she had trouble staying mad at Mike Murray for very long. "Did you see that van almost run me down?"

"Yeah. It came around from the back like something was chasing it. I thought it was going to hit you. You okay?"

"It just startled me," she said. "I've had enough for one night. Good night."

"Come on. I came all the way over here. I want to talk to Carmela."

"She'll be asleep by now, which is what I intend to be very soon."

"I'm coming anyway," Mike said, and he followed her into the building and up the stairs.

She ignored him and continued to the second floor landing. The door to Gladys's apartment was ajar.

She stopped, frowning.

Mike caught up with her. "What's going on?"

"Gladys wouldn't leave the door open."

She pushed the door open. Gladys lay slumped on the floor. A chair lay on its side. The coffee table was turned over.

"Oh my God. Gladys."

She ran to the woman and felt for a pulse. "Call for an ambulance. Tell them she's unconscious."

She went to the bedroom, calling for Carmela while Mike dialed.

The bed clothes were on the floor. A water glass was in pieces by the bedside table. There was no one there.

She went back to the living room. "Call Detective White's direct line too. Carmela is gone."

Gladys moaned and opened her eyes.

Alex raced to the kitchen, coming back with a wet towel. She put a throw pillow under Gladys's head and pressed the towel against a cut on her forehead.

Gladys struggled to sit up. "There were two of them. I tried to fight, but they hit me, and I fell. I guess I went out."

"Stay still until help arrives."

A few minutes later, she heard an emergency vehicle pulling into the lot, siren blaring, and looked out the window to see three paramedics jump out. A squad car and White's unmarked vehicle pulled in behind it, and the paramedics came up the stairs and into the apartment followed by White and a uniformed officer.

White didn't take the news about Carmela well. She called for a crime tech after making her own quick search of the apartment, then stood tight-lipped while the paramedics worked. "It looks like she put up a hell of a fight."

"She's stable, but she needs stitches," the lead paramedic said. "We're taking her to the ER."

"I need to ask her a few questions first, if she can talk."

"I'm all right," Gladys said.

"Can you describe your attackers?"

"They were wearing ski masks. One was a big guy. The other was smaller, wiry with snake tattoos on both arms. The big one had a gun. He hit me. I don't remember anything else until Alex got here. I said I'd protect Carmela. This is my fault."

Alex took Gladys's hand. "You did everything you could. It's our fault for leaving you alone with her."

White motioned to the paramedics to move Gladys and turned to the officer with her. "Go with her to the hospital and get a statement."

"I'm going too," Alex said.

"Not yet. I have more questions for you," White said. "You can catch up with her later. What happened when you got here?"

"It's okay, Alex. You stay," Gladys said as the paramedics strapped her to the stretcher.

Alex watched the paramedics maneuver the stretcher through the door and down the stairs.

"A van almost ran me down coming out of the parking lot, about a half hour ago. Two men were in the front, but I couldn't make out what they looked like. Do you think Carmela was in there?"

"Did you get the license?"

"I didn't. I couldn't see much because the street light was out, but it was dark blue I think, with paneled sides, no lettering. It was the kind of van they tell young girls to stay away from. Mike saw it too."

"I didn't get the license either," Mike called out from the bedroom.

White pulled out her cell and called it in. Alex heard her say to someone at the station, "The fire was a diversion and I fell for it."

White hung up, her expression thunderous and went into the bedroom. Alex followed.

"What the hell do you think you're doing in here? This is a crime scene," White said.

Mike held up a black bandana. "I found this. Looks like the kind of bandana those bikers in Rag Town were wearing."

"You're contaminating evidence."

"Aren't you at least glad to know where the bandana came from?"

CHAPTER ELEVEN

It was late afternoon when Vargas arrived in Dalton. He stood in the doorway of El Caballero's well-appointed office, Cuchillo behind him. He glared at El Caballero. The man did not look happy to see him and that at least was satisfying.

"*Señor* Vargas, this is a surprise. There was no need for you to come all this way. I have everything under control."

Vargas ignored the *gringo*'s outstretched hand and surveyed the plush red Oriental carpet on the polished wood floor, the mahogany desk, and the credenza. A gilt-framed oil painting of a three-masted schooner adorned the wall. He looked at Cuchillo. "El Caballero is doing very well, is he not?"

El Caballero rubbed his temples. "We're making progress. My people will have the cleaning lady by the end of the day."

Vargas brushed a tiny piece of lint from his slacks. "I hear that there's another *puta* missing, and I had to find that out on my own. What else are you not telling me?"

"I was going to tell you the next time we talked. It's not important. We'll get her too."

The desk phone rang. El Caballero reached for it, listened. "Good. Where are you?" He frowned. "You can't keep her at your house. Take her to the farm."

Vargas watched El Caballero with narrowed eyes.

"I told you this would work out. I've got Billy Williams here. He has Carmela Flores."

"I want to talk to him."

El Caballero switched on the speaker phone. "Tell *Señor* Vargas all about it, Billy."

Billy's drawl filled the room. "The two of 'em was in this apartment, the Flores *puta* and that fat broad I followed last night from the clinic. Marvin and me had to bash the fat one up aside a' the head to shut her up, but we got the Flores woman."

Vargas frowned and pushed his face close to the phone. His words came out in a hiss. "Another *puta* got away. Do you have her too?"

The phone was silent. "No, sir. Not yet, sir," Billy said.

El Caballero raised his voice. "*Señor* Vargas just arrived from Mexico, Billy. What is Carmela telling you about the other girl?"

"She ain't said nothin' 'bout nothing. Just hollers every time we try to talk to her."

"Tell her we'll give her more money if she gives up the girl," El Caballero said.

"Tell her we'll kill her if she doesn't," Vargas said.

A sharp report sounded in the background.

"What in God's name was that?" El Caballero said.

They could hear men yelling, a woman screaming, the sounds of a scuffle, another scream.

"Billy?"

Billy came back on the line, breathing hard. "Damn bitch pulled Marvin's gun right out of his belt, and the gun went off. I got the gun off her, and Shirley's sitting on her, tying her up good. Got to go."

El Caballero's hand shook as he replaced the receiver. "The good news is that we have Carmela Flores. Billy and Marvin are the two best men I have. They'll take her to a place in the country I know about and get her to tell us how to find the other woman. We have everything under control."

Vargas's left eye twitched. "Nothing is under control."

He stormed out of the office, ignoring El Caballero's protests. Cuchillo followed. Once he was seated in the rented Mercedes, he dialed his cell, tapping his foot while it rang.

"Everything's fucked up here," he said when Diego answered. "What's going on with Lucky Dan?"

CHAPTER TWELVE

It was past midnight when Alex pulled into the lot in front of her condo. Mike parked his Mustang beside her. A party was in full swing at the neighbors' apartment next door. Music from an electric guitar vibrated through an open window, along with sporadic howls and whoops. She got out and waved goodbye.

Mike got out of his car. "I'm coming with you. I want to make sure you're safe."

"You're as tired as I am. Go home."

He stood firm, arms crossed, looking at her with that crooked grin. "My mom raised me better than that. I'm seeing you to the door."

She smiled in spite of herself and pulled open the lobby door. This day would not end. Her body ached. She longed for a hot bath and a quiet night's sleep. She thought yesterday was bad. Today had been worse. She knew Mike was trying to be nice. A little pushy, but she supposed that was part of being a reporter. She just wanted to go to bed.

She reached the landing. "This is far enough. Good night."

He was still behind her.

Really, he could be irritating. He seemed to think she was going to invite him in, and that wasn't going to happen.

"I'm fine. Please go home."

She turned toward her door, key in hand, and stopped dead. The door was ajar. A ribbon of light fell across the landing.

"Did you lock the door when you left?" Mike asked.

"I'm sure I did, and I turned off the lights."

"There's no sign of a break-in. Who else has a key to your apartment?"

"My parents, but they're home in bed."

"Wait," Mike said. "I'll call Keisha."

She held up her hand for him to be quiet and looked through the crack. Her eyes adjusted to the light. Papers were spread all over the floor. The television was on. A roar erupted as Jeter scored a home run. Travis Bingham was slouched in her favorite chair, drinking a beer.

She pushed the door open. "Travis, what the hell are you doing in my apartment?"

Travis looked up, shirt collar unbuttoned. The offending bow tie hung loose around his neck. "Hello, Alex. It's about time you got home."

"How did you get in my apartment?"

"Let myself in. Remember I have a key from when I helped you move last year. Where've you been? I cleaned out the fridge waiting for you."

"That's none of your business. How dare you come in here? Get out."

Travis leaned back in the chair, grinning. "Aw, Alex. Be nice."

A sudden throbbing pain seized the left side of her head. "I want my key back now."

Mike stepped in front of her. "The lady asked you to leave."

Travis raised his bottle in salute and hiccupped, then he looked at Mike and his eyes narrowed.

"I know you. You're a reporter. I've seen you around the courthouse." He looked back at Alex. "This guy's bad news. He's the one writing about your center. He'll be writing about you next."

The two men glared at each other over Alex's head.

"I don't need advice from you, Travis. Get your things and leave."

"Your problem, Alex dear, is that you don't know who your friends are. I'm only here to help."

"Out."

"I'm also here because your mother asked me to look in on you."

"You lie."

"After you ran out of the club tonight we talked for a long time. She's worried about you, and after Mexico City, you can't blame her."

"Travis, what do I have to do to get you out of here?"

Travis stood up, swaying on his feet, and braced himself on the arm of the chair.

She walked to the door and held it open.

"Alex, you never used to be like this. You've changed since all that happened to you." Travis gathered his papers and stuffed them into a red accordion file folder in no hurry to leave.

Mike moved forward. "Speed it up, buddy."

Travis took a swing at Mike and missed.

"Travis, damn it. The police are coming," Alex said.

Travis stumbled, caught the arm of the couch, and looked from Alex to Mike and back. "Okay, I'm going. But you know how to find me, sweet cakes."

Travis was gone before she realized that he still had the key. This was what her mother wanted her to marry?

"What a dumbass," Mike said.

"He is, but I let him get to me. All my life my parents and his have been pushing us together. They even went in together and hired a limo to take us to the senior prom before I said I'd go with him. I went to a movie with a friend instead. They were mad at me for weeks."

In the distance a siren wailed. Mike's cell rang.

"Hey, Keisha. Call 'em off. Some friend of Alex's got into her apartment. He's gone now."

"Is she upset?" she asked when Mike hung up.

"Let's just say I couldn't put her response in a family newspaper. Detective White is not in a good mood tonight."

"Thanks for your help with Travis, but I really wish you'd go now. I'm dead on my feet."

"I think I should stay. Bingham could come back. Besides, I'm starving."

She followed him into the kitchen. "Really, I can handle Travis. Please go home."

Mike opened the refrigerator and looked in. "You got anything good in here?"

She rubbed her stiff neck. "There's nothing left but Diet Coke and spring water. I haven't had time to go shopping."

He opened a bottle of water for himself and another for her.

"No food?" He poked his head into a cabinet, emerging with a PowerBar, ripped off the wrapping and bit down, chewing slowly.

"Damn. Tastes like a cross between peanut butter and straw. How can you eat these things?"

She sighed and went back to the living room, collapsing on the couch. "Finish that, and then go home."

Mike was still chewing when he came out of the kitchen. He pulled the easy chair next to the couch. "What do you make of all this?"

"I don't know. A lot of stuff doesn't make sense. What do those men want with Carmela?"

Mike lowered himself into the chair and propped his long legs on the ottoman. "She must know something, or she did something to make someone mad. Late last night, after most of the equipment was gone from the fire and the neighbors left, I went back to *Mi Tienda*. The old lady came out to talk to me."

He stopped to finish his water. "I wanted to ask about a girl she talked about that morning, someone who came to her market with Mariana. She said the two looked alike, one a little older and protective. She guessed that they were sisters. She thinks Elena knows where the younger woman is because soon after Elena and Victor got to her house last night, Elena took Victor and went back out. The old woman saw them take food from the market. They came back an hour later without the food. Carmela's cousin must know where the other girl is."

Alex felt herself go cold. "This really is about human trafficking, isn't it?"

"If it's human trafficking, this may be the biggest thing to happen in Dalton in years. The FBI will be all over it. My gut tells me this is my big break."

Alex thought of Cristina. Tears filled her eyes, and she shrank back into the couch pillows.

Mike didn't notice. "A few years back nobody wanted to hear about human trafficking. Now you see it everywhere you look: television shows, news articles, posters in airports. It's big business, growing all the time. Some say it's a thirty to forty billion dollar industry."

Alex reached for a tissue from a box beside the lamp. "If there's a woman out there hiding from human traffickers, we have to help her."

Mike looked at her. "You okay?"

"Yeah, this all brings back a bad time for me. If Victor went somewhere with his mother, he might know where the girl is."

"Why didn't I think of that? I'll go back to Rag Town tomorrow."

"Will you call me as soon as you find him? I'll be at the center, cleaning up."

She stood and yawned.

"Okay, I'm gone." He smiled. "Unless, of course, you want me to spend the night. Make sure Travis doesn't come back?"

"No thanks. I'll put the chain on the door."

She saw him out, then shut and locked the door. The living room was a mess. A file folder lay on the floor where Travis had left it. She set it on top of the armoire and went to bed.

Mike was almost to his car when Travis Bingham climbed out of a BMW coupe and stood in his way.

"Alex told you to get lost," Mike said.

"You're not from around here. The Harringtons are powerful people, and they're not going to have a piece of shit like you hanging around their daughter."

"I'll give you five seconds."

Bingham tried to hit him.

Mike placed both hands on the man's chest and shoved, sending him stumbling backward against the car. "You're right, I'm not from here. Where I come from folks don't start a fight when they're out-classed. You're out of your league, buddy."

Bingham righted himself and lunged.

Mike threw an upper-cut, connecting with Travis's jaw. Bingham went down.

Mike walked away toward his car.

"Stay away from Alex, you hear?" Travis yelled, struggling to sit.

"As long as there's a story, I'm not going anywhere," Mike said.

A siren sounded. An unmarked police car pulled into the lot, and Officer Craven got out. "What's happening, gentlemen? Ain't you boys out a li'l late? Prob'ly need to be movin' along home."

"Good evening, Officer Craven," Bingham said. "Mr. Murray and I were just having a little conversation."

"Oh it's you, Mr. Bingham. Sure there's no problem?"

Travis pulled off his tie and stuffed it in his pocket. "None at all. Mr. Murray and I are just leaving."

Craven squinted at Mike. "Murray? That you again?"

"Yeah, it's me. You know us reporters. Always around. Bad hours, bad company, and if we're lucky, bad coffee. Just like cops."

Mike climbed into the Mustang and drove out of the lot onto the street. He looked back at Officer Craven in the rearview mirror. Convenient the way that Craven had just happened to show up.

He glanced at Alex's apartment window. Bingham was right about one thing. The Harringtons wouldn't be happy to know that their beautiful daughter was hanging out with a kid from the wrong side of the tracks. Screw 'em. He hoped he was going to get to know Alexandra Harrington a whole lot better.

CHAPTER THIRTEEN

Vargas checked his watch. Lucky Dan was running in the Texas Classic Futurity in Grand Prairie in less than an hour, and he should be in the owner's box surrounded by beautiful women, not stuck here. If he had lieutenants in the U.S. that he could trust, he would be at the race. He threw the *Dalton Herald* onto his hotel room floor, slammed his hand on the table, and turned to El Caballero. "There is a story about the dead woman in the paper. This reporter won't stop."

"He's just a young buck, trying to make a name for himself. Thinks he's a hotshot investigative reporter. Don't worry about him," El Caballero said.

"In Mexico reporters are afraid for their lives. Those who won't back off when we tell them, feed the buzzards."

"I'll deal with it. A word from me to his editor and the story will go away."

Cuchillo's dark eyes moved from Vargas to El Caballero. "You want I teach the reporter a lesson?"

CHAPTER FOURTEEN

Mike eased the Mustang onto the dirt beneath the old oak in Rag Town for the third time in less than twenty-four hours. No sound broke the Sunday morning hush. The CLOSED sign still hung on *Mi Tienda*'s door, and shades covered the windows of the upstairs apartment. Next door at the unpainted house nothing stirred. The acrid smell of charred wood hung in the humid air. Damn it was hot, had to be close to a hundred already.

Alex was probably sleeping, something he wasn't doing much of lately. If he didn't hit it big with this story soon, his editor would have him back covering traffic accidents and school board meetings. Roush wasn't happy with him as it was, reminding him that he'd lost his job in Arizona for not doing what he was told. "Being a great writer will only get you so far," the editor had warned.

To hell with Roush. Somewhere out there a girl was hiding, and who knew what was happening to Carmela Flores, assuming she was still alive. This was his story, and he wasn't giving it up even if he had to find another job.

Yellow crime scene tape hung across the front of the burned-out building. When he got closer, a movement inside caught his eye. Someone or something was in there. He walked closer and peered in. Smoke curled from the charred wood. He choked on the acrid air.

"Who's there?"

He heard a crunch and saw a figure dart across the dark space. Someone short. A kid maybe.

Blackened beams creaked above, shifting. The sharp crack of breaking wood was followed by a thunderous crash. Dust poured out. He heard a cry, muted at first, then louder. He broke through the crime scene tape and stumbled across fallen boards and broken glass toward the sound. A boy was pinned on his back beneath a fallen beam, moaning. It was Victor. Mike lifted one end of the beam, bracing it against his shoulder, and reached out to the boy with his free arm.

"Hey Victor, you all right? Can you move?"

Victor looked at him through glassy eyes and whimpered.

"Crawl toward me. Take it slow."

Victor hoisted himself up on his hands and feet and began to drag himself forward, his face contorted in pain. It took several minutes before he was clear of the beam.

Mike lowered the beam and gave the boy a hand, helping him to his feet. He put one arm around the boy's waist. "One step at a time. Easy does it."

They stumbled over pieces of charred wall frame and tiles from collapsed sections of the roof, reaching the sidewalk just as the beam broke loose and thundered to the ground, carrying what remained of the ceiling. A cloud of ash poured from the site, covering them from head to foot.

Mike wiped sooty sweat from his eyes and picked bits of plaster from Victor's hair. "What were you doing, climbing around a burned-out building?"

Victor's shoulders sagged. Tears rolled down his cheeks. He ran a sleeve across his face, smearing ash and tears.

"Promise you won't do anything that dumb again?"

Victor nodded and held up a broken picture frame. Two little girls smiled from behind shattered glass.

"What've you got there?"

Victor rubbed his shoulder where the beam hit him. "A picture of my mama and *Tía* Carmela when they were little. Maybe that will make my mama feel better."

"You're hurt. Let's get you home so your mama can clean you up and get a doctor to look at your shoulder."

"No. I'm okay. Please, mister. I don't want to go home." The boy swallowed hard. He pulled himself up to his full four-and-a-half feet and crossed his arms.

Mike looked at him for a minute and then nodded.

"You hungry? I passed a Pancake House about a block from here. How about breakfast? I haven't eaten anything in hours, and I bet you're hungry too."

Victor's face lit up. Mike led the way to the Mustang.

"This is a cool car. Where'd you get it?"

"How old are you?"

"Nine. Almost ten."

"This car's older than you are. I bought it in Arizona where I grew up, from a drug dealer who was going to prison. I'm sorry about your house. How's your mama doing?"

"Not too good. The cops came last night. They talked for a long time about *Tía* Carmela. They think my mama knows something, but Mama says no."

He let Victor pick a booth near the video game machines and waited while the boy decided between blueberry and apple pancakes. He ordered a plain waffle.

Victor's small eyes brightened, and he pointed to the video games. "Can I play with those?"

Mike nodded and fished some change from his pocket.

When the waitress set an impressive stack of pancakes on the table, Victor wriggled back into his seat and poured syrup over the pancakes.

"Your mother left *Mi Tienda* after the fire. Where did she go?"

Victor looked up, frowning. "How do you know that?"

"The old woman from the market told me. She's worried about you."

The boy stuffed a large spoonful of pancake into his mouth and chewed. "My mama wouldn't like me talking to you."

"I'm only trying to help. You might feel better if you tell me about it."

The boy looked at the video game, then at the pancakes, and

shrugged. "Everything is bad. *Tía* Carmela is gone. We don't have no place to live. My mama goes out and don't say nothing. She takes food and stuff to some girl and comes back all upset."

"Tell me about this girl. Who is she?"

"Somebody *Tía* Carmela was helping. Mama took me with her last night when we got the hamburgers, before our apartment burned down." He rubbed a dirty fist across his eyes.

"You saw the girl? What does she look like?"

"She's older than me. And real pretty. She comes from Mexico, like us."

"Can you take me to the place where you saw her?"

"It's near where *Tía* Carmela works. I'll take you there if you promise not to tell my mama."

"Okay. Finish up. You can show me where you saw the girl."

"Deal."

Mike sipped his coffee and checked his phone messages while Victor devoured the stack of pancakes. When the boy was nearing bottom, he made a call.

Alex answered on the fourth ring.

"Good morning. Did you get some sleep?"

"Oh, hello." She lowered her voice. "I'm at the center with Gladys. The doctors discharged her from the hospital this morning, but she won't rest. She insists on cleaning up. Where are you?"

"I'm on my way to the center with Victor. I have an idea where the girl is hiding. Be there soon."

He hung up before she could argue, and hustled Victor out of the Pancake House and into the car.

"We're going to the place where your Aunt Carmela works. My friend Alex is there. Maybe you can tell me where you went to with your mama."

————

Alex took one look at Victor when Mike walked into the center with the boy and jumped up from her chair.

Gladys stopped mopping. "You're both a mess. Where's Victor's mama? She'll have a heart attack when she sees him."

Gladys took Victor's arm and led him, howling, toward the bathroom.

Mike looked after them. "Gladys looks better than she did last night, though I can't say her disposition's improved any."

"Where did you find Victor?"

"Kid was digging around the burned-out apartment building and almost got himself killed doing it. A few video games and some pancakes fixed him right up though. He told me that Carmela hid a girl someplace around here. Hopefully, he can show us where."

"Why would Carmela do that? Why not bring her here along with Mariana?"

"She must have been afraid of someone."

"Mike says that Carmela was helping another girl besides Mariana, and that Victor knows where she's hiding," Alex said when Gladys marched back into the room, leading a still-protesting but much cleaner Victor.

Victor let out a yelp. "You promised not to tell."

Mike put his hand on the boy's neck. "We have to tell Alex and Carmela about the girl so we can help her. We've got to find her before someone else does. Show us where you took the food."

"We'd better call *Señora* Casas first and tell her that you're here," Gladys said.

Victor looked at her in horror. "No. Don't call my mama. Please. She's gonna be mad at me. She told me not to tell nobody about the girl."

Alex smiled and knelt down beside him. "We'll talk to your mama so she won't be mad at you. What kind of place was it that you took the food? Was it a big building, a church maybe, or a house like this one?"

Victor shook his head. "It was a little house with lots of bushes that smelled sweet."

"Sweet like flowers? The goldenrod is in bloom all over the neighborhood," Gladys said. "Can you describe the house?"

"It's white with a little door. It has a horse on top."

"That's got to be the carriage house. The horse is the weather vane on top. Carmela stores her cleaning equipment there. It's out back," Alex said, and ran into the garden.

Mike led Victor by his good arm. Gladys limped behind.

In the garden the boy stopped. "That's it," he whispered. "That's where we took the food."

"Do you know the girl's name?" Alex asked.

"Mama called her Teresa."

Mike opened the carriage house door and looked into the musky interior. Crickets screeched at them from the bushes. There was no other sound. He stepped inside. The smell of mold and decay was overpowering. When his eyes adjusted to the dark, he could make out a vacuum cleaner and several mops, a chair, and a small cot. In the back, a slight girl was crouched on the floor.

Alex was behind him. He stepped aside for her. "She may be less afraid of you."

Alex nodded and called out from the doorway in Spanish, "Teresa? We're Carmela's friends. We're here to help you. Victor is here too, Carmela's nephew."

Teresa backed further into the corner and sat down on the floor, curling into a fetal position and covering her face with her hands.

"The poor girl's clearly terrified. We've got to coax her into the center," Alex said.

"Where's Victor?" Gladys said, looking around.

CHAPTER FIFTEEN

Alex stepped over the cleaning equipment, careful not to make any movements that might frighten Teresa even more. There would be hell to pay when the police found this woman was hiding in a building belonging to the center, especially if the girl was a human trafficking victim.

She crept closer. "Teresa? My name is Alex."

Teresa couldn't be much older than eighteen, if that. Alex thought of the women in the warehouse, remembering their terror, so like this poor woman's.

"Teresa, please come out. We want to help you."

The girl shrank back against the wall, shoulders shaking. "*Quiero a mi mamá.*"

When at last Teresa agreed to come out of the carriage house, Alex led her into the clinic and helped her to the couch in the reception area.

Gladys brought her a glass of water. "The poor girl's little more than a teenager and scared to death. I called Elena Casas. Maybe she can help. We need to call the police too. The girl may be in danger."

"I'm not sure that's a great idea," Mike said. "Think about it. Who else besides the cops knew where Carmela was last night?"

"I trust Detective White," Alex said. "She blamed herself when Carmela disappeared. I don't think she had anything to do with it."

"Okay, go ahead and call Keisha. I'm going back to the garden to look for Victor," Mike said.

Alex was tucking a blanket around the trembling girl when the front door flew open, and Elena and the old woman from *Mi Tienda* came in. They stopped when they saw Teresa on the couch.

"*Dios mío.* If they find her, they will kill her like they did her sister," Elena said.

Teresa shrank back into the couch, tears streaming down her cheeks.

"She knows about Mariana?" Alex asked.

"When we brought her food and clean clothes last night, I told her that her sister is with the angels," Elena said.

"No wonder she's terrified," Gladys said.

Teresa began to sob.

The old woman settled herself beside the girl and patted her back. "Do you remember me, Teresa? You came into *Mi Tienda* with your sister."

Alex's throat tightened. The men who took Carmela must be trying to find this girl. Nothing else made sense. Once they knew where Teresa was, they wouldn't need Carmela anymore. She fingered the white streak in her hair. They had to find Carmela, and fast.

The old woman spoke to Teresa in Spanish in a low voice for several minutes.

Elena shook her head. "Her sadness is too much. Maybe she will talk to us later."

Alex nodded. "We need to talk." She took Elena by the arm and led her into her office. Gladys followed, leaving Teresa with the old woman.

"You do have to tell us everything you know now. Your cousin's life depends on it."

Elena paced back and forth, wringing her hands. "My cousin made me promise never to tell."

"Do you want to see Carmela again?" Gladys asked.

Elena's shoulders sagged. "Some bad men kept women, many from our country, in a house near here. They paid Carmela to bring the women to the center when they got sick."

Alex tried to stay calm. "Your cousin took money from those people? They paid her to bring their victims here? We patched them up and sent them right back to hell. We could have saved them from the traffickers. Carmela betrayed us."

"Put yourself in Carmela's place, Alex. She was terrified and probably afraid we would go to the police," Gladys said.

"She would have been right too."

Elena nodded. "Carmela thought they would hurt her if she didn't do what they said. She told herself she was taking care of the women. Then she met Teresa and Mariana. They came from a town in Mexico near where our family lives. She wanted to help them. On Friday Teresa came to Carmela. Mariana needed a doctor. You know the rest."

"We have to call the police now," Gladys said.

"No, no. The police will arrest my cousin."

"Would you rather she was dead?"

Elena started to cry.

CHAPTER SIXTEEN

While she waited for Keisha White to answer, Alex watched Mike through the window, moving around the garden, searching for Victor. The phone went to voicemail. Alex left a message. "We have Mariana's sister here at the center. Please come as soon as possible."

The French doors opened, and Mike came through, holding a wriggling Victor by the neck.

Elena's face reddened. "You bad boy. Where have you been?"

"*Señora* Casas, your son is a brave boy. I asked him to help us to find Teresa so that we could help her. I promised him he wouldn't get into trouble. Please don't blame him," Alex said.

"Tell them what you saw, Victor," Mike said.

Victor looked from Mike to his mother. "There's a van parked in the driveway of a big, white house back of here. I saw a woman with yellow hair and two men take women out of the house and into the van."

"What color was the van?" Alex asked.

"Dark blue," Victor said.

"What if it's the same one I saw leaving Gladys's parking lot?"

"It all ties together. Teresa and her sister probably came from that house," Mike said. "We got to get over there."

"Alex called the police. We have to wait for them," Gladys said.

"Gladys is right. We can't go in on our own. What if they're keeping Carmela there? We need the police. I'll call Detective White again."

"I'm going over," Mike said. "You wait here and bring Keisha."

———

"Thank God, you're here," Alex said when Keisha White came into the center's front hall twenty minutes later. "What's this about? I was clear across town when I got your first message about finding a sister, then another one about someone getting away."

In a few words Alex told Keisha everything that had happened since the fire, ending with the discovery of Teresa in the carriage house.

"Victor found the house where we think Mariana and her sister came from. The people were packing up, taking other women with them. Mike's over there now."

Keisha looked at Teresa who was still huddled on the sofa next to the old woman from *Mi Tienda*. "Is that the sister? She should be able to tell us about the house."

"She's too afraid to talk."

"We need a warrant. And back-up," Keisha said, and pulled out her phone.

Alex ripped off a piece of paper from a notepad and handed it to Keisha. "I looked up the address of the white house."

Keisha spoke into her cell. "Yes, I know it's Sunday. Try the golf courses if you have to, and send someone here to stay with the sister." She hung up.

"An officer's on the way to take care of the sister. She may be a witness to Mariana's murder and heaven knows what else. Someone has to stay with her until then."

"Gladys can do that. Follow me," Alex said. "Let's hope we're not too late."

Within minutes they reached a large, white Victorian house whose wraparound porch, steeply pitched roof, carved trim-work, and porte-cochère spoke of better days. The driveway was empty. Keisha looked at the address and called it in. Mike stepped out of the bushes at the side of the house. "They're gone. The van was leaving just as I got here. I got the license number this time."

"Was Carmela with them?" Alex asked.

"I didn't see her."

Two police cars turned into the drive and stopped in front of the house. A baby-faced officer climbed out of the first car, followed by another who looked almost as young. Officer Craven joined them from the second car.

"We're not waiting for the warrant. Front door's open. We're going in. I'll get the first floor and the basement. You're with me," she said to one of the young officers. "You two take the upstairs. Craven, you case the neighborhood. Find out what the neighbors know about this place."

White turned to Alex and Mike. "Wait here."

"Aw, Keisha. You wouldn't even know about the house or the girl without us. You need us. I promise not to publish anything without your approval."

White glared at him. "You have a hell of a nerve, Murray. I'm ordering you. Stay out."

Mike squeezed Alex's arm and put a finger to his lips. The officers disappeared into the house and Craven walked toward the street.

"I'm going in," Mike said.

"Not without me."

Alex followed Mike up the sagging steps and through the once grand oak doorway into the front hall. Voices came from what she guessed had once been a parlor.

They tiptoed to the end of the hall and peeked in. The officers were too focused on their search to notice. A chair lay on its side. Newspapers and magazines covered the floor. In the kitchen beyond, piles of dirty dishes filled a chipped enamel sink and covered a yellow Formica counter. Trash spilled out of a metal trashcan that stank of coagulating Chinese food cartons and moldy pizza crusts.

"This place is God-awful," White said.

Mike pulled Alex back into the hall just as White turned in their direction. The detective studied the hall for a second, shrugged, and moved through the archway on into the dining room. Alex crept back into the room, followed by Mike, and peered after White. Red flocked paper covered the walls and a threadbare Oriental carpet lay on the floor. Glass beads divided the dining room from a living room beyond.

"Looks like Hollywood's idea of a Victorian whorehouse," the officer with Keisha said.

White grunted and walked ahead to the stairs to join the two officers above. The other officer followed.

Alex and Mike could hear White and the officers moving through the upstairs bedrooms. They snuck up the stairs and peered into what must have been a master bedroom. Discarded underwear, a beaded necklace, makeup bottles and lipstick tubes, and an empty box of condoms were strewn around the room. The rooms smelled of cheap perfume, sweat and moth balls.

They could hear White and the officers searching the other bedrooms.

"Can you believe this place," one of the officers said. "There are bare mattresses in every room and a load of moth-eaten army surplus blankets."

"In the bathroom," another officer called. "I got prescription bottles filled with antibiotics and morning-after pills. If they kept illegal drugs here, I'm not finding them."

"Probably took the illegal stuff with them," White said.

Someone shouted from the front hall. "Hello. Forensics."

"Up here," White yelled and turned to the officers. "Let's let the crime scene techs work up here first while we look around the basement."

Alex and Mike waited in the shadows until the technicians had reached the far bedrooms, then crept down the stairs and out onto the porch.

Alex inhaled the sweet, late-afternoon air. "God, it's good to be out of there. Those poor women."

"We've got to be looking at human trafficking. A Mexican reporter I know tells me there's a network that goes from Mexico across the U.S. These guys move women and children through fast. This house probably doubles as a whorehouse and a transfer site," Mike said.

"Why didn't anyone see what was happening and do something?"

"Because no one wanted to see, most likely."

White came out onto the porch with the officers. "Looks like the girls lived upstairs. There are a couple of decent enough bedrooms downstairs for entertaining johns. The rest of the place, where they kept the women, is a pit. First pass I didn't see that they left anything useful behind. Let's hope the techs find more."

"Funny. The front of this place isn't so bad. Green trees, mowed lawn, even some flowers. From the street you'd never guess what this is," the baby-faced officer said.

Craven rounded the corner of the house and climbed onto the porch. "I talked to folks on both sides. They said people came and went, just kept to themselves, quiet-like."

"You'd think there'd be a lot of traffic in and out of a place like this," White said.

"The neighbors didn't want to get involved," Craven said.

"What about the businesses in the neighborhood?"

"The guy at the convenience store on the corner said girls came in every week, rarely the same ones twice, mostly Hispanic but some Asian. He saw cars drive up to this house, nice cars sometimes. Never asked questions, said it was none of his business."

"Did you get descriptions?"

"A blonde woman, some men who came in and out, nothing specific."

White punched a number into her cell.

"Find out everything you can about this house. Who owns it? If it's a rental, what name is on the lease? Get someone to open up the files today. I don't care if it's the weekend." She clicked off the phone. "Let's see how good the guys in the precinct are. I'm going back to the center to see what I can find out from the sister."

———

Alex and Mike were waiting when White arrived back at the Center with the other officers.

"Where's the girl?" White said.

Alex nodded toward the waiting room. "She's on a couch in there, but I doubt you'll learn much. She won't even talk to Carmela's cousin. She told us her name, and that was it."

"Does she speak English?"

"Not much, but we can translate if you can get her to talk."

White crossed the lobby into the reception area and knelt down beside Teresa. "We want to help you, but you have to help us too."

Teresa covered her face.

"She's afraid of the bad people who killed her sister," Elena said.

White put her hand on Teresa's shoulder. "We're going to take you to a safe place where no one will hurt you."

The girl shrank back into the couch, shivering, her eyes welling with tears.

"She's terrified. After her sister's death, it's no wonder," Alex said.

"She'll have to come with us."

"No. No. She can stay with me," the old woman from *Mi Tienda* said. "She should not go to jail. She's done nothing wrong."

"We're not arresting her. She's a material witness to a murder. She can identify the people who brought her here from Mexico and those who killed her sister. She needs our protection. You can't take care of her."

"You said my cousin would be safe," Elena said. "You said you would protect her. Why should we believe you?"

"We're this girl's only chance. These people don't leave witnesses. You can help by keeping quiet."

White glared at Mike. "That means you too, big guy. One word of this on the paper's blog or in print and you get nothing from us ever again, understand?"

"Got it, but you know it's gonna get out eventually."

Keisha turned to the officers. "Take her to the safe house and stay there with her."

Teresa sobbed uncontrollably as the officers led her to the squad car. Craven left with them.

Elena wrung her hands as she watched Teresa leave. "What will happen to her? Bad people are looking for her. They want to kill her."

White started to answer when her phone rang. She answered and listened. Her eyes traveled to Alex. "You sure about that?"

She hung up. "Have any of you heard of the JoVille Group?"

Alex frowned. "It's a real estate company with a lot of property in Dalton and other places around the country. Why?"

"The JoVille Group owns the white house. The name of the general partner listed on the deed is Alexander Harrington."

"That's my father. Are you saying my father owns the brothel?"

CHAPTER SEVENTEEN

Alex stood still, her stomach twisting in knots. The room was overly bright. Sounds ran together. People seemed to move in slow motion around her. There had to be a simple explanation. Her father couldn't have anything to do with human trafficking.

Señora Casas and the old woman from the market corralled Victor and gathered their things. They pushed the boy ahead of them toward the door.

Mike Murray opened his mouth to speak, saw Alex's stricken expression, and turned toward the door. "See you, Alex."

She nodded and looked away.

Gladys gave her hand a squeeze and followed Elena.

Keisha White was the last to leave. She seemed about to ask a question.

"Can we talk later, detective?"

White nodded and left.

Alex was alone. She took a deep breath, trying to slow her racing thoughts. Her father had always been there for her, fixing her favorite doll when Travis cracked its head open with a hammer, helping with her math homework, and cheering for her at track meets. He'd even taken her side against her mother when she refused to be friends with the daughter of a socially prominent family because the girl had called their new Hispanic maid stupid for speaking poor English.

Heart pounding, she dialed her parents' number. Her mother answered.

"I can't talk now. The fundraiser's tomorrow night. I need you here by three to help set up. Your father will be home. You can talk to him then."

She felt herself flush. With all that had happened since Friday night, a fundraiser for the incumbent governor was the last thing she wanted to think about.

"Damn it, Mother. This involves my center. Does Daddy own the white house behind us?"

"I have no idea, and do not use profanity with me, young lady. We will discuss this later."

Alex began to say that she wasn't going to the fundraiser, but stopped. She did want to talk to her father face-to-face. "Okay, I'll come," she said and hung up without saying goodbye.

———

Much as she hated to turn patients away, Alex canceled the Monday clinic. She and Gladys worked hard, giving the center a thorough cleaning. They were both exhausted when the hall clock struck four.

"Shouldn't you be heading for the fundraiser?" Gladys asked.

"I forgot all about that. You can tell how much I don't want to go."

She dashed home, pulled a sleeveless linen dress from her closet and put it on, washed the dirt from her hands and ran a comb through her hair. Once back in the car she hit the gas and drove toward the country club section of town. She didn't see the cruiser, sitting behind a stand of pines until its lights swirled and the siren croaked. She pulled over and waited.

"What's the hurry, miss?" the young, uniformed officer said when he reached her car. "I clocked you at forty-five in a twenty-five zone."

She forced herself to smile. "I had no idea I was going that fast, officer. I am so sorry."

The officer looked at her license and registration, and then looked up, meeting her eyes. "You know you could crack up your car and get really hurt, driving like that."

She tried to look contrite. "Yes, sir."

The officer considered her for a minute. The corner of his mouth twitched. "I'm going to give you a warning this time if you promise to slow down."

Her smile broadened. She glanced at his name badge. "I'll do that, Officer Dunham. Thank you."

She could see him watching as she pulled away from the curb. The last thing she needed was another speeding ticket. That would be three this year.

She slowed when she reached her parents' house. Sleek, top-of-the-line cars filled the circular drive. She parked where the attendant indicated and sat, looking around. Guests climbed out of BMWs and Lexuses, all faces she recognized from the club, greeting each other with squeals of delight as if they hadn't met in years.

Brightly lit lanterns festooned the old oaks and magnolias in the front yard. Music came through the open front door of the house. She could see her mother standing on the front step.

She took a quick look in the visor mirror, tucked her hair behind her ears, and climbed out of the car.

She was halfway to the front door when a squad car pulled alongside and stopped, blocking the driveway. Keisha White and Craven got out.

Alex sprinted for the front door to warn her mother.

"Where have you been? We expected you hours ago. Look at you. You need more makeup."

"Mother, the police are here. I think they want to talk to Daddy about the white house."

"Now? That's outrageous. The governor will be here any minute."

Keisha White came up the steps behind Alex. "Mrs. Harrington? I'm Detective White, and this is Officer Craven. We would like a word with Mr. Harrington."

Renee Harrington's eyes darkened, her eyebrows folded into a deep crease, and she stood in front of the door, blocking the way. "I won't allow it."

Alex's father appeared in the doorway. "Renee, dear, whatever this is, I'll deal with it. You carry on here."

He turned to the officers. "Please follow me."

White walked into the house with Craven following, past a table in the front hall filled with plastic name badges.

Alex looked at her mother's horrified expression. "I'll go with them."

In the front hall a young woman stepped in front of her. "Miss, do we have your name on the list?"

"I live here, or at least I used to," Alex shot back as she pushed past the woman. By the time she reached the library, her father was holding Keisha White's card and offering seats.

"I'll stand, thank you," White said and glared at Craven who was about to sit down. "Do you own a house at 800 York Street in Tryon Park, Mr. Harrington?"

"York Street? I really don't know without checking. That's near my daughter's center, isn't it? What's this about?"

Alex stepped forward. "We found a girl, Daddy, Mariana's sister. She was hiding in our carriage house. She and Mariana may have come from the house on York."

"You're listed as the principal owner of record for the house. Do you still say you know nothing about it?" White said.

From somewhere in the house a band struck up "The Old North State."

Scott Foley appeared at the library doorway. "The governor's car is coming up the drive. Renee needs you at the front door, Sandy. I'll take over here."

Sandy Harrington handed White's card to Foley. "Detectives, please excuse me while I greet the governor. This is Mr. Foley, our family attorney. He can help answer your questions."

Travis came in behind Foley. "And this is Travis Bingham, a family friend and an assistant district attorney," Sandy said before he dashed from the room.

Travis slipped across the room to Alex and put a hand on her shoulder.

She shook it off and glared at him.

Foley positioned his considerable girth in front of Keisha White.

"This isn't a convenient time for you to talk with my client, Officer White, is it?"

"It's *Detective* White."

Foley's beady eyes drilled into the detective's. "If necessary, I will schedule a time in the office during the week. Please call my assistant for an appointment. Meanwhile, I will have to ask you to leave through the side door to avoid the governor's entourage and the press."

Craven turned to go. White grasped his arm. "We'll wait here until Mr. Harrington can see us. A woman has been murdered and another is missing. We don't have time to waste."

Foley's face turned an unhealthy shade of purple. He nodded to Travis who took out his cell phone and began to dial.

"You don't know who you're dealing with. Nothing justifies creating an awkward situation for the Harringtons, much less for the governor."

"I have Chief Odom on the line," Travis said.

Foley took the phone, stepped into the hall and talked, keeping his voice low.

White watched through narrowed eyes, her mouth set.

Foley handed the phone to White who listened, and then, in a strangled voice, answered, "Whatever you say, sir."

Very slowly White handed the phone back, without looking at anyone, and walked stiffly toward the outside side door. Craven hurried behind to catch up.

"How could you do that?" Alex demanded when they'd gone. "She's trying to find out who killed Mariana."

Travis moved close to Alex for a second time and put his arm around her shoulder.

She pushed him away and stalked out the side door after White and Craven.

"That young lady is getting to be quite a handful," she heard Scott Foley say.

Halfway to her car she met Mike Murray, coming up the drive. He turned to walk with her. "What's going on? Keisha just charged out of here like an enraged bull."

Alex climbed into her car and said over her shoulder, "I've never been so embarrassed in my life."

She took off, leaving deep ruts in the manicured grass.

CHAPTER EIGHTEEN

Alex was still seething a half hour later when the doorbell rang. "Hang on," she called, silently swearing at whoever had the nerve to show up tonight. She looked through the peephole. Mike Murray smiled back at her.

She opened the door. "This really isn't a good time."

"Thought you might be hungry. I got a pizza, pepperoni on one side, vegetarian with feta on the other. Brought some wine too."

He opened the box with one hand so that she could smell the warm pizza.

What was this guy thinking, showing up like this? She looked from the pizza to Murray's plaintive expression. The pizza was tempting. She hadn't eaten anything since breakfast.

She shrugged and stepped back from the door. "Okay. Come on in."

Mike strode to the kitchen and put the pizza box and the wine on the counter. He began opening drawers. "You got a corkscrew?"

"Bottom drawer on the left. I warn you, I'm not in a good mood."

"You'll feel better after you eat something. The wine will help too."

He got plates and wine glasses from the cabinet.

She watched him. "You do this on a regular basis, just move in and take over?"

"My nature, I guess. What was Keisha so upset about?"

Mike handed her a plate with a piece of vegetarian pizza.

She took a bite. "This really is good."

He poured the red wine into glasses. "I figured you'd need something after the weekend you had. What happened back at your parents' house?"

She took a sip of wine. "Come on into the living room."

Mike followed her to the couch, put the wine and pizza box on the coffee table, and sat down.

She sat down next to him. "Keisha White came to talk to my father, and Scott Foley and Travis Bingham treated her like dirt. They even called the police chief to demand that he make her back off, and he did it. I don't blame her for being mad."

"Foley's a big deal real estate lawyer and developer, tied in with all the big projects around here and at the coast, too. His name is on the white house title too."

"I went to the fundraiser tonight to talk to my father, but I didn't get a chance. He can't know what the white house was being used for, especially after human traffickers tried to kidnap me in Mexico City."

"You were kidnapped by human traffickers?"

She took another bite of pizza, chewed slowly, and swallowed. "I escaped, but only at the cost of another woman's life, a woman named Cristina. I called my father from the police station. He used all his influence to get help for Cristina, but we were too late. My father paid for Cristina's funeral. He's not involved in human trafficking. He even gives money to anti-human trafficking organizations."

"I had no idea. Here I've been talking about my big story, and for you it's personal. What a jerk."

She smiled. "You couldn't know. Besides, telling people about human trafficking may be the best way to fight it. Let's talk about you. How did you get to Dalton? You don't sound like a southerner. Where are you from and how come you know Spanish?"

Mike moved a little closer. "I'm from a small town in Arizona nobody's ever heard of. I picked up enough Spanish from the Hispanic kids in the neighborhood to get along. After college I went to work for the local paper, but it didn't work out. I wanted to write about important stuff, and the editor-in-chief had other ideas. I didn't know enough to keep my mouth shut. Guess it's a theme with me. What about you? Did you grow up in that big house?"

"I lived there until I went to college. Jobs were tight when I graduated so I came back here and started working for the center. That's when I got my own apartment. Not a very exciting life really."

"You seem pretty exciting to me, and that white streak in your hair makes you look downright exotic. Is it for real?"

"If you mean is it natural, yes. I've had it all my life. I hated it as a kid, but I kind of like it now."

The doorbell rang. A man's voice called through the door. "Alex, are you in there?"

She jumped up, hitting her wine glass with her hand. "Daddy."

Mike caught the glass.

Alex opened the door. "I want to talk to you."

Sandy Harrington leaned against the door frame, his face pale, creased with new lines. "I know, baby. That's why I'm here."

"Come on in. There's still some pizza left."

"Good evening, Mr. Harrington," Mike said.

"Mike is just leaving," Alex said.

She closed the door behind Mike and turned the deadbolt. Her father looked terrible, and for the first time in her life she was afraid to hear what he had to say.

CHAPTER NINETEEN

Vargas had been in this hellhole for two days. Lucky Dan had come in second in the All American Futurity, and he'd missed it. That reporter was still writing stories in the local paper about human trafficking. The local police had called in the FBI. El Caballero hadn't found the missing girl, and that stupid bitch of a *puta* wasn't talking. He'd see that she talked today. What a God-damned mess.

He drove the rental Mercedes into the dirt yard of an old house and got out. Cuchillo climbed out of the passenger side and Diego came out of the back. The two followed him up onto the well-worn porch steps to the open door. Red dust clung to his polished boots. He grunted and bent down to wipe them with his handkerchief.

El Caballero was waiting for him on the porch, his face drawn. "Good afternoon," El Caballero said, pulling a roll of antacids from his pocket and popping one in his mouth.

"You know Billy, *Señor* Vargas. Marvin's in there with him. Billy and Marvin are two of my best men. They always work together, some kind of cousins though they don't look at all alike. Shirley's in there too, trying to get Carmela to tell us where Teresa is."

Vargas's eyes narrowed. He walked inside and looked around. Carmela Flores sat tied to a metal chair in the middle of the room, blindfolded. Billy Williams and another biker-type, a slightly built man with arms covered in tattoos, leaned against the back wall. The woman El Caballero called Shirley stood beside Carmela, a cigarette bobbing in her creased mouth.

Shirley blew smoke in Carmela's face. "We pay you good money to take these girls to the clinic. What the fuck do you think you're doing?"

Carmela Flores remained silent.

Shirley slapped her.

Vargas shoved Shirley out of the way and stuck his face close to Carmela's. "You're from Mexico. You know what we do. We cut you to pieces, one piece here, a piece there. We put your body inside a barrel filled with acid and watch you dissolve. You have a family. This will happen to them too. ¿*Me entiendes*?"

Carmela Flores shook her head. "I cannot tell you. The Virgin Mary came to me. She told me she would forgive my sins if I protect Teresa."

"The Virgin Mary can't help you here."

Vargas nodded to Cuchillo.

Cuchillo smashed his fist into Carmela's face. The chair went over backwards. Carmela lay with her feet in the air, tied to the chair, sobbing.

Cuchillo kicked her ribs, over and over. Vargas motioned to him to set Carmela and the chair back up and turned to El Caballero. "You see how this is done, *Señor*?" Vargas said.

Cuchillo thrust a knife under Carmela's chin.

She fainted.

Vargas gave her unconscious body a kick in the ribs.

"For pity's sake, stop," Marvin cried out "You'll kill her. One dead woman is enough."

Vargas laughed and kicked Carmela again.

Marvin rushed forward, pushing between Vargas and the woman.

Diego pulled his gun from the small of his back and aimed it at Marvin.

"No," Billy yelled and rushed at Diego, too late.

Diego's gun flashed.

Marvin's eyes widened. He rocked back and crashed to the floor, emitting a low, guttural noise. His shirt turned from white to bright red.

Shirley raked her hands through her straw-colored hair and looked at the still figure on the floor. "What the hell was he doing?"

Billy knelt down beside Marvin and reached for his cousin's hand. His big body shook. "You had no cause to shoot him. He had a good heart, is all."

"He was in a damn funny business then," Shirley said.

"What am I gonna tell his mama?"

"Tell her that her son had shit for brains," Vargas said.

Diego pointed to Billy. "Do I kill him too?"

"No, don't," El Caballero said. "He's too valuable and he's related to most of North Carolina. You shoot him and we'll have his kin coming from everywhere. It's going to be bad enough dealing with them over Marvin."

Vargas kicked Marvin's foot. "Get this *mierda* out of here."

Billy gave Vargas a look of pure hatred, turned his back, and gently closed Marvin's eyes.

"I want it out of here," Vargas screamed.

Billy's skin was slick with sweat. He still didn't move.

El Caballero put a hand on Billy's shoulder. "I know Marvin was your cousin, but you have to do what Mr. Vargas says. Take him somewhere where no one will find him and give him a decent burial."

Billy staggered to his feet, shoulders hunched, and stared at his boss, his eyes blank.

"Billy, please. Nothing you do will bring Marvin back now," El Caballero said.

Slowly Billy bent down and took hold of Marvin's shoulders. Tears ran down his cheeks and off the end of his nose as he dragged the body across the floor and out the front door.

Vargas's cell rang. As he listened, his eye began to twitch.

A voice on the other end said, "The police found the girl. They're taking her to a safe house."

CHAPTER TWENTY

Alex pulled a light jacket over her sleeveless blouse and ran a comb through her hair. She'd stayed up late talking to her father and had overslept. The center was open again. Work, with its rhythm of patient visits, scheduling and paperwork, would be a relief after the last three days. Nothing had been routine since Carmela crashed through the French doors on Friday afternoon.

She looked back at her messy apartment. The refrigerator was empty. A pile of dirty clothes needed attention. She'd deal with it later. The *Dalton Herald* lay on the mat. No time for that. She threw the paper on the hall table, turned the key in the lock, and went out into a wall of warm wet August air. As she ran down the stairs she could hear could hear the ringing of the land line that her parents insisted she have on the unlikely chance that her cell phone wouldn't work for some reason. She was late already. Whoever it was would have to leave a message.

"Alex." The center front door flew open before she had gotten her key in the lock. Gladys pulled her inside. "Where have you been? I've been trying your home phone and cell for the past half hour."

"Sorry. I heard the house phone ring, but I didn't want to stop. My cell's been off since last night when Daddy came over after the fundraiser."

"You talked to him? Did he tell you why his name is on the deed?"

"He says that the house is in some real estate portfolio he owns as part of the JoVille group, that's all. His brokers take care of the real estate portfolio, and managers deal with the tenants. He and Scott Foley are meeting with Keisha White this afternoon. I'm sure they'll sort it out."

She stopped. "Why were you looking for me?"

Gladys handed her a copy of the *Dalton Herald*. "I take it you haven't seen this."

She read the headline aloud. "'Local Executive Involved in Sex Trade.' I don't believe it."

"Keep reading."

She read down the page, feeling herself flush. "My father's name is there and references to the center are all through it."

"Look at the byline. Your reporter friend isn't doing anybody any favors. It's all there. Mariana. The fire. Carmela's kidnapping. How we found Teresa. He says it's all connected to human trafficking."

"How could he write this? I was with him last night. He brought a pizza and wine. We talked about all kinds of things. Daddy warned me not to trust him. So did Keisha White."

The phone rang. Gladys answered, listened, and handed the phone to Alex. "It's Detective White, looking for Mike Murray. She wants to talk to you."

Alex took the receiver. "He isn't here. I doubt even he'd have the guts to come here after today's article."

She hung up, promising to let White know if Mike showed up.

"I forgot to tell you, your mother called a few minutes ago," Gladys said.

Alex rolled her eyes. "I'm sure she's livid."

She had just picked up the phone to call her mother when Mike walked through the front door, smiling.

She clenched her teeth so tight that pain shot up her jaw. She held up the paper. "When did you write this, before or after our glass of wine?"

"Don't be upset. You've got to understand, I write the news. It's my job."

"You put my father's name in the paper, and you connected the center to human trafficking."

"Everything in the article is true. I never said that your father was involved in criminal activity, only that he owned the house where the women lived. Mariana was a patient at the center. Look at it as a positive. Could be the article will make people come forward with information about the traffickers. Maybe it'll inspire the cops to work harder."

Keisha White came through the open clinic door.

"You're a jerk, Murray. We don't need inspiration from you. Did it even occur to you that your article could put Carmela Flores in even greater danger?"

Mike's eyes flashed. "That's not fair. Without me, you'd have a lot less than you do now."

Keisha looked around the room, her eyes moving from the reporter to Alex. "I need to ask you some questions about the center."

"I keep telling you, the center has nothing to do with any of this and neither does my father."

"Your father is a principal in the JoVille Group. He's also a member of the center's board of directors. What's the connection between the center and the JoVille Group?"

"There is no connection other than that my father belongs to both."

"The FBI is convinced that this is about human trafficking. They're on the case now too."

White handed Alex an envelope. "I told the sheriff I'd deliver this since I was coming here anyway. It's a subpoena, requiring you, as director of the center, to bring all of the requested documents to the city attorney's office in two weeks."

Alex took the subpoena and started to read, trying to make sense of it.

Mike reached for it as soon as Keisha White left. "Can I see that?"

Alex pulled the document away. "Absolutely not. We don't need this in the paper too. Now get out."

Mike flinched and retreated to the door. "I'll call you," he said.

She slammed the door behind him and picked up the newspaper again. "Everyone will think the center's involved in human trafficking. They'll read that the center took care of trafficked women on a regular basis and that one of our board members, my own father, owns the house where the women lived."

"Technically, that's right, you know," Gladys said.

Alex walked to her desk and collapsed into her chair. "The only way out of this mess is to find the people who really are behind this. We can't count on the police and the FBI to do it. They're looking at us instead of trying to find the real culprits."

CHAPTER TWENTY-ONE

Alex's eyes were bleary from looking through center files when she came across a file she'd never noticed before, marked "Schools Project." She leafed through it, frowning at a brochure about some sort of school in Mexico, then put it aside for later.

She was still in the office several hours later when her father called. She cradled the phone against her shoulder. "How did it go with the FBI, Daddy?"

His voice was strong, like his old self, more confident than last night. "I got through it with Scott's help, but I could tell that this human trafficking issue is a big deal for the FBI. It's not just in Dalton. They're looking across the whole country."

"What did they ask you?"

"They wanted to know about the house on York Street. They think I knew what was going on there. A tall black FBI agent named Silva, ex-Marine by the looks of him, questioned me for over two hours, but I held my own."

"I'm sure you told him you had nothing to do with it."

"Of course, but I don't think he believed me. He showed me a record of the rent on the house—four times above the going rate—and wanted to know why we charged so much. I told him I didn't have anything to do with the rental agreement. I promised I'd talk to the rental agent, but I knew the answer. We charge whatever the market will bear. If tenants are dumb enough to pay more than the going rate, that's what we charge."

"Did he tell you the FBI and the police think there's a connection with the center?"

"It's pretty clear that they're looking at both the center and the JoVille Group. They spent a fair amount of time trying to tie the two together. From their questions, I think they suspect the center of involvement in money laundering as well as human trafficking, but they won't get anywhere. There's nothing to find."

"I know that. Our books are audited annually. When the FBI looks at the center's financial records, they'll see that."

"They want access to the JoVille books too. Foley objected. There's no probable cause for anything. We're going to fight them."

"There's something else, Daddy. I found a file about a school in Mexico. Do you know anything about it?"

The phone was silent.

"Daddy, are you there?"

"Yes, I'm here. I vaguely remember something about a schools project from way back, before we started the center. That would be ten or twelve years ago. As I recall, a group of us gave money to poor children at some orphanage in Mexico City. It's not relevant to a trafficking investigation, I'm sure of that. Let Scott handle it. You have enough to do, running the center."

"Keisha White called me today. She was a lot nicer. She needs my help. She thinks if Elena Casas goes with her to see Teresa, she'll have better luck getting her to talk. Thing is, Elena won't go without me."

"That's good. You go with them. As soon as the police hear Teresa's story, they'll know the center isn't involved."

She felt a churning in the pit of her stomach. "We are involved though. Carmela was bringing women from the white house to the center for medical care. Apparently the traffickers were paying her. That's how Mariana got to be a patient here in the first place."

"You were just helping women in need. Don't worry about it."

She heard noise from the street. "Wait a minute, Daddy. Something's going on outside."

She put down the receiver and looked through the window. A large crowd was gathering on the sidewalk. She opened the window a crack. The crowd was shouting something.

"I'll have to call you back."

She hung up and turned back to the window. More people were getting out of parked cars. Several held up signs that read, STOP HUMAN TRAFFICKING.

She opened the door and addressed the crowd. "We're on your side. We take care of families, women, and children. We would never knowingly have anything to do with any illegal activity."

The protesters formed a circle around Alex. One woman shoved the *Dalton Herald* in her face. "It's all here."

Other protesters pushed pamphlets on her.

"Please leave," she said.

Gladys came out onto the steps. "Enough. I've called the police."

"We're not going away."

Gladys pulled Alex back inside and closed the door.

Alex was shaking. "The patients will be afraid to cross a picket line if this keeps up. How do I convince those people that we're on the same side?"

CHAPTER TWENTY-TWO

Alex was in the back seat of an unmarked police car. Keisha White and Elena were in the front. They were meeting with Teresa and Alex was eager to hear what the girl had to say.

The car stopped in front of a square, gray house in a quiet working-class neighborhood. No one would take it for a Dalton police department safe house. White stepped out and opened the door for Elena, and Alex climbed out of the back. Just as they reached the front door and were about to knock, a late model American car parked behind White's car, and a well-built African-American man of around forty got out and joined them. The man's dark gray suit, regimental tie, and white buttoned-down collared shirt gave him a military look.

"This is Agent Silva from the FBI Task Force on human trafficking," White said.

Alex saw Silva look at White with raised eyebrows.

"Ms. Harrington is joining us because Ms. Casas has specifically asked that she be here when she meets with Teresa."

Alex extended her hand. "I'm just here to help."

Silva gave a curt nod, shook Alex's hand, and turned to Keisha White. "You think the girl's going to talk to us today?"

"We can only hope. Nothing else has worked."

A slightly built officer who looked even younger than Alex opened the door. Her holster was unsnapped.

"Good morning, Pam. How's Teresa today?" White asked.

"She seems calmer. She's even eaten a little breakfast."

When they were all inside, White turned to Alex and Elena. "This is Officer Lea. She's been with Teresa pretty much every day since we brought her here three days ago."

Lea led them into a sparsely decorated room. Teresa sat on a couch in front of a small television, watching a Spanish language soap.

"Hello, Teresa. *Señora* Casas is here. Do you remember her from the center?" White asked.

The girl kept her eyes glued to the set.

White walked around her and turned the television off.

"You know Alex Harrington, and this gentleman is Agent Silva from the FBI. We all want to catch the people who killed your sister. Carmela Flores is missing. We need you to help us."

"Please, help me. We have to find my cousin," Elena said in Spanish.

Slowly, Teresa turned to look at them. She opened her mouth and spoke for the first time, her voice barely above a whisper. "They will hurt my family."

"We won't let them. The Mexican police won't let them," White said.

Teresa shook her head. "The police are bad too. They take money. They do not help us."

Silva walked to the couch. "I promise that the FBI will work with the Mexican *Federales* to protect your family. You want to help us catch the people who killed your sister, don't you?"

White sat down on the chair next to Teresa's, reached in her bag for a small package wrapped in tissue paper, and held it out in the palm of her hand. "This belonged to your sister. I thought you should have it."

Teresa took the package and slowly unwound the paper. A tiny gold cross fell out in her hand. Her face crumpled.

"Please tell us what happened, Teresa," White asked.

Teresa brushed away a tear and bowed her head for several seconds before looking up and straightening her shoulders. "I will tell you what I know."

Alex thought of Cristina and swallowed hard. These poor women had been through so much.

"Let's begin with how you met these people," White said.

The girl began to speak. Her words, halting at first, became stronger.

"A man and woman came to our village. They met my sister, Mariana, when she was at the market and began talking with her. They said they were looking for people to work in the U.S. and asked if she would like to hear more. They promised that if she went with them, she would have a job and money to send home. She would have pretty clothes and ride in a big red American car. When she told me about it, she was so happy. There would be money for our family and lessons in English too. She wanted me to come with her to have a better life."

"When was that?" White asked.

"Maybe three months ago. I don't really know for sure. Our mother didn't want us to go. She knew that Mariana was not strong. My sister had a fever in her heart when she was a little girl, but our family needed money. Finally, my mother agreed that we should go."

Teresa's eyes filled with tears. "Our mother said I should make sure Mariana was all right. Now Mariana is dead, and it is all my fault."

"It's not your fault, Teresa," Alex said. "It's the fault of those evil people."

Teresa's shoulders shook. The room was silent except for the groan of the air conditioner.

It was several minutes before Teresa could speak again. "Those people lied to us. You must catch them and make them pay."

"That's what we're trying to do, with your help," Silva said. "Tell us what happened next."

"A big car came for us. We had never been away from our village before. The car took us a long way to a warehouse."

Alex shuddered.

"Do you have any idea where the warehouse was?" Silva asked.

"The driver said we were in a place called Tenancingo. There were many women there, some from Mexico, others from Guatemala, I think. There were children, too. They were crying."

Teresa's voice cracked. "The next day a man took Mariana and many others away. They left me alone with another girl. When

Mariana came back, her mouth was swollen, and she had marks all over her body. She said many men raped her, many times. When she tried to resist, they beat her."

Teresa was still, unable to continue. A fly buzzed on the window sill.

Alex ran to the kitchen, coming back with a glass of water that she handed to Teresa.

"The next day a truck came. Mariana and I were squeezed into the back with many women and some children. In the day it was so hot. The smell of sweat and pee made me sick. At night it was so cold. We huddled together to stay warm."

"Where did the truck take you?" White asked.

"We rode all day and all night and another day. At last the truck stopped in a place that was all rocks and stones, the desert I think. It was night. Men we hadn't seen before took us out of the truck. They made us walk. We walked for hours. We were hungry and thirsty. The men gave us only a few bottles of water to share and some crackers. They led us into a very long, dark tunnel, and when we came out, another truck was waiting."

Teresa stopped talking. Her eyes were far away. Elena patted her shoulder. "What happened then?"

"We went in the truck for another day and a night until finally, the truck stopped. The back doors opened, and a woman with yellow hair pulled Mariana out of the truck. Mariana screamed for me. She was afraid the men would separate us. The woman yelled to a man on the truck, and he pulled me out and threw me on the ground. The woman walked around us and said we should both stay. Then the truck drove away, and the woman took us into a very big white house."

White laid two mugshots on the foot stool in front of Teresa. "Here are pictures of the people whose fingerprints we found at the house where you lived with your sister. Do you recognize them?"

Teresa looked at the pictures. She pointed to the woman. "The men called her Shirley. She took us from the truck. She is the one who beat my sister."

"Her full name is Shirley Hodges. Tell us about her," White said.

"She hurt anyone who did not do what she said. Sometimes men would come to the house, but more often the girls would go out in the van to a hotel or a truck stop. Mariana would cry and say she did not want to go, and Shirley would hit her."

"They didn't take you with them?"

Teresa covered her face with her hands. Her body rocked back and forth. "I heard them say that they had plans for me."

White pointed to the other mugshot. "Would you look at this picture please? Who is this man?"

Teresa looked at the picture. "That's Marvin. He was nicer than Shirley. One day when no one was there he took us to a market where there were Mexican people. Shirley was angry when she found out. She screamed at him and took Mariana away. When I saw Mariana again, she had bruises on her arms and legs."

"Who else was in the house with you?" Keisha asked.

"There was a big man with a beard. Shirley called him Billy. He mostly watched us so we could not leave. And sometimes there was another man too. Shirley said he was a rich guy."

"Can you describe this rich guy?" Silva asked.

"I never saw his face, but I heard him talk. He was a *gringo*."

"You think he was an American?"

Teresa nodded.

"What happened the night Carmela brought Mariana to the center?"

"Mariana and I were upstairs alone. Shirley brought me a clean white dress and said to put it on. Mariana asked why, but Shirley just slapped her. I put the dress on, and Shirley led me to a room where some men were waiting. She told me to walk in front of the men so they could see me. One of the men said a number, then another man said a number. Shirley lifted my skirt. I started to cry."

Alex dug her nails into the palms of her hands.

"What happened then?" Keisha asked.

"Mariana ran into the room. She called Shirley names. Shirley hit her and dragged her from the room. The men were angry. They said the neighbors would hear and call the police. They all left."

"Then what?"

Teresa twisted her shirt and looked out the window.

"Billy took me upstairs and locked me in a room. I could hear Mariana screaming downstairs. I beat on the door and begged to get out. No one came. In the morning I wanted to see my sister. Billy said no. Later, in the afternoon when it was all quiet, Marvin came. He took me downstairs to a first floor room next to the kitchen where my sister lay on a little bed, moaning. She had blood on her face, and her clothes were torn. Marvin told me that I could stay with her for a while and went away."

"How did you escape?" Silva asked.

"I was desperate. I remembered a Mexican woman named Carmela who worked at the clinic behind us. She took Mariana to see the doctor there sometimes. I hoped she would help us. There was a window in the room. Long nails stuck in the window frame, but they were old and rusty. I banged them with my shoe until they fell out. I thought someone would hear, but I was lucky. Nobody came. Maybe they were all out somewhere. I climbed through the window and found Carmela coming out of work. I told her that Mariana needed a doctor and begged her to come."

"Carmela came back with me. She said that she could never get into the house through the small window so I had to sneak her into the house through a door to the kitchen. I was afraid Shirley would come, but she didn't. She must have gone out. I heard Marvin and Billy laughing in the living room. I could smell something sweet, like marijuana. They didn't hear us."

"Mariana could walk a little. Carmela helped me get her through the hall to the kitchen and out the back door. My sister was very brave. She tried not to cry out, but it hurt her to move. We got her to the garden behind where Carmela works, and Carmela told me to hide in a little house. She took Mariana into the clinic. I could not see anything from the little house, but I heard sirens. Nobody came. I was all alone for many hours. I prayed for my sister."

Teresa stopped and looked at Elena. "Later you brought me food. That's all I know."

"Thank you, Teresa. That's very helpful," White said.

Outside, White turned to Silva. "That was good. We got a positive identification of Shirley Hodges and Marvin Moore, and we know to look for someone named Billy."

When they reached White's car, Silva looked at Alex. "Teresa said there was a man, probably American, who appeared to be running the operation. Do you know anything about that?"

"I know that it isn't my father, if that's what you're insinuating. Teresa didn't say anything that implicated either the center or my father."

Silva gave her a hard look. "The only thing we know for certain is that we're dealing with human trafficking, and someone in Dalton is behind it."

CHAPTER TWENTY-THREE

Mike stared at his computer screen. Newsroom phones rang around him, voices buzzed, people yelled. It was all background noise. He was in a world of his own. He answered greetings from passing colleagues in a daze. His head ached. His neck hurt. He closed his eyes and leaned back in his chair. Last night things had seemed to be going pretty well. It was just his rotten luck that the story had led where it did. He was sure he'd blown any chance he had with Alex.

"Great story," the reporter at the next desk said. "Where are you going with it?"

"Good question. I think it leads directly to Mexico."

He looked at the row of glass-walled offices where the editors sat. Roush waved him in.

"Looks like the boss wants to see you," his neighbor said. "He doesn't look like a happy man. Good luck."

Mike got up and walked toward the glass office, mentally rehearsing his argument for taking the trafficking story to Mexico. Murder, a kidnapping investigation, growing interest in trafficking, important players, FBI involvement. This story had it all. He took one look at the scowl on his editor's face and shelved the pitch for another day.

"We're getting heat about that piece of yours," Roush said, pulling on his suspenders. "Close the door. I had an attorney from Foley and Forebush on the phone this morning, hollering about disparagement, libel, business interference."

"Everything in that story is absolutely true."

"Yeah, but we're talking about the movers and shakers of Dalton, the whole damn state really. These people can cause a lot of trouble. You stirred up a fuckin' hornets' nest, Murray. Unless there's some breaking news, I want you to back off."

"No way. There's a federal grand jury looking into human trafficking, and I'm talking to a reporter in Mexico who's writing a series on it from his end."

"You want a job here or not? I'm ordering you to back off. There's plenty else to cover. Besides, I can't afford to keep you on this. We're too thin."

Roush handed him three new assignments. "Try not to kick shit in the face of every god-damned big shot in the state, would you, please?"

Back at his desk Mike collapsed into his chair and ran a hand over the stubble on his chin. No way in hell he was going to back off. He looked at the three new assignments: a fight at the local high school, a fire in a tenement, and complaints from irate citizens about cameras at traffic lights. All on deadline. He'd blitz through them and get back to his story.

He picked up his pad and was about to head for the elevator when his phone rang. The display read Espinosa: the Mexican reporter.

"I read your story. Good stuff. You have anything more?" the reporter asked.

He gave Espinosa the short version of everything that had happened. "I need proof of a connection between Dalton and Mexico."

"You say the dead woman came from the south of Mexico? The traffickers are active there because people are so poor. They promise these girls, young men too, jobs and education. Find out what town the woman came from. Maybe I can figure out what traffickers are operating there and if there's a connection between them and the real estate group you wrote about. Be careful, my friend. These people do not like reporters. Many are dead because they got too close."

———

Mike's watch read midnight when he pulled up in front of the little rented house he'd called home since moving to Dalton two years before. Three articles in one day was a lot, even for him. He'd finished, turned them in, and swung through Rag Town on his way home. *Mi Tienda* was closed, and there was no sign of activity at the unpainted house.

The street light in front of his house had been out for weeks. Dalton wasn't too good about fixing busted street lights in his part of town. He walked to the door, looking for the stray cat. The gray tabby was usually waiting by the door when he got home, ready to dash into the house, but tonight it was nowhere in sight. He missed the little varmint.

He'd recorded a game and was looking forward to kicking back with a cold beer before bed. When he put his key in the lock, the door swung open. His mind had been on the center and Alex when he'd left this morning. Had he forgotten to lock the door? He thought of Espinosa's warning. He couldn't afford to be sloppy. He could call the cops and give Keisha a good laugh. No way.

He pushed the door open and nearly fell over the pile of newspapers he'd been meaning to take to the recycling bin. Funny, he didn't remember putting them there. The tabby was inside, meowing. He could swear he'd put the cat out this morning. His neighbor had been complaining about the cat walking all over his car, even threatened to take it to the pound. Maybe the guy had thrown the cat in the house to prove a point.

He shut the front door and listened. The cat cried again, hungry most likely. He checked the kitchen and the coat closet and then the bathroom. There were a few magazines scattered across the floor, but the cat could have done that.

He went into the kitchen and poured a handful of dry cat food into a bowl on the floor. The cat ignored the food and continued to meow. What was the matter with him?

He shrugged and opened the refrigerator. Nothing in there but a jar of peanut butter, some strawberry jam, and an out-of-date loaf of white bread, and here he'd had the nerve to make fun of Alex's fridge.

At least there was beer. He fixed a sandwich, grabbed a beer, and went into the living room to turn on the game. The cat followed close at his heels, still crying.

The blow, when it came, sent a lightning strike of pain from the back of his head down his spine.

He heard a voice he didn't recognize. "That'll teach him to keep his nose out of where it don't belong."

He passed out.

———————

The ceiling fan came into focus. Craven's sallow face loomed above him. "You must've made someone real mad, boy. Lucky for you your neighbor found you and called us. Said your cat was driving him nuts running back and forth from his house to yours. You could've been here a long time."

"Did you see who hit you?" Keisha White asked.

Mike tried to speak. His voice came out in a croak. His head throbbed.

"Don't try to talk," White said, and turned to Craven. "Get him some water and a washcloth, would you?"

The water helped.

Two uniformed cops came out of his bedroom.

"Anything?" White asked.

"Someone was waiting for you. There's a cigarette butt ground into the carpet."

"Bag it," White said. "Maybe we'll get lucky."

She helped Mike to his feet. "You okay? You've been out for a while by the look of it. It started to rain over an hour ago, but there are no wet footprints in here, yours or anyone else's."

"I didn't see a thing and then, wham."

"You've got a nasty bump on the back of your head that you need to get checked out," White said.

"This is a warning," Craven said. "If someone wanted you dead, you'd be dead."

"He's right. You might consider cooling it for once in your crazy-ass life."

"No way. I'm fine," Mike said, struggling to sit up. "I got an article to write."

CHAPTER TWENTY-FOUR

Alex sat cross-legged on the office floor, surrounded by documents, some of them going back ten years. It had been a long, dreary day. A copy of the subpoena lay in her lap.

"Mike's article today was all about a break-in at his house. Someone hit him on the head. He says it was because of his human trafficking articles. Who would be dumb enough to think a knock on the head would shut Mike Murray up? He'll only go at it harder."

"You need to forget about that guy. He's nothing but trouble," Gladys said.

Alex picked up a stack of files and handed them to Gladys. "I'm sorry he got hurt, but you're right. We have more to think about than Mike Murray." She held up the subpoena. "This doesn't make sense. Why would they want paperwork relating to countries outside the U.S.? Do they mean Mexico?"

Gladys lowered her stocky frame into the desk chair. "The center doesn't have a connection to Mexico that I know of."

"Maybe it does. I came across a file about some kind of a school in Mexico City."

Gladys held up a file. "Is this it? It's labeled 'Schools Project.'"

"That's it. I asked my father about it. He says it's an old project that some of the board members were involved in years ago."

Gladys leafed through the file and held up what looked to be financial statements. "Looks like someone gave a whole lot of money to some school that's part of an orphanage, hundreds of thousands of dollars. Where's the money coming from?"

Alex reached for the file and flipped through the contents, then turned back to the beginning.

"It lists the Foleys and Binghams as contributors. Here's a record of contributions from the JoVille Group and some other businesses I've never heard of," Gladys said.

"There does seem to be a school and some kind of orphanage. There's a brochure here. It's called, 'Suffer the Little Children.'"

"I almost forgot. Mr. Foley called earlier to say he was coming over today. Maybe he knows something," Gladys said.

Alex put the folder aside and was about to tackle another stack of papers when the clinic door burst open and Renee flew into the room.

"They're going to arrest your father. I just know it."

She'd never seen her mother like this, hair a mess, mascara smeared, and wearing shoes that didn't go with her outfit.

"What are you talking about, Mother?"

"Two men were at the house this morning. FBI agents. They were asking all kinds of questions about your father. They wanted to know where he is. What are we going to do?"

"That doesn't mean they're going to arrest him. Where is he, anyway?"

"That's just it. I don't know. He never tells me where he's going these days. I've called everywhere. Do you think he's in jail?"

Scott Foley came through the door behind her mother and put his hands on her shoulders, moving her firmly into the room.

"For heaven's sake. Why would he be in jail?"

Renee began to pace, pulling at the fronds of an asparagus fern until the whole plant lay in pieces on the floor. "He's been nervous as a cat lately. Something's bothering him."

Foley mopped his forehead and turned to Gladys. "Little lady, would you be so kind as to get us all something cool to drink? Some sweet tea would be nice. Mrs. Harrington looks like she could use some, and I could too."

Alex scrambled up off the floor before Gladys could react. "I'll go with you."

Gladys marched into the clinic kitchen, her lips pressed together. "It's been a long time since anybody called me little lady, little anything for that matter!"

"I know. Just ignore him. He's a bit old fashioned."

When they came back with the tea, her mother was perched on the edge of the leather chair, and Foley was sitting in Alex's desk chair.

"Sandy could just be worried about the center. He dotes on Alex, and we all know the dear child is having a difficult time. Did these men show you an arrest warrant?" Foley asked.

Renee took a mirror from her purse and fixed her makeup, and then patted her hair into place. "No, they did not."

"I thought not. They have no grounds to arrest Sandy or anyone else. Besides, we have over a week before we have to produce anything on that subpoena. They're just trying to rattle you."

"Well, they succeeded." She swiped a hand over the table beside her and inspected it for dust. "I thought you said you cleaned this place, Alex."

"I did." Alex handed her mother a glass of sweet tea. She put another glass in front of Scott Foley.

"Well, you didn't do a very good job."

Alex ignored her. "While you're both here, could we go through the files? I have some questions."

"Anything at all," Foley said, rocking back in the desk chair while he sipped his tea.

"I know your firm wrote the articles of incorporation and by-laws. Who set up the financial structure and the bank accounts?"

"We did. Everything is in order. I review the audit and the IRS filings myself every year with the outside accounting firm. There's never been a problem. Don't worry your pretty head about any of this."

Alex stiffened. "Please don't patronize me."

The "Schools Project" file lay on top of the stack on the floor. She picked it up. "What's this about?"

Foley reached for the file and made a show of studying it. "That's just an old charity. It's not relevant to the subpoena. I'll take it with me so it doesn't confuse things."

She reached for it. "There has to be some reason it was in our files."
Foley snatched it away from her.

"Give it to me."

She was struggling with Foley for the file when two men in dark suits came in through the center's front door.

Renee stood up. "Those are the agents from this morning."

"That's Agent Silva. I know him," Alex said.

Silva gave Renee a curt nod and turned to Alex. "We have some questions for you."

Foley moved forward. "I represent the center and Ms. Harrington. You'll have to make an appointment. Here's my card. Call my office to set up a time."

Alex walked around Foley and held out her hand. "Agent Silva and I spent an afternoon together with Teresa at the safe house."

Foley stepped in front of Alex. "As chair of the board and attorney for the center I must insist that you talk with Ms. Harrington another time and in my law office."

"I can talk with them now," Alex said.

Her mother shot her a warning look. "I'm feeling ill, Scott. I need you to take me home."

"Let me handle this, Alex, honey. That's what lawyers are for," Foley said.

Alex flushed. She wasn't some little girl who could be told what to do.

Before she could protest, Silva took the card that Foley held out to him. "I look forward to talking with Ms. Harrington very soon."

She watched the agents leave. "I can handle this. I know more about this than either of you."

Foley gave her a dismissive shrug and held out an arm to her mother. "Time to go, Renee. We'll find Sandy, and everything will be fine."

"I have to apologize for my daughter, Scott. I don't know what's come over her."

"That's quite all right," Foley said. "Alex is one of my favorite people, but she mustn't talk with anybody about this investigation unless I'm with her, for her own protection as well as for the center."

Alex shut the door behind them and snapped the deadbolt.

"To think I liked that man once."

"Bet that was a long time ago," Gladys said.

CHAPTER TWENTY-FIVE

Everywhere Vargas turned, the news was bad. There was an FBI task force. His whole operation was falling apart. As if that wasn't bad enough, Lucky Dan had broken his right hind leg in training runs for the next race. Those idiot veterinarians wanted to put him down. They weren't even trying to save him. He'd called them. "I don't care how much it costs. If you care about your life and your family, you will make it so he can run again."

It was close to one o'clock when Vargas and Cuchillo walked past El Caballero's astonished secretary into his plush office.

El Caballero jumped to his feet.

Vargas walked to the desk while Cuchillo stayed in the doorway, keeping the secretary from following.

"You can go to lunch now, Barbara. It's all right," El Caballero said.

No one spoke until the door of the outer office closed.

El Caballero forced a smile. "Good afternoon, *Señor*."

A small vein throbbed in Vargas's forehead. His eyes narrowed. "You told me only the local police were involved."

"You're talking about the FBI? I was going to tell you as soon as I saw you. As I understand it they're focusing on the center and the house on York Street. They're not looking at you or the network."

"Idiot. The house is part of the network. What if your FBI connects what happened there to our operations in other cities?"

El Caballero gripped the edge of his desk. "You have to believe that we're doing everything we can think of here."

"I do not have to do anything," Vargas said.

Cuchillo took a step forward, hand on his knife.

Color drained from El Caballero's face. "Please. We're all under a great deal of pressure, *Señor.*"

"You know what will happen if you fail me."

El Caballero reached in his breast pocket for a silk handkerchief and wiped his forehead. "I assure you, *Señor*, I will do whatever you say, but these things take time."

Vargas's eyes raked El Caballero from head to feet. He'd had it with this stupid *gringo*. One day his operations would stretch across the U.S. He would have the connections he needed, and fools like this one would be out of his life for good. Only strong, loyal, smart people would work for him. He would spend all his time with his beloved horses.

The outer office door opened. Billy Williams came in, carrying a brown paper bag, and stopped short, looking at Vargas and Cuchillo. "Boss, I got you a turkey Reuben."

El Caballero came around the desk, reaching for the bag. "Come in, Billy. *Señor* Vargas and I are having a friendly chat."

Vargas stepped in front of El Caballero. "Yes, do come in. I understand that you have been with El Caballero for a long time, and you know our operations here very well. Dalton is the model for my network, and I am not at all happy with the way your boss is managing things. So I'm taking over. You will take orders from me now."

Billy looked from his boss to Vargas, his mouth dropping open.

Vargas walked past him, out of the office.

Cuchillo followed. "What if he goes to the FBI? Suppose he makes a deal with them? He knows too much about our operations."

Vargas stopped. "Maybe we should give El Caballero another taste of what will happen if he betrays me."

CHAPTER TWENTY-SIX

The next morning a blue van sat next to the dumpster behind Alex's apartment building. Her car was only a few yards behind it. Mud covered the numbers on the van's license plate. Alex frowned. It hadn't rained in weeks. With its darkened windows, side panels, and absence of logo, the van looked like the one that had peeled out of Gladys's lot the night Carmela was kidnapped.

The driver's side door of the van opened, and a thin woman with sunken cheeks and a scarf around her head stepped onto the pavement and looked around, then drew on a cigarette, pulling the thin lines around her lips together like an accordion. A stream of smoke circled her head.

Alex watched the woman walk toward the building. Something about her looked familiar. A new neighbor or someone visiting, maybe? Since Mexico she didn't trust anything out of the ordinary. Maybe her mother was right, and she was paranoid. She pushed all thoughts of the van and its driver out of her mind, got into her car, and drove to work.

When she got home at night the van was gone. She went inside, ready to tackle the mess she'd left that morning. Her cell chirped to indicate she had a voice mail. She listened to Mike Murray's voice. "Please call me, Alex. We need to talk."

Maybe she was being too hard on him. He was just doing his job, and, as Gladys said, there was some truth in what he was writing. Still, she was going to make him sweat a while before she'd call him back.

She poured herself a glass of wine and wandered around her apartment, unable to settle down. She wasn't coping at all well. She forced herself to sit. She had to pull herself together.

They hadn't found Carmela. What if those men killed her? Even though she'd lied about the women she brought to the center, Carmela didn't deserve to die.

Alex looked at the clock. Seven o'clock, plenty of time for yoga stretches before bed. She had just finished changing into comfortable clothes when the doorbell rang.

Half hoping to see Mike Murray, she peered through the peephole.

"What are you doing here?" she asked, unlocking the door and pulling it open.

Travis Bingham stood in the doorway, holding a dozen long-stemmed red roses. "Please? I owe you an apology. Could we talk? There's something you need to know."

"Not tonight, Travis."

"The roses are for you. You shouldn't be upset with me."

"So it's my fault?"

"Come on, Alex. Are you going to leave me standing on the doorstep? Surely we're better friends than that."

She sighed. "I don't have time to talk. I want to work out before bed."

Travis eyed her glass of wine. "Really? You drink before working out? I seriously doubt that. I've been in court all day. Please let me in."

She shrugged and carried the flowers to the kitchen. When she returned, Travis had pulled the hassock in front of the armoire.

"What do you think you're doing?"

"Nothing. I thought this might look better over here."

She put the flowers on the coffee table. "So now you're rearranging my furniture?"

"You know us lawyers. We're all a little compulsive."

"Thanks for the flowers, but you need to go."

"Give me a couple of minutes. I heard a story today that I think you'll want to hear. It's about this schools project you keep asking about."

"How do you know I was asking about the schools project?"

"Scott Foley told me. I started working for him this week."

Alex gave up and took the couch.

Travis sat down, put his feet on the coffee table, and cleared his throat. "Some time ago the Foleys decided to combine a business trip with a vacation in Mexico. They were staying in a hotel on the outskirts of Mexico City when a major earthquake struck the downtown area, killing thousands of people and injuring many more. Over a hundred thousand people were left homeless."

Travis paused to check her reaction.

"Go on."

"Everything was fine where the Foleys were staying, but they couldn't believe what they were hearing on the news about the rest of Mexico City. Needless to say, they couldn't go on with their vacation because transportation was a mess. Then they heard the story of more than a dozen infants pulled from the rubble of collapsed buildings. Many were found beside their dead parents, all in the poorer areas of the city. Everyone was amazed at their survival, and they soon came to be called the Miracle Babies."

"When was this?"

Travis looked away. "I don't remember exactly. Ten years ago, maybe more. Scott and Dixie wanted to do something. They gave money to the International Red Cross, but they knew the babies and children would need help for many years to come. So the Foleys worked with a local children's hospital in Mexico City to raise money. In time they decided to set up a school connected with a Catholic orphanage."

"And that's the schools project? What does it have to do with the center?"

"I'm getting to that. About the time your parents were talking about setting up the center the Foleys were raising money for the school. They worked together on both projects. That must be why the schools project file was at the center. The Foleys' own money covers expenses for the Miracle Babies who went to the school and for other victims of the earthquake. Your parents contributed to the school, and in return the Foleys supported the center. That's the only connection between the two. The schools project has nothing to do with your dead patient or with the subpoena."

"Why have I never heard about this? I'm executive director of the center."

"Now Alex. You're making way too much of this. I didn't know about it before now, either. Probably because the Foleys are so modest. They want their work to be anonymous."

He opened an envelope. Several glossy shots of children fell out on the floor. He leaned down to gather them and handed them to Alex.

She looked at the pictures. "Are these the earthquake victims?"

"They are. The Foleys are wonderful people. For their sake, you have to stop asking questions. That's all I came here to say."

After Travis had gone, Alex returned to the living room. She looked at the hassock. She didn't believe for a minute that Travis had moved it for aesthetic reasons. She'd interrupted him, doing something. She climbed on it and ran a hand over on top of the armoire. The accordion file folder Travis had left the last time he was in her apartment was still there where she'd put it. She'd forgotten all about it. So that's what he was after.

She opened the folder and rifled through it. It was a file about the schools project. The first few pages were copies of the papers Scott Foley had taken away with him, but there was more. There were lists of recent donations and expenditures that she hadn't seen before.

She set the file on the coffee table, reached for her laptop and started typing. "Miracle Babies" and "Mexico City" produced stories about the great Mexican earthquake of 1985, long before the founding of the center. The story was a crock. A cold, shaking fury was building within her. Did Travis think she wouldn't check? She pushed her chair back from the computer and hit speed dial. The phone rang several times before her mother picked up.

"Mother, Travis just told me the biggest bunch of crap I've ever heard. Would you please tell me what the schools project is all about?"

"Alex, your language is deteriorating by the day."

"Just answer the question, please."

"It's nothing to get so worked up about. It's something from a long time ago. You're blowing this way out of proportion. I've had a long day. We'll talk another time. Good night."

"No, don't hang up."

The phone clicked. Damn the woman. Alex slammed her cell on the counter. The clock read ten-thirty. She gave up for now and headed for bed.

CHAPTER TWENTY-SEVEN

Alex was up by six the next morning. She shoved clean workout clothes into a bag and drove to the gym. It felt like forever since she'd been there. Exercise always made her feel better. An hour of punishing deadlifts, power cleans, and pull-ups followed by an all-out one-mile run on the treadmill and the endorphins took over. She'd been hitting the gym at least three times a week since Mexico and could tell she was stronger, more agile and athletic. The brutal workouts plus running and self-defense classes took up most of her free time, and she liked it that way.

"Hey, Alex, looking hot."

She kept walking. "Hey, Ron. You're not. You have a ways to go. Really shows."

"You free later?"

Idiot didn't even get that she was blowing him off. In the changing room she stripped off her sweat-soaked clothes and ducked into the shower. She was leaner and with greater muscle definition than she'd had in years. She hummed and let the hot water pound her exhausted muscles for ten minutes before toweling off and heading back to her locker.

She could hear Lupe and another woman from the cleaning crew at the far end of the locker room. Lupe was crying and the other woman was trying to comfort her. "The police will find your niece and bring her home. Everything will be all right."

Alex stood still. She couldn't believe what she was hearing. She and Lupe had talked many times over the past year, about Mexican food and Lupe's family.

"The police don't do nothin'. Nobody is looking for her. Some men took her right off the street when she was going to a movie with her boyfriend. When her boyfriend tried to fight them, they killed him. They'll kill her too when they get tired of her."

Alex closed her eyes. Their talk brought it all back. The pungent cologne of the man who'd dragged her from the bus. The agony in Cristina's face when the bullet hit her. Cristina's blood-soaked blouse. The fear and the remorse.

"*Perdonen*," she said, approaching the cleaning crew. "Lupe, I couldn't help hearing. Where was your niece when she was kidnapped?"

Lupe wiped away her tears and tried to smile. "She was in my town in Mexico. These people make girls like her work or become *putas*. Nobody cares."

"I care. The same thing happened to me in Mexico. Some men tried to kidnap me, but I was lucky. I got away. Many are not. The traffickers are everywhere, even here in Dalton. The police and the FBI *are* trying to stop them. If you give me your niece's name and description, I'll tell them about her. They will want to talk with you. They can help you look for her."

Alex's hair was still damp when she walked into her favorite coffee shop a half hour later. She felt shaky. She had to do something.

She looked around for Keisha White. She'd received a text from the detective when she was leaving the fitness center, asking to meet this morning, alone. No doubt Scott Foley wouldn't like it, but then he wasn't being exactly forthcoming himself.

The shop was unusually empty even for a Wednesday morning, a good thing since she'd just as soon that no one saw her meeting Detective White. Cinnamon and chocolate mingled with the aroma of hot coffee. She stepped up to the counter.

The manager greeted her with a broad smile. "Hey, Alex. It's been over a week. We missed you,"

"Good to see you too, Joe. I've been pretty busy."

"Yeah. So I hear." He lowered his voice. "There's a cop here says she's waiting for you. I put her in the back booth."

Alex got her *café con leche* and walked toward the back past an elderly man playing solitaire and a student staring at a computer. She slid into the booth across from White.

"I've got to tell you what I heard just now at the gym." She told the detective about her conversation with Lupe.

"Unfortunately, that's a pretty common story," White said. "The poor girl could be anywhere by now, but I'll give the information to the FBI. I'm glad you told me. I wanted to talk to you more about this anyway. That's why I asked you here."

"Do you really think I would have anything to do with human trafficking?"

"No I don't, especially in light of what happened to you in Mexico City, but I believe someone connected with your center is, and you can help. Talk to me. In the year that you've been in charge, did you ever see anything suspicious at the York Street house?"

"I told you I saw Carmela with Mariana and Teresa once in back. I also saw her talking with a blonde woman, maybe a month ago. Carmela said it was a neighbor from the house behind us. Maybe it was Shirley Hodges, the one Teresa identified. I didn't see anything else."

"How come you and your medical staff didn't suspect that you were treating trafficked women? Many of them must have shown signs of abuse."

"I've been asking myself the same thing. We get abused women all the time. We urge them to file complaints, and tell them about shelters where they can go. Sadly, a lot of them just go back for more of the same. None of the women that Carmela brought in would talk to us. I blame myself for not asking more questions. I should have tried to get them to tell us who hurt them. Reported it to the police."

"You should have, but you can make up for that by helping us now. We have the forensics back from the York Street house. Ever heard of a guy named Billy Williams? His prints were all over the house."

Alex shook her head.

"Williams works for the JoVille Group, for your father. We asked your father about him, but all he said was that Williams was some sort of handyman."

"My father's companies have a lot of employees. It's not surprising that he doesn't know all of them."

White sat back and looked at her. "Did you know that Scott Foley traveled to Mexico twice this year and your father five times? Even your mother went there once."

"My father has businesses in Mexico and real estate holdings. My mother enjoys being pampered. There's a spa there she likes. I really can't tell you anything about Scott Foley, but I don't believe my center has anything to do with human trafficking other than what Carmela did."

"You really believe that?"

Alex stared into space. She hoped she was right. She thought of her conversation with Travis last night and the file she'd found about the schools project. Could it have anything to do with what happened to Mariana? Her gut told her something was wrong, but maybe that was because she couldn't get a straight answer from anybody. She wasn't going to tell White about it. It would just cause more problems for the center. She had to find out for herself.

"Is there anything you're not telling me?" White said.

There was a time when Keisha White would have intimidated her. Not anymore. She'd survived Mexico. Nothing could be worse than that. She picked up her bag and stood.

"All I can tell you is that you're wasting time if you think my father had anything to do with this. He's the best person I know."

CHAPTER TWENTY-EIGHT

Mike worked the trafficking story every chance he got. Roush would tell him to leave it alone if he found out, so Mike didn't tell him. He frowned at his computer screen, trying to decide where to go next. The newsroom was winding down. He waved good night to a fellow reporter and went back to his notes when the phone rang. Expecting Espinosa, he picked up. Not Espinosa. Another **Spanish-accented** voice that sounded familiar.

"You the guy asking 'bout the dead woman?"

"That's me. Who's this?"

"Meet me at midnight behind *Mi Tienda*. Jus' you."

The line went dead before Mike could negotiate a better place. He didn't like that one at all. He guessed that the caller was one of the Hispanic gang from Rag Town, and none of those guys were what you'd call friendly.

An hour later, he was groping his way around to the back of the market in the dark with one hand over his nose to block the smell of rotting food and taking care not to bang into garbage cans and cardboard boxes. Roaches scampered from his path. He tripped over something that looked like a rusty crowbar. He bent down and picked it up and moved forward into the shadows. The building blocked the light from the street. He stumbled in the dark, and turned on his flashlight, not happy to be making himself a clear target.

"Hello. Anyone there?"

He gripped the crowbar. Minutes passed. He waited. Something ran across his foot, a rat most likely. He wasn't afraid of taking on one teenager. He'd stayed in pretty good shape since Afghanistan. Much of his time there had been spent as an embedded reporter, but there'd also been grueling workouts, running, climbing walls, bars, pull-ups, push-ups, and he'd kept it up after he got out.

"Hey. You called me. I'm not waiting forever."

Small animals scampered across the rubble.

He turned toward the street. "Okay. I'm out of here."

Someone spoke from behind the shack. "You alone like I tol' you?"

"Yeah. Just me. You wanted to talk, so talk. Fast. This place stinks."

Mañuel stepped out of the shadows and limped toward him, eyes shifting from side to side, searching the shadows.

Mike waited. Mañuel's arm was in a sling.

"I got something for you," Mañuel said. "But you don't tell no one where you got it, right?"

"That's correct. I won't reveal a source even to the cops. What've you got?"

Mañuel looked around the lot again. "Some guys been comin' around, making like they in charge. They're runnin' women through here from Mexico, like the one you was asking about who got killed."

"How do you know that?"

"I jus' know."

"Who's behind this? Someone in Dalton?"

"I don't got a name, but there's a local boss. A *gringo* who keeps the police and *Federales* away. Good deal for him until that woman got killed. The real *jefe*, the top guy's from Mexico. Mad as hell. He come here with these guys I'm talking about."

"Do you have a name for the local boss?"

"Jus' know he's rich, very important, but I hear he's afraid of the top guy."

"You know anything about the big *jefe* from Mexico?"

"Yeah. He makes the *gringo* here do what he say. His guys come into Rag Town. They say they gonna make us do what they say."

"How many people are you talking about?"

"Four, maybe five guys from Mexico," Mañuel said.

"And there's the two bikers you fought with in front of *Mi Tienda*?" Mike asked.

Mañuel rubbed the arm. "Yeah, them too. We didn't do too good this time."

"Why did you call me?"

He looked around the lot again. "Cause they cut up our leader Javier pretty bad, and they busted my arm. They say they gonna bring more guys from Mexico and wipe us out if we don't do what they say."

"What do they want you to do?"

"They say we help with the women. We don't want to do that."

"Who else knows you're talking to me?"

"Nobody but me. You jus' write a story about those guys, and say they're movin' women through here so the cop'll make them go back to Mexico."

"It's not that simple. I'd like to help, but I need more information. I need corroboration, someone besides you to tell me this is happening. I want all you can find about these guys. Who is this local *jefe*? What's the connection with the big boss in Mexico? Get me names and find out how they get the women here. Then we're in business."

He heard footsteps on the rough ground and turned toward the noise. Three figures, backlit by the light from the street, came toward them. Mañuel was over the wall in seconds.

The leader of the Hispanic gang came out of the shadows with two other gang members Mike recognized.

"Mañuel, you idiot, get back here."

Mañuel scrambled back down from the wall and slunk toward his gang, hands stuffed in his pockets.

The leader's eyes were blackened, and a large gash ran across his forehead. His right arm was in a sling.

"You're Javier?" Mike asked.

"Yeah. You help us and we give you people in Mexico who can help you blow this whole thing up."

CHAPTER TWENTY-NINE

When Alex parked in front of her apartment at seven o'clock the following night, the lot was empty of all but the cars she recognized. Her muscles were in knots. She was like a coiled spring, wound tight from too little sleep and too much caffeine. She needed to run. She took the outside stairs to her apartment two at a time, fumbled with the lock, threw open the door, and dashed into her bedroom.

She pulled on her running shoes, and minutes later she was back outside in shorts and a sports bra. The days were cooling down earlier, the shadows getting longer. Fall would be here soon. It felt less like she was breathing through a wet washcloth. She waved at a neighbor on the way down the stairs and ran around to the back of the building toward her regular running path around the reservoir. Her father always fussed that the route was too secluded. She carried a can of mace on her waistband, she told him. She was fine.

The sun sat low in the sky, its light glinting off the rippling surface of the reservoir. She ran along the trail until it reached the highway and jogged in place, waiting for the traffic to clear. A blue van flashed by. Her heart jumped sideways. She forced her breathing to slow. There must be hundreds of blue vans around. She was being ridiculous.

She crossed the road and continued around the reservoir, running up on a flock of crows devouring a dead raccoon. The crows flew up in her face, screeching in protest. She jumped back, chest heaving, and stopped. The bushes formed a solid purple mass against the fading light. Crows cawed at her from the trees. The crows lived here. She was the intruder. She had to get a grip. She headed for home, picking up the pace.

She felt the earth shake under her feet. Someone was behind her on the path. Runners, she hoped. She turned to look over her shoulder. There were two of them—big guys, youngish, one black, one white, and they were gaining on her. She ran faster, muscles straining with each step. Her chest was tight. She wasn't going to be able to outrun them. At the bend they caught up. Both were wearing the same blue and white shirts, Dalton University colors.

"Lady, you're really hauling," one of them called as he passed her.

"We could use you on the team," the other yelled. Laughing, they continued on ahead.

Smiling, she settled back into her normal rhythm. By the time she circled back to the path that led to her apartment building, she was ready for a shower and something cold to drink. She reached the clearing leading up to the parking lot and stopped to stretch. No one was around. The day's tensions were gone. The pollen-heavy scent of goldenrod saturated the air. She paused, savoring the endorphin rush, taking long slow breaths until she heard the squeal of tires.

A blue van rounded the corner of the building and sped toward her. The ground pitched beneath her. She rallied, fumbling for the can of mace. The can slipped through her sweating hands, hit the ground and rolled. She dove for it, grasping it just as the van slammed to a stop. A big, bearded man jumped out and lunged for her. She clutched the mace can and sprayed. The man howled, clawing at his eyes. She dodged under his arm and ran toward her building.

A second man, younger, faster, flew at her, catching her by one ankle. She pitched forward. The pavement ground into her cheek. The man had wrapped one arm around her neck, bending her back until her vertebrae cracked. He rolled her over and put a knee in her chest. The pain was crushing. The bearded man, tears still streaming, wound duct tape around her wrists.

She twisted away, trying to break free and tore off her tennis bracelet. The big man bound her feet, pulling the tape so tight that she lost all feeling in them. They picked her up and tossed her into the back of the van. She landed on her right shoulder. Searing pain shot through her arm.

The van doors slammed shut. She lay on the floor in the dark, fighting for breath, her head throbbing, blood seeping into her eyes. The engine started. The van backed up fast, then turned and skidded out of the parking lot. Traffic noises grew louder as the van left the parking lot and drove along a paved road for several miles. She could hear cars honking, truck noises, a train whistle.

She fought to control her panic. This couldn't be happening, not again. What were the chances of being abducted twice? She fought the urge to throw up. For one awful long moment she gave up. Then she thought of Cristina and Mariana. She owed it to them to live, to avenge their deaths. Whoever these men were, they would not win. She rolled onto her knees.

A weak stream of light came from around the doors. Her eyes adjusted to the dim light. The van reeked like the sour smell of rotting fruit. The tape dug into her wrists and ankles. She inched across a heavy plastic drop cloth. Her skin, wet with sweat, stuck to it. Were they going to kill her? She fought back another wave of nausea.

The van took a corner fast. There was nothing to hold on to. She slid across the plastic, slamming against the side panel. Reds and greens and yellows flashed. Blood trickled into her eyes. She wiped the blood away with her bound hands and leaned back, gulping putrid air while the van spun around her. The back of the van seemed miles away. She pushed herself onto her hands and knees and began to crawl through dried leaves, empty cardboard cartons caked with food, and cans reeking of stale beer. Exhausted, she reached the back corner. She needed a weapon. She patted her hands around the floor until she found a glass bottle under an old army blanket. She gripped the bottle and waited. The tires bumped along the broken pavement. The doors rattled.

The van banged over potholes and broken pavement. She raised the bottle above her head and smashed it hard on the edge of a metal drum. The glass cracked. She sat back against the side of the van holding the broken bottle between her knees and worked the duct tape on her wrists back and forth across the jagged glass. The tape broke, and she moved on to the tape around her ankles.

The van turned onto dirt. The whoosh of traffic quieted, replaced by the grumbling of a gravel road. Tree branches smacked against the truck. The van slowed and the engine cut out just as her ankles broke free. She heard the driver's door open. One foot hit the dirt, then the other. Two more landed on the other side of the truck. Voices came around to the back of the van, two men. Her heart thudded. She sprang into a crouch. The handles rattled, and the doors swung open, filling the van with fresh air.

Her abductors appeared in the opening, silhouetted against the dusky light.

"Where the hell is she?"

A third man pushed the two aside and climbed in. He came toward her. She smelled the strong, musky cologne first. Then she saw his face and gasped. She would never forget that face and the puckered scar that dissected it. This was no random kidnapping. Mexico hadn't been random either. These men were after her. Why?

Scar-face came toward her, his small eyes shining. "I been waiting a long time for this, *puta*. We gonna teach you a lesson."

She shrank back against the van wall.

Scar-face came closer. She lunged, aiming the bottle directly at the shoulder. The raw edge of glass sank deep into soft flesh. She threw her weight into it. Blood spurted from the wound. She pulled the glass out.

Scar-face grabbed his arm and fell backwards against the side of the van, howling.

She scrambled over him, still clutching the broken bottle, and jumped at the bearded man, aiming the sharp glass at his face. Before she could connect he fell back. She had an opening. She jumped out of the van and landed in the dirt. She looked around. An old farmhouse stood in one direction, the road in the other.

She took the road. With a quick look over her shoulder, she saw her two abductors scramble into the van. She took off, running flat out. If she could make it to a main road, someone might help her. She put several hundred yards between herself and the van before she heard the sound of revving engines. She turned. Two Harleys were racing toward her. She dove into a ditch, rolled to her feet, and took off through a wooded area.

The Harleys leapt the ditch, coming fast. She ran toward a laurel thicket, dodging the trees. The bikes came faster. They were on her in seconds. The bearded man jumped off and ran after her. She tripped over a tree root, stumbling. Before she could regain her balance the man was on her, bringing her down. She shot her hands out, aiming the broken bottle at his eyes.

The younger man twisted her arm, hard, making her cry. "You stabbed Diego. You gonna pay."

She screamed and dropped the bottle, kicking backwards.

The man picked her up and slammed her on the ground.

She screamed again.

The man let out a low, dirty laugh from deep within his chest. "Save your breath, *puta*. Only birds and rabbits out here."

The bearded man tied her wrists and ankles so that the rope cut into her skin. She lay on the ground face down, helpless.

"Get her shoulders," the younger man said and took her feet. They carried her to the bikes. The one with the beard held her while the dark-skinned man climbed on his bike and threw her across the seat to put her in front of him. The two men kicked the Harleys into gear.

In seconds the bikes reached the porch. The men dismounted and pulled her off the bike. They carried her into the farmhouse, up a flight of wooden stairs, and through a narrow doorway into a small, dark room where they threw her on a metal bed. She felt the prick of a needle in her arm.

"That'll hold her," the dark-skinned man said.

CHAPTER THIRTY

Mike left Rag Town, playing back in his mind everything he'd heard from Javier and Mañuel. Espinosa was right. The human trafficking story went way beyond Dalton. There was a network that led from Mexico to Dalton and probably to other places in the U.S. He had to convince Roush to let him work on this full-time. Maybe he could talk his editor into tapping into the *Herald*'s dwindling funds to send him to Mexico. He and Espinosa could work on this together.

If only Alex would talk to him. Her office and cell both gave him computerized messages. She couldn't stay mad forever, could she? He wanted to tell her about Espinosa and what he'd learned. At around one in the morning he gave up trying and went to bed. He'd go to the center in the morning. She'd have to talk to him.

It was past nine when he got up the next morning. He was still tired but determined to find Alex. He put the gray tabby outside and drove to the center. He was sure of a cold reception. Maybe he deserved it, but he'd deal with it.

Gladys was sitting behind Alex's desk, cradling the phone between her ear and her shoulder when he walked into the lobby. She covered the receiver and waved him in, actually looking relieved to see him.

"Mr. Murray. Thank God. Do you know where Alex is?"

His jaw dropped. "The last time I saw Alex she was with you here. Remember, she threw me out?"

"You haven't seen her since? She wasn't at the staff meeting this morning, and that's not at all like her. There's no answer on her cell. I've left messages everywhere. No one's seen her."

"What about her parents?"

"I have her mother on the phone now. She doesn't know where she is either, and she's raising hell, like it's my fault that I bothered her."

"Did you check your messages?"

"Of course. There are no messages. Nothing on her calendar."

Gladys turned back to the phone. "Yes, Mrs. Harrington. I'll call you as soon I know anything."

Gladys hung up and glared at the phone. "Damn woman's more put out that I woke her up than that Alex didn't show up for work."

"Maybe she just slept in. She seemed pretty strung out the last time I saw her," Mike said.

"Unlike her, but that was my first guess too. She's been going at it pretty hard lately, but by ten, I got worried. I tried phoning her apartment. No answer. That's when I tried Renee Harrington. I made the mistake of saying I was going to call Keisha White. That really sent her into orbit."

"It's only eleven o'clock. Alex probably forgot to tell you about some meeting out of the office."

Gladys leaned forward on her arms. "Maybe, but this isn't the only thing going on around here that doesn't make sense. Can I trust you?"

"Sure. I'm a friend of Alex's; at least I'd like to be."

"Even though you're a reporter?"

"Nothing goes into print, I promise."

Gladys cleared her throat. "Do you know what happened to Alex in Mexico City?"

He nodded. "Alex told me about her escape, and about a girl she called Cristina. You think her not showing up has something to do with what happened in Mexico City? That was months ago."

"I know it isn't rational. Alex isn't even in the same country. It's just that there are a lot of ties to Mexico; first Carmela disappears, then there's Mariana and Teresa, the fire, all of it connected to human trafficking. Makes me wonder."

"What's going on?" Keisha White said from the doorway.

Gladys started. "How long have you been there?"

White came into the office and looked around. "Since you started talking about Alex and Mexico City. Where is she?"

"Not here."

"I can see that. Has anyone checked her apartment?"

"I've called, but I'm short-staffed. I can't leave the clinic."

"I'll do it," White said, heading out the door.

Gladys followed her. "Please ask Alex to call when you find her."

————

Mike followed White to Alex's apartment and pulled in beside the unmarked car. Alex's car was in the lot in her usual space. White and two uniformed officers knocked on the apartment door. He was halfway up the stairs when Renee Harrington opened the door.

"We're looking for your daughter, Mrs. Harrington."

"I told Gladys not to call the police. This is all a mistake. I'm sure my daughter is visiting a friend or getting her hair done."

"May we come in?" White asked, pushing past Renee Harrington into the apartment, leaving the door open.

Mike continued on up the stairs and stood on the landing, listening.

"Really. This is intrusive. You can't come in here like this."

"Your daughter's car is in the lot and she's not here. Where is she?"

"I have no idea," Renee Harrington said. "She isn't with any of her girlfriends. I've called all of them."

"You don't mind if I look around," White said. She left the living room and was back ten minutes later.

"The bed's not been slept in. It looks like she came home, changed clothes, and went out. There are work clothes on the bed, leather pumps on the floor. A dresser drawer is open. What does she usually keep in there?"

"How should I know?" Renee Harrington's mouth grew tight. "Maybe she went for a run. She does that sometimes."

"On a work day when nobody in the office knows where she is? That doesn't sound like your daughter. Why aren't you more concerned, Mrs. Harrington? Is there something you're not telling me?"

132

"Certainly not. She hasn't even been gone for twenty-four hours. This is not police business. I insist that you to leave us alone."

"Under ordinary circumstances, I might, but there is nothing ordinary about this case. We've had a murder, arson, and kidnapping in less than a week. Also she's been kidnapped before."

———————

Mike was standing in the hall outside of the apartment when Keisha White came out.

"Damn it. You followed me, Murray. You were listening."

"You think something's happened to Alex? What's up with her mother? Isn't that a strange reaction when her daughter's missing?"

"That's three questions, and I don't have answers to any of them. Now get out of my way so I can do my job."

White opened her cell. "Put out an all-points bulletin on Alexandra Harrington, age twenty-five, medium height, brown hair with a white streak, green eyes."

Mike followed White down the stairs. "Can we print her picture in the paper? Get it on round-the-clock local news? Someone must have seen her."

"Back off. I've got this. Nothing's public until we say so. Got that?"

"Will you let me know if you find something?"

Without answering, White got in her car and drove off in the direction of police headquarters.

Mike got back in the Mustang. Who else might know where Alex had gone? He tried calling her gym. Nothing. He thought of Travis Bingham. He didn't want to think about Alex with him, but he had to try. He pulled out Bingham's business card, dialed, and waited.

"Bingham here."

"Do you know where Alex Harrington is?"

"Murray? That you? I don't know where Alex is, and I wouldn't tell you if I did."

CHAPTER THIRTY-ONE

Moonlight streamed through the narrow window and fell across Alex's face, waking her. She had no idea where she was or how she had got there. Slowly, it came back to her—the faces of her abductors, the van, the dirt road. She remembered two men dragging her into an old house, cuffing her right wrist to the head of a metal bed, sticking her with a needle. Now she lay on a mildewed mattress in a hot and airless room with unfinished walls and the sloping ceiling of an attic. Handcuffs held one arm above her head, wrenching her shoulder. Her back ached. She was caked with dirt and dried sweat, and she had to pee. She moved her arms and legs, one at a time. Nothing was broken.

She heard a sound from across the dimly lit room, like the whimper of a frightened animal.

"Miss Alex. It's me, Carmela."

"Carmela? Have you been here all along?"

"*Sí.* Two men bring me here from Miss Gladys's. More men are downstairs."

"How many are there?"

"There is a mean woman and a big man with a beard. Also, many men from Mexico."

"You helped those men. You took money from them."

"I was afraid of them."

"Why didn't you come to me or Gladys?"

"I am so sorry. I try to make it better. I help Mariana and her sister.

The men hurt me, but I don't tell them where Teresa is. Is she okay?"

Alex felt her anger toward Carmela soften. The poor woman was clearly terrified and genuinely sorry.

"Teresa's in a safe place now where no one can hurt her."

"The men say the police find Teresa. They don't need me no more. I think they will kill me."

"Are you free? Can you move around?"

"A big rope ties me to this bed, but I'm rubbing it against the bed frame."

Alex craned her head to look out the window. She thought about the route they'd covered in the van and what she'd seen when she tried to get away. The farmhouse was at least ten miles from town.

"I hear them talk. They say they catch you in Mexico City, but you got away. The big boss wants you."

"I know. We've got to get away fast. Both of us."

Carmela rolled her plump legs over the edge of the mattress and planted her feet on the floor with a triumphant thump. "Miss Alex, I did it. I got my rope off."

"Great. Help me with these handcuffs."

A noise came from the hall. The doorknob turned.

"Quick. Get back in bed. Make it look like you're still tied up," Alex said.

The door swung open. A woman stood in the doorway, glaring at them, the woman from the parking lot, without the head scarf. Alex recognized her easily now as Shirley Hodges from the mugshot.

"What's goin' on in here?"

Alex sat up. "You have no right to keep us here. Let us go."

Hodges crossed the room and slapped Alex so hard that her neck snapped back. "Diego'll be here right soon to teach you a lesson for what you done to him in the van. He'll take care of your friend too. If Mr. Vargas wasn't fussing so much about them horses, she'd be dead already."

Alex felt a shard-like pain tear through her neck. The room spun.

"No more sass," Hodges said and she walked out the door, slamming it behind her.

Carmela's shoulders shook.

Alex heard footsteps in the hall. She tensed, listening.

"Hey, Diego, What's happening?"

Alex held her breath. Scar-face was back.

"Another shipment's due here tomorrow. Mostly women. Some workers. We're passing them on to New Jersey."

Footsteps retreated down the stairs, a door closed, and the house fell silent.

Carmela's voice quivered. "They're going to kill us."

"We aren't going to give them the chance."

Alex was looking out the window, trying to work out a plan when the door opened again. The big man from the van came in, carrying a box that he put on the cot beside her. He stood looking at her, scratching his belly.

She studied him. Dark, curly hair covered every inch of his body that she could see. He'd wrestled her to the ground, kidnapped her, and now he was bringing something to her, his little eyes blinking with expectation.

She didn't move.

The man bent down, opened the box, and pushed it across the bare mattress toward her.

The box was filled with glazed and sugar doughnuts.

She gasped.

"Eat," the man said.

She thought of refusing, but she was weak from hunger. She grabbed a doughnut and tore into it.

"Carmela needs one too."

She studied the man while he carried the box across the room to Carmela. She'd seen him somewhere before. She thought back to what Keisha White had said about the fingerprints in the white house.

"You're Billy Williams, aren't you?

The man looked at her and nodded.

"You work for the JoVille Group. For my father."

He nodded again, and his expression turned almost friendly. "I been with your father a long time."

Odd that her father hadn't seemed to know Billy.

"Would you please take these things off? I need to go to the bathroom."

Billy grunted and pulled a small key from his jeans pocket. He unlocked the handcuffs and walked across the room to an old chest of drawers, coming back with a ceramic chamber pot.

"Turn around," she said.

When she was done, and had come back to the cot, Billy picked up the pot and emptied it out the window. He made no move to reattach the handcuffs.

She got up and crossed the room to Carmela, still keeping an eye on Billy Williams.

Billy spoke, his voice low and gravelly. "That bunch are gone to get supplies, all 'cept for me and Shirley and Diego whose shoulder's not feeling too good and who's all doped up. You got to go now."

"First you kidnap me, now you're being helpful. Why?"

Billy's mouth grew tight. "They killed Marvin. He didn't deserve to die, not like that. This is payback."

"Who's Marvin?"

Billy shook his head. "My cousin. Go out the window and over the porch roof. I'll keep Shirley busy."

Billy went out of the room, leaving them alone. Alex waited. Listening. The house was quiet. This could be some kind of trap, but they didn't have a choice.

"Come on Carmela. Time to get out of here." Carmela shrank back against her cot. "You go, Miss Alex. I can't keep up."

For a split second Alex was tempted. She had a much better chance of getting away on her own. Then she remembered Cristina. She'd left her to die alone. She couldn't do the same to Carmela, no matter what the woman had done. "Get up. They'll kill you if you stay here."

She pulled Carmela to her feet, picked up the rope beside the cot, and started toward the window. "If we can tie the rope to the bedframe, we can hold it while we slide down the porch roof, then climb down the gutter to the ground."

Together they pushed the bed below the window. Alex tied the rope to the bed frame and lowered it to within two feet of the porch roof. "I'll go down first."

Carmela followed her to the window and looked down, her body shaking. "I'm scared of heights."

Alex climbed out onto the window ledge and gripped it. "We hold onto the rope and go down hand over hand. Once I'm down, you follow. I'll catch you."

She climbed on the ledge and looked down. The tin porch roof was only a dozen feet below, easy enough if it weren't for Carmela.

"See, it's not so far. All you have to do is hold onto the rope and walk your feet down the side of the house."

Carmela covered her eyes. "I cannot do that."

"You must, Carmela. I'll go first and catch you." She gripped the rope and lowered herself to the tin roof below, motioning for Carmela to follow.

Carmela squeezed her plump body through the window and froze. "You heard Shirley. The men will kill you."

Carmela's face twisted in terror. Shaking, she took hold of the rope, swung against the wall, and lost her grip, crying out as she fell and crashed onto the roof beside Alex.

Shirley Hodges had to have heard that. Sweat poured down Alex's back.

She pushed Carmela down and lay flat against the roof, cupping a hand over the woman's mouth.

"Who's there?" Shirley called from the door directly below.

She heard Billy's voice. "I don't see no one. Tree limb prob'ly fell on the house."

Alex waited, barely breathing, for footsteps, a shotgun blast. A minute passed. Sweat trickled down her back. No one came onto the porch. The front door slammed.

"Quick. Before they come back."

Carmela held up hands that were raw from rope burns. "Please. I cannot."

"I know it hurts, but the men will be back any minute."

She put one arm under Carmela's and helped her across the slippery roof to the edge.

"It's not very far to the ground from here. There's a rain barrel next to the porch. I'll hold onto the gutter and climb down to the barrel. You follow, and I'll catch you."

Carmela curled into a fetal position and shook her head.

Alex sighed. There was no way she could carry Carmela down the gutter. "There's got to be a ladder somewhere."

She climbed down to the barrel and jumped to the ground. There was a shed within a few yards of the house. The door was open. She pressed her back against the wall, inched her way toward the shed and stopped. No one came out of the house. She ran for the shed door and ducked inside. A wooden ladder lay on the floor. She tried to pick it up. It was too heavy and cumbersome to carry. She'd have to risk the noise of dragging it. She picked up one end and pulled it out of the shed. The ladder clattered along the dirt for a dozen feet before catching on a tree root. She pulled. The ladder stuck. Her shoulder was still aching from the van. She gritted her teeth and gave the ladder a hard yank. The ladder broke free and slid onto smoother ground. Step by tortuous step she dragged it toward the porch, sure that each clatter would bring Shirley running. When she reached the porch, she looked up the drive to the road, heart thudding. Nothing yet. She summoned up all the strength she had left to upend the ladder and lean it against the edge of the roof.

Carmela looked down at the ladder, eyes round with terror.

Alex climbed up and grabbed Carmela's arm, and, ignoring her sobs, pulled her to the edge of the roof. "We're running out of time."

"I can't, Miss Alex."

"Yes Carmela, you can. Now move."

An eternity later, Carmela was on the ground beside her. Their best chance was to run to a stand of tall pines thirty yards from the house in the opposite direction from the drive. The memory of that other escape through tall grass paralyzed her. She could see Cristina lying in the dirt.

"Miss Alex, what do we do?"

Alex shook herself. "We run." She took Carmela's arm and set off for the trees, across the high grass, keeping low, catching Carmela each time she tripped.

When at last they reached the trees, she looked back at the house; still no sign of Diego and the others. Carmela stopped, panting, and leaned against a tree, her face flushed. "No more, Miss Alex. I need to rest."

"There's no time. You heard what Shirley said. Vargas is coming."

CHAPTER THIRTY-TWO

The officers and detectives of the Dalton P.D. stared intently at the television screen. Mike slipped into the squad room, unnoticed. Pictures of Alex from earlier times flashed across the screen: her high school graduation, a horse show, a debutante ball.

He ran a hand over the stubble on his chin. The girl in the pictures was smiling, relaxed, not at all like the intense Alex Harrington he knew. Had Mexico City done that to her?

He walked up behind Keisha White. "Any news?"

"You look terrible."

"You don't look so hot yourself, detective. It's been three days. You've got to have something. I'm going crazy."

"We have the DNA back on the cigarette butts from your house. Whoever attacked you isn't in any U.S. database."

"I don't care about me. What do you know about Alex?"

White's face softened. "You really care about her, don't you? You're dead if you breathe a word of this. We found a tennis bracelet in the parking lot behind her house. Looks like she put up a fight. The FBI is all over this now. It's official. We're calling it a kidnapping."

"Any demand for ransom?"

"Nothing yet. This is connected somehow with Mariana's murder and Carmela's kidnapping. I'm sure of it."

Mike flinched and looked at White. "Do you think she found something at the center that made her a threat to somebody? She's been digging through the files and asking a lot of questions."

"I met her for coffee the day before she disappeared. She really wanted to clear the center and her father. I think she'd have told me if she'd found anything that would help. Her parents keep calling the chief and the governor. All they're doing is making everything a whole lot harder."

The door to the squad room opened, and Chief Odom walked in and joined the group watching the television. Pictures flashed up of people walking along country roads, tramping through the woods.

"Volunteers are out searching for miles outside of town. I came here to tell you we're setting up a hotline," Odom said.

A newscaster broke into the coverage of the search. "With us in the studio are Mr. and Mrs. Harrington, the parents of the missing woman."

Renee Harrington's face was immobile, Sandy Harrington looked distraught. A number flashed across the screen. "Please call the police hotline if you know anything about our daughter. We're offering a twenty-five thousand dollar reward for any information that leads to finding her," Sandy Harrington said.

White turned to the chief. "We're not staffed up for a hotline. The phones will be ringing off the hook with that kind of reward. We're working twenty-four seven now."

"This is the Harringtons' idea. They think it will help. We don't have a choice. The governor himself called me at home last night. He's a family friend, you know. I'm to call him if anything breaks, and he said *anything*."

"What do you expect to get from the hotline, Chief?" Mike asked.

Odom's face turned an alarming brick red. "Who the hell let a damn reporter in here? Get him the hell out of here."

Mike opened his mouth to protest when Officer Lea rushed into the squad room. "The search team found a body in the woods about three miles south of town."

———

Mike knew the coldness inside him was fear. He'd covered the crime beat here and in Arizona, but never when he felt personally involved. He got out of his car behind Keisha White and followed the detective into the woods, trying to be professional and failing miserably.

"I'm going to catch hell if the chief finds out I let you come along, Murray. Stay out of the way," White said.

"I owe you, Keisha."

"Keep it to yourself."

They trudged through dense woods in silence for half a mile, climbing over fallen logs and pushing aside branches until they saw one of the forensics team walking toward them.

"No need to rush. Body's been there a while. Looks like somebody buried it. Animals dug it up and must've fought over it. A part of an arm is missing, and the face and hands are gnawed beyond recognition. Identification's not going to be easy."

"Man or woman?" White asked.

Mike held his breath.

"Male, Caucasian, medium height, slender build. That's about all we can make at this point."

White looked at Mike. "Not Alex."

He swallowed, then exhaled slowly.

Keisha turned back to the forensics tech. "Where's the body?"

"Up ahead, thirty yards or so. I'm going back for more equipment. The M.E. is there with the team."

Mike followed White in the direction the man had indicated, his steps lighter despite the rough terrain.

When they reached the scene a tired medical examiner got up stiffly from next to the body and took off rubber gloves.

"Afternoon, detective. This guy's been dead a few days, a week at most. Hard to tell exactly with a body left outside in this heat. Could be tough getting a print after all the animals have done to him."

Keisha White leaned over to look at the body. "With all the decomp and animal damage, without the tattoos his own mother wouldn't recognize him. Any chance this was an accident?"

"Not hardly. He was shot. Looks like a small caliber, fired at close range, but not here. There's no blood. He was shot somewhere else."

Mike leaned against a tree, writing furiously on his pad while the

M.E. directed the removal of the body and the forensic team completed its initial a search of the area and secured the scene. The sun was disappearing behind the trees by the time they were done. White looked exhausted when she joined him.

"What about the homemade wooden cross at the head of the man's grave?" he asked

Keisha White nodded. "The cross is crude, made of two sticks tied together. Looks like whoever buried him cared about him."

"You'd think someone would have reported him gone by now," Mike said.

"I've checked. No one meeting this guy's description has been reported missing in Dalton in the last month." White reached down to scratch an ankle. "Damn these bugs." She slapped a mosquito and looked at the blood on her hand. "Let's get the hell out of here."

CHAPTER THIRTY-THREE

Alex moved from tree to tree. Carmela followed, grumbling. The afternoon shadows grew longer. Alex's watch said six o'clock, only an hour or so before sunset. Their cover would be better, but she worried whether Carmela could manage in the dark. She was pretty sure they were south of town. She remembered that the van had traveled over a heavily trafficked hardtop surface before turning onto the dirt road that led to the farmhouse. She thought they'd crossed over the Hawk River Bridge so Highway 15 wasn't far away. She hoped they were heading toward the highway now. If they couldn't find it soon, she had a backup plan. From her Girl Scout days, she knew there were caves around here somewhere. Worst case, they would find one and hide there. These people had killed Cristina. They had killed Mariana. They were not going to catch her again, and she was not going to let them kill Carmela.

They hadn't gone more than a mile when Carmela's knees buckled. "You go on Miss Alex, please."

Alex struggled to control her frustration. "No way I'm leaving you. Come on. You can do it." She helped Carmela to her feet and half carried, half dragged her to a stand of dense trees and settled her behind a large boulder. "Keep down and don't move."

Wind rustled the tall pines. Small animals scampered through the underbrush. So far no one was behind them.

They stumbled on for another ten minutes when the warning call of birds came from the direction of the farmhouse.

She stopped to listen. A man yelled. Another man answered. She dove behind the boulder, pulling Carmela with her. Voices called out in the forest, coming closer. Someone shouted something in Spanish. She heard people crashing through the undergrowth. The men came into view. She counted six of them including Diego, and she crouched down further next to Carmela. She recognized Billy Williams's voice.

"How long is this gonna take? These woods is full of bears and snakes. It's getting dark."

"We've got to keep going. Vargas'll kill us if these *putas* get away."

Diego stopped a few feet in front of where they were hiding and stared into the foliage. Alex's heart thudded against her rib cage. Her mouth was dry. She held her breath.

Diego turned and moved off. "Nothing over here. We've got to try another direction."

She watched through the trees as the men disappeared into the woods, arguing about which way to go. Their voices grew faint, fading until all she could hear were the birds.

She hugged Carmela. "We can't count on their not coming back. We've got to get out of here."

Carmela's eyes were wide. Her face was flushed. She jumped to her feet and followed Alex for the first time without protest.

Alex moved from tree to tree, navigating by the moss on the north side. "You're doing great, Carmela. I think there's a river ahead and a major road. That's our best chance of finding help."

They made steady progress. Neither spoke, both focused on moving quickly and quietly. Then suddenly Carmela shrieked.

Alex stopped, her heart in her throat.

Carmela was pulling at her skirt, trying to free the material from a jagged branch.

"For God's sake, Carmela. Come on, we've got to keep moving," Alex said, breaking off the branch.

They started again, Alex in front, setting the pace as fast as she thought Carmela could go. Her tank top was soggy with sweat and stained with Diego's blood. A mosquito whined in her ear. She swatted at it and trudged on, glad of the coming darkness.

Carmela panted behind her. Branches tore at their arms and legs. They stumbled over fallen trees and exposed roots. When they had covered another half mile, the ground fell off sharply ahead. It was some kind of ravine. The river had to be close.

A man shouted, no more than a half mile away. She strained to listen. The voices grew closer. She recognized Diego's voice, and Billy Williams', and there were at least three more men than before, all Mexican judging by their accents.

Alex's heart beat fast. Blood rushed in her ears. She pushed Carmela behind the trunk of an old poplar.

The voices came closer.

"Hey. Over here. What's this?"

"That's a piece of cloth. Don't look like it's been there long. They're around here," one of the men said.

Alex tensed. Carmela's skirt. She pulled the woman back further into the trees.

Four men walked past them and stood looking down into the ravine.

She heard Billy Williams speak. "No way she's gonna get that fat old broad down there."

One of the men yelled, "Hey, I got more cloth."

They climbed back up the path toward the women. Alex could hear them a dozen yards away. She crouched down and looked through the leaves. Her heart was pounding so hard it was a wonder the men couldn't hear it.

"It's black out here. We'll never find them in the dark. We need dogs."

"Hey, Billy. You've got to know where to get us some dogs."

"Sure do. Won't take more 'n an hour to get 'em either."

"Someone should stay here and watch for them," Diego said.

"I ain't staying out here all night and get eaten up by bugs. The *puta* can't go anywhere in the dark."

"You're right. Let's get out of here and find some dogs. We got their scent on the cloth. The dogs'll find 'em a lot faster than we can."

The men left, crashing through the underbrush. The light was gone. An owl hooted overhead. Relief washed over Alex. They had another chance, however small.

Carmela sank down to the ground, hugging herself. "We are safe for tonight? We can find somewhere to rest?"

Alex stood up. "No way. They'll be back soon. Come on. We'll hold on to each other."

She gripped Carmela's arm and pushed ahead through the heavy brush in the direction of the ravine. A full moon rose above the trees. She could just make out the path ahead.

The ground dropped off suddenly. She slipped on loose stones and her feet went out from under her. She grabbed a branch to keep from falling and found her balance. Breathing hard, she pushed thick branches aside and looked down at the jagged rocks of a deep ravine. She could see the river several hundred feet below.

She thought she heard dogs far in the distance. She looked around in desperation.

"We're on some kind of path along the ravine. There has to be a way down to the water somewhere."

She held onto Carmela and felt her way along the ravine's edge. Sticky threads of spider web clung to her face and hair. She wiped her face with both hands and continued on. Each time she leaned though the trees to check the ravine, the sides seemed steeper.

She heard the dogs again, closer now. Her heart sank.

Carmela tripped, sprawled on the ground, and began to sob. Alex helped her up. "We have to keep going."

A woodchuck ran in front of them toward the ravine. Alex ran ahead to see where it had gone. When she parted the brush, her spirits soared. A narrow dirt track ran through a stand of small trees. She tested it with her foot. The earth was solid. The trees thinned. She followed the path down to a rocky ledge. A fast-moving river was only ten feet below.

She went back for Carmela. "It's not too far now. Stay with me."

When they reached the rock ledge, she stopped and looked around. A path, probably made by animals, led from the far side of the ledge down a steep rocky incline.

"Okay, Carmela. We're going down backwards. Stay right by me, and I'll guide you."

Inch by painful inch they made it down the rugged path, at last standing on solid ground beside the river. Alex's hopes rose. They just needed to find some way to cross.

They picked their way along the uneven bank in the moonlight, slipping on moss-covered rocks for what seemed like hours.

Carmela stumbled, caught herself on a branch, and stopped, facing the stream. "Look, Miss Alex. Lights."

Alex could just make out the flash of cars through the trees somewhere on the other side of the river. The air seemed to lighten. They were going to make it. They'd found the road. She climbed down the bank to the water's edge. Her foot hit cement. They had reached a spillway. Thank God it was summer now. There was no water going over the top.

"We can crawl across."

Carmela backed away, whimpering.

Somewhere dogs barked.

Carmela shuddered.

"Just do what I do."

Alex went down on her hands and knees and began to crawl across the top of the spillway, wincing as the cement scraped her skin.

The dogs sounded closer, somewhere at the top of the ravine. She crawled faster. "Hurry, Carmela."

Carmela was close behind, breathing hard, but still coming.

Alex reached the end of the spillway and stood with difficulty. She turned to help Carmela. "Okay, up we go. The road is only a few yards above."

She led Carmela up the grassy bank to the edge of the road. Highway 15. She was dizzy with relief. A big rig came around the bend. She stepped into the road and waved.

The truck's brakes screeched. The truck stopped. The driver's side window rolled down and a jolly, red-faced man leaned out. "Can I help you?"

"Can you take us into Dalton?"

Keisha White drove Alex and Carmela from the hospital to the Harringtons' house after the emergency room doctors had patched them up and pronounced them healthy except for a few cuts and bruises and a little dehydration.

Alex was asleep when the car turned into driveway. Her parents were waiting on the front steps. Sandy Harrington ran to the car and opened the back door. He touched his daughter's shoulder. Alex opened her eyes.

"Alex, honey, you're home, thank God."

Her father's voice was hoarse. He looked ten years older.

She fell out of the car into his arms. "Daddy, they were the same men who kidnapped me in Mexico. Billy Williams was one of them. They were after me. Their boss from Mexico was there too, a man they called Vargas. I told the police."

Her father's face turned white. "I can't believe it."

Renee Harrington pushed her husband aside and grasped Alex's arm. "We're never going to let you out of our sight again, and we insist that you stay here until the police sort this out."

Alex pulled away. "I'll be fine. I told the police everything. They know how to find the farmhouse. It'll all be over soon."

Renee Harrington held her daughter at arm's length. "You and Carmela each need a bath and clean clothes. You look simply terrible, and you smell worse."

CHAPTER THIRTY-FOUR

Vargas scanned his men, watching them squirm in their skins. They should be scared. The woman had made fools of them and of him. No one made a fool of Emilio Vargas and lived. The men had let her go. They would pay. At home he would take away their money. Shoot some of them in front of the others. Here he had a problem. He needed them all to keep the locals in line. Their punishment would have to wait, but that made him look weak, and he hated that more than anything. If the men thought him weak, they would turn on him. A *jefe* could never relax. Even more than usual he would have to watch these men twenty-four hours a day.

No one spoke. Not a board creaked. Even the old house knew to keep still in the face of his wrath.

Cuchillo alone had the guts to speak. "The dogs picked up their scent. We were closing on them. Then they were gone."

Vargas looked at him. "You've killed many powerful men in your day, and yet you let one unarmed girl and a fat old women get away. What good are you? Any of you."

Cuchillo shifted his weight from one foot to the other. "The Harrington *puta* is a tough bitch and knows the area. She and the old woman got to have made it to the road and got help."

Vargas scowled and began to pace. Dalton was a dangerous place now. The *puta* would go to the police. The police and the FBI would look for him everywhere. The dead woman's sister, Teresa, was an even bigger problem. That one wouldn't keep quiet forever. She could identify Shirley Hodges as her sister's killer, and the minute the police got a hold of Shirley, the woman would talk. Shirley was a liability.

He looked at Billy Williams. Billy's knowledge of the operation and of Dalton could be valuable, but Billy was El Caballero's man, and he still seemed pretty mad about his cousin's death. Cuchillo said that Billy kept to himself and would only do what he was told when threatened. Maybe they should have killed him along with his cousin.

"You were here. You tell me how the *puta* got away."

Billy held his hands up and shook his head. "I don' know nothin', Mr. Vargas. I was inside, changing Diego's bandages. Just ask him."

Vargas swiveled to Diego whose shoulder was still wrapped in gauze and adhesive tape from the stab wound.

"Billy's right. He was with me when Shirley started screamin' that the *puta* was gone," Diego said.

The front door flew open. Shirley Hodges burst in and stopped. "I take it y'all didn't find 'em."

Vargas's words came out like bullets. "You were in charge. You let them get away. It's your fault."

"Now don't you go blaming me. We was all together downstairs when them bitches climbed out the window. Who would've thought they'd do a thing like that?"

Vargas's phone vibrated in his pocket. He pulled it out and read the vet's number on the display. The multiple surgeries Lucky Dan had endured on his right hind leg weren't helping. Vargas turned away from the group and took the call, his stomach sinking. The vet said the horse now had laminitis in the left hind leg and was suffering. Vargas's eyes filled with tears. They were going to have to put his beautiful horse down.

"Don't do it until I get there," he shouted into the phone.

Cuchillo and Diego exchanged glances and stepped back.

He hung up, shaking with rage. He looked from his men to Shirley. "Kill her. Now."

Shirley threw her hands up in front of her and backed away, screaming.

Cuchillo moved forward, knife in hand. Diego pulled a gun from his waist and closed in from the side. Hodges backed toward the door, shaking her head, eyes wide, and stumbled over a chair.

Cuchillo locked an arm around her neck and sliced the knife into her stomach and up under the ribs.

She slid to the floor, screaming and writhing in pain. Diego put the gun against her temple and fired. Her head fell back against the floor, silent. Blood pooled around her head.

Cuchillo rolled her over with one foot, squatted down, and pulled out the knife. He wiped the blood on her skirt and shoved the knife back in his belt.

"Jesus," Billy said.

Vargas turned on him. "You want to be next?"

Billy shook his head and backed away. "No, man. No problem."

"Get her out of here, and burn this house down."

He looked at Cuchillo. "You're in charge. Lucky Dan is bad. I have to go back home. Clean this mess up. Get the sister and shut her up for good."

CHAPTER THIRTY-FIVE

The day after the escape Alex was on the sunporch of her parents' house, on orders from her doctors to rest. She leaned back against the flowered cushions of an over-sized wicker chair and tried, without much success, to focus on a book. A glass of sweet tea sat on the table beside her, untouched. Her mother sat back in a wicker chair next to hers, working on a crossword puzzle and complaining without stopping about the volunteers who were helping her with the charity fashion show she was hosting at the club. Her father was in the library with Scott Foley, talking about some kind of business deal.

Across the room Carmela leaned back against the chaise lounge, eyes closed. With her father's support Alex had overcome her mother's objections to Carmela's staying at the house. She'd argued that the kidnappers were still out there, and Carmela needed protection.

The farmhouse, the woods, the dogs. She'd made it out alive. She hadn't left Carmela behind. She felt strong for the first time since Mexico, calmer. The police were getting closer to finding the people responsible for Mariana's death. They were the same ones who had dragged her off the bus in Mexico City. They had killed Cristina.

She'd told the police and the FBI how to find the farmhouse and the human traffickers and what she'd heard about an upcoming shipment. She'd given them descriptions of her kidnappers and that they had referred to their boss as Vargas. She'd answered their questions. No doubt even now the traffickers were moving women into the U.S.

She knew now that these men were targeting her. She had to know why, or she would live in fear the rest of her life. The deaths of Cristina and Mariana were connected to her too. The only way she'd be able to live with that knowledge was to find their killers and do everything she could to see that other women didn't suffer the same fate.

"You could have been killed. We almost lost you," her father had said over and over. He had always been overprotective, but now he wouldn't let her out of his sight. Her mother remained aloof, seeming to hold her daughter responsible for everything that had happened.

The doorbell chimed. Her father's voice resonated from the front hall. Seconds later he came out onto to the porch followed by Keisha White and Agent Silva. Foley was behind them.

"Honey, Detective White and Agent Silva want to talk to you and Carmela. I've asked them not to stay long." He turned to look at Keisha White. "Fortunately our attorney, Scott Foley, is here this morning. Scott will be sitting in on your session with Alex. I believe you've met him already, detective."

"I'm familiar with Mr. Foley."

"Really, Daddy. I don't think we need him," Alex said.

"I'd just be more comfortable if he were here."

Alex pressed her lips together, then shrugged and got up. She shook hands with Silva and smiled at Keisha White. The detective had become far more sympathetic to her since the kidnapping.

"Did you find the farmhouse?"

"What was left of it. Your directions were good. We back-tracked from where the trucker picked you up, but the kidnappers were gone. They'd burned the house to the ground and all trace of them with it. I have a team scouring the area, and there's a nationwide alert for them. We need to ask you some more questions. The sooner we know why they kidnapped you, the better able we'll be to catch them and shut their whole network."

Renee stood. "I think this is preposterous. Don't you realize what my daughter and her employee have been through?"

Sandy put a hand on his wife's shoulder. "We need to cooperate, my dear. Scott will be with them."

"We just have a few questions. Is there somewhere we can go to talk?" Silva said.

"Now wait just a minute," Foley said.

"Sure. I'm ready. Come on Carmela," Alex said, ignoring Foley.

Carmela sat up, eyes wide. "No, no. I cannot."

"It's all right, Carmela. No one's going to hurt you."

"These two ladies are under great stress. You already talked to them at the police station. They've had enough," Renee said.

"I'm sorry, but we do have to talk to them. There may be things they remember now that they didn't before. Even small details could be helpful. The sooner we talk with them, the better chance we have of apprehending these people," White said.

Alex took Carmela's hand and led her into the library. "We may think of something that will help, Carmela. I know you want to get those people as much as I do."

Foley followed, and White shut the library door. Unlike the last time in this room, today she was in charge. Alex and Carmela sat together on the leather couch. White and Silva took the two wing chairs across from them. Scott Foley insisted on standing.

"Let's start with the abduction, Alex. We know you tried to fight back, we found your bracelet in the parking lot," White said.

"I tore it off before they threw me in the van. I hoped you'd find it."

"That was smart. I know you've gone over this at the hospital, but take us through it again."

"There was a third man waiting for us at the farmhouse. I knew him. He was one of the men who dragged me off the bus in Mexico City. They called him Diego. When he came for me in the van, I stabbed him with a broken bottle. He killed Cristina. I wanted him dead."

"Now, Alex, you don't mean that. You would never intentionally kill anybody. You were only defending yourself," Foley said.

"I do wish I'd killed him for what he did to Cristina."

"That's enough. I insist we stop this conversation right now."

"I want to talk with them, Scott. We have to find these people."

"Alex, I'm warning you."

Silva ignored Foley and turned back to Alex. "There was never a ransom demand. This wasn't an ordinary kidnapping. Why do you think Diego and the others were after you?"

"I don't know."

"I'm sure it was a coincidence," Foley said. "Alex was just in the wrong place at the wrong time. Kidnappings are common in Mexico."

"This is no coincidence. These are the same people who kidnapped her in Mexico," White said.

"Scott, butt out," Alex said. "I can handle this."

White looked at Carmela. "Alex told us that you were taking money from the traffickers before Mariana died. Who paid you?"

Carmela's eyes were fixed on the rug. "The yellow-headed woman, Shirley Hodges."

"I don't represent Ms. Flores, but I think she should have an attorney present."

"It will go a lot easier for her if she cooperates now," White said.

Carmela's eyes fluttered as if she were going to faint.

"Carmela, please, tell them what you know," Alex said.

Carmela began in a small, shaky voice. "Shirley tried to make me tell her where Teresa was. There were others there too. The big boss from Mexico and a boss from here too."

"Can you describe the bosses?" Silva asked.

"The Mexican boss, yes. He was thin, and he had a very mean face. The boss from here stayed in the back so I never see him."

"Would you recognize his voice?"

She shook her head. "He didn't talk much. When he did, it sounded funny, like he had his hand over his mouth."

"That's interesting. I wonder if that means you would recognize him otherwise. Tell me more about the Mexican boss, the one Alex told us the men called Vargas. We think he must be Emilio Vargas, one of the biggest traffickers in Mexico. He fits your description. What else did you see?"

Carmela continued, growing more confident. "This Vargas is the *jefe*, the big boss of the whole thing. He called the boss from Dalton an idiot."

"Why would this Vargas be here in Dalton if he's such an important guy?" Scott Foley asked.

"My guess is the Dalton operation has some greater importance for Vargas than the death of one woman or he wouldn't be here. He'd let the locals handle things. Could be he doesn't have confidence in his man here," Silva said.

"Which is good. Maybe he'll make a mistake," White said.

Silva put a mugshot of Marvin Moore in front of Carmela. "What about him? Was he there?"

Carmela's shoulders began to shake. "They called him Marvin. A man called Diego killed him."

"Diego? The guy that Alex stabbed in the van?" White asked.

Carmela nodded. "Diego works for Vargas."

A loud crash from outside made Carmela jump. Angry voices erupted, growing louder. Alex got up and ran to the window just in time to see Travis Bingham taking a swing at Mike Murray.

She ran into the garden. White and Silva followed.

Alex looked at Mike. "What are you doing here?"

Mike ducked. Travis tried again. Mike landed a punch on Travis's jaw. Travis went down hard, winded.

Mike brushed himself off. "I'm here to see you."

Travis got to his feet and took another swing at Mike.

Mike punched Travis in the gut, sending him flying.

Travis struggled to sit up, gasping for breath.

Mike looked at Alex. "I've called and left messages. I tried to see you, but your father wouldn't let me in. I just want to know that you're all right."

"This clown was hanging around. He won't leave you alone," Travis said.

"I'm fine, Travis. Why are you here?"

Travis looked at her, red-faced. "I'm protecting you from this moron."

"For God's sake, you're the moron. I don't need your protection, from Mike or anyone else."

Sandy Harrington appeared from around the corner of the house. "I heard a lot of noise. Travis, is that you? What are you doing sitting on the ground? Are you sick?"

"Only in the head," Alex said.

Travis pointed to Mike. "That reporter's bothering Alex."

Sandy pointed a finger at Mike. "My daughter is not talking to reporters. Get off my property or I'll have you arrested."

White gave Mike a thin smile. "Murray, you're clearly not welcome. I'm ordering you to leave."

Mike stood his ground for a minute, looking from Sandy to Keisha before turning to Alex.

"Call me when you can, Alex. Please. We need to talk."

Alex watched him walk toward the road, shoulders hunched, hands in his pockets. She wasn't mad at him anymore. She thought of everything that had happened since she'd met him. What had he learned since she'd seen him last? Maybe he'd been right all along. If they worked together, they could catch these people.

White interrupted her thoughts. "Come back inside, Alex. We have more questions."

Silva's cell phone rang. He took the call, then said, "Detective, we have to go. We have a problem."

CHAPTER THIRTY-SIX

Mike was not happy with the way things had gone at the Harringtons'. He was desperate to see Alex and was afraid that wasn't going to happen any time soon. The code for "officer needs assistance" squawked over the police scanner on the seat beside him. He pushed thoughts of Alex aside and listened. Sirens sounded in the distance, coming toward him. Squad cars and an ambulance streaked past. He stepped on the gas and followed.

He parked the Mustang behind the ambulance and ran toward the noise. There were police cars everywhere.

The baby-faced officer he recognized from the search of the York Street house stood on the perimeter, his face ashen.

"What's going on?"

"It's the safe house. Pam Lea and Craven were guarding a witness. Neighbors heard shots, a lot of them, but now there's nothin'. The house is quiet. No one's come out. Lea's not picking up."

"Is that Craven over there in front of the house?"

"Yeah. He went to get lunch and left Lea there by herself. There'll be hell to pay, that's for sure."

Craven stood back from the rest, round shouldered, his narrow face drawn.

A squad car stopped in front of the safe house. Chief Odom got out and stormed toward the group of cops and paramedics. "SWAT team's on the way. No word from Lea?"

"We tried the bull-horn. No response. The shades are drawn. We can't see inside."

A black van pulled in front of the chief's car, and the SWAT team poured out of the back.

The chief looked at Craven. "What the hell were you thinking, leaving her there alone?"

"Nothin' was happening. I was starving. Pam said it wasn't a problem."

Mike stood back, watching.

Suddenly, the SWAT team rushed the house, breaking down the front door, sweeping inside. One of the team appeared back at the door and yelled for the paramedic, who raced up the walk, disappearing into the house.

Several minutes passed. The medics emerged, carrying a stretcher, moving fast toward the ambulance.

A growing group of officers watched, visibly shaken.

Mike turned to see Keisha White coming toward them, two steps ahead of Agent Silva.

"Where's Teresa?" he called to her.

"Press corps behind the line," White snapped and disappeared into the house.

He walked back to the young officer he had approached earlier. "Who's that in the ambulance?"

"It's Lea. She's in bad shape. She held her own, looks like. Took out two guys before someone shot her."

"Hey, rookie. Stop talking to that guy. He's a reporter. Send him to public affairs," another officer yelled.

A television news truck pulled up and reporters from other outlets converged on the safe house. Mike stepped back into the shadows and phoned the story to the *Herald*.

Five minutes later two more medics came out.

"Who's in there?" Mike asked the young officer.

"Two guys. Mexicans I hear. They fit the description of some guys who've been hanging out in Rag Town lately."

"Shut the hell up," the officer yelled again.

Mike moved closer to the house. A shout came from the back yard.

A group of officers raced around the house in the direction of the noise. Mike followed.

Two officers were supporting Teresa, one on each side. The girl was pale and visibly shaken.

"She was hiding in the garage. Must have run out when the suspect came in the front," he heard one of them say.

White came out through the back door of the house and, spotting him, yelled, "There's a press briefing out front, Murray. Get moving."

Back in front of the house a police media relations woman was speaking to the growing crowd of reporters. Cameras rolled, panning from the body bags to the flashing lights of the ambulance and the open door of the house.

"A Dalton police officer was shot at 3:45 today when two suspects attempted to enter a residence. The officer is being transported to Dalton County Hospital. You'll get an update as soon as we have more information. Two persons were fatally wounded in an exchange of gunfire. Their identity is not known at the present time. That's all we have for now."

The media swarmed after her, yelling questions.

"I promise to let you know as soon we have more information. Thank you," the woman said and retreated to a waiting police car.

Mike stood apart from the rest of the press, looking for Keisha White. He spotted her helping Teresa into an unmarked car. He caught up with them. "How did those two know where to find Teresa?" he asked White as she helped Teresa into the back.

"Murray. You're worse than a rat terrier. An officer has been shot today. Give us a break."

He watched the car pull away. He had to tell Alex about this. He tried her cell, hoping this time she'd answer.

CHAPTER THIRTY-SEVEN

"Please let me know as soon as there's more, and thanks for calling," Alex said and hung up.

"What was that about?" her father asked.

"Some men, maybe the ones who kidnapped me, broke into the safe house. They shot Officer Lea. Teresa's all right."

"You were talking to that reporter, weren't you? I keep telling you to stay away from him. We don't need any more media attention, especially while your kidnappers are still out there. It's not safe."

"I can't hide forever. I'm not going to be safe until Emilio Vargas and his gang are in jail."

"Honey, I'm begging you to be careful."

Her father had aged visibly. His hands trembled, and the skin on his face and neck had begun to sag.

He forced a smile and handed her an envelope. "I think you need to get away from all this. Your mother and I have a surprise for you. Here, take a look."

She took the envelope and slipped an index finger under the flap. Two printouts fell onto her lap. First class to London, leaving in two days.

"For you and your mother. You girls deserve a treat. You can go to the theater, shop, tour some historic sites."

"I can't go to London. Suppose the police find my kidnappers? They'll need me here to identify them."

"Carmela can do that. You know the police are being lenient with her in exchange for her cooperation. Let her cooperate. This is for your protection and our peace of mind."

Renee swept into the room, carrying three champagne flutes and a bottle of Dom Perignon on a silver tray, smiling for the first time since Alex had come back.

"This calls for a celebration. Tomorrow, we pack. There's so much to do."

"I'm not going, Mother."

Renee exchanged glances with her husband.

"What do you mean? You don't have a choice. Think of us for a change. You've always been stubborn, ever since you were little. You'd rather be spanked than do what you were told. We've been through a terrible time, worrying about you."

"Now, Renee. That's a little harsh," Sandy said.

"Don't you 'now Renee' me. You always take her side." Renee stormed out of the room.

Alex watched her mother leave and sighed. She gave her father a hug. "I'm so sorry, Daddy. I know you're been through a lot, and I'm not ungrateful. It's just that there's more that I have to do here."

She woke early the next morning, ready for war. She'd start with the schools project. She pulled out her cell and dialed Peaches Bingham's number.

"Alex, sugar, it's so good to hear your voice. To think you were kidnapped and escaped all by yourself. It doesn't bear thinking about."

"Mrs. Bingham."

"It's Peaches, sugar. Call me Peaches."

"I know you've been involved in the center from the beginning. Have you ever heard of the schools project?"

"I can't remember much these days. I think the Foleys collected money for poor children in Mexico. We gave them a little bit of money, but that was a very long time ago."

Alex remembered seeing notations in the file Travis had left at her apartment of sizable recent donations from the Binghams. She tried the other board members. All of them said the same thing. If they had made contributions to the schools project, they were small and long ago. No one had heard anything about the project in several years.

She took her purse and car keys, leaving a note for her parents that said she was going to her apartment for some things she needed, which was actually true. She needed Travis's file folder.

When she got to the apartment, everything was as she had left it, but the file wasn't there. She was sure it had been on the coffee table the last time she saw it. She searched everywhere. Travis must have come back for it. Scott Foley still had the center's file copy. She'd have to work from memory.

A visit to the accounting firm of Haskins, Haskins and Haskins was next on her list. Ambrose Haskins, C.P.A., leaned back in his desk chair and folded his arms across his ample belly. His full head of gray hair was combed in the front in a pompadour. An array of precisely aligned diplomas and credentials hung on the wall behind his head. His desk was so highly polished that his round face was reflected in the surface.

"As you know as executive director, we've given the center a clean audit every year since its inception. I'm sure you're not suggesting there's anything improper about your finances."

Alex met his gaze. "What do you know about the schools project?"

Haskins' chins wobbled. "I haven't heard about that in years. Why do you ask?"

"I found a file that showed recent large contributions."

Haskins cleared his throat. "I'm sure there must have been, but it has nothing to do with your center."

"Then how come Peaches Bingham and the rest of the board say they haven't heard about it in years?"

A flush crept from his neck across his face. "No doubt there's a simple explanation. I just don't happen to know it. Why don't you ask Scott Foley?"

"Mr. Foley hasn't been very helpful. Do you know whether a school even exists?"

"Of course it does. It's a school that's attached to an orphanage somewhere in Mexico City."

"I'd like the address of the orphanage, please."

Haskins pulled a handkerchief from his pocket and wiped his forehead. "I'll get it for you, but I think you're making a fuss about nothing. I have every confidence in the Foleys and you should too, Alex. Trust me. This is not something that need concern you."

———

Mike Murray threw open his front door and pulled her inside. "God, you're a beautiful sight."

Alex smiled and took the cup of coffee he offered her, aware that she was glad to see him too.

"Have a seat," he said, pushing the cat off a well-worn sofa.

A loud squawk erupted from the kitchen.

"What was that?"

"Police scanner. I keep it on over the weekend in case something breaks. You get used to it after a while."

"It's funny, a noise like that would have made me jump a while ago. You'd think I'd be worse after what just happened, but I'm better, less jumpy, fewer nightmares."

"It's no wonder. Look what you were able to do on your own, no help from anyone. You're a strong woman."

She waved him aside. "Where are you on the human trafficking story?"

He filled her in on everything he'd learned from the gang and from Espinosa. "Next stop, Mexico. What about you? I hear that the farmhouse where the kidnappers held you belongs to the JoVille Group. What's up with that?"

"My father says it's just land bought for speculation years ago. The house was supposed to be vacant. He thinks the kidnappers were squatting there. I know it looks funny, especially when the group owns the white house too, but they have hundreds of properties. My father is really upset. He's started a full investigation, and if anyone inside the group is even remotely involved, the investigation will uncover it."

She told Mike about the schools project, ending with her conversation with Haskins.

"Any time anyone says, 'trust me,' I don't," Mike said. "Give me the address of the orphanage. I'll see what I can find out when I'm in Mexico."

"I'm going with you."

"No way. Your kidnappers are still out there."

"I have to go. I know firsthand not to leave it to the Mexican police. The truck driver who picked me up in Mexico City dropped me at the closest police station. I pleaded with the police to help Cristina and the other women in the warehouse, but they stalled, pretended they had jurisdictional problems. My guess is they were on the take. It was only after I called my father and he called the American Embassy and officials in the Mexican government that the *Federales* arrived. By then it was too late. Cristina was dead and the men were gone, taking the other women with them."

Mike stared at her for several seconds. "I'm not going to talk you out of going, am I? Espinosa, the Mexican journalist I've been talking to, agrees with you about the police. He was adamant that I not tell them the names that I got from the gang in Rag Town. He says that even if the U.S. law enforcement officials are honest, they may share the information with their counterparts in Mexico who aren't."

"How much do you trust Espinosa?"

"He hasn't given me bad information yet, and he's offered to introduce me to people in Mexico City who can help with my story."

"So we're on. When do we leave?"

"Your parents will never let you go. I'm surprised that they let you out of the house today."

"They didn't."

The police radio cracked, an all-points bulletin: "Woman missing from the country club section of Dalton. Description: Caucasian woman, age twenty-five, five feet seven inches tall, one hundred and twenty pounds, brown hair, green eyes. Name: Alexandra Harrington."

Mike leaped to his feet. "Holy crap. Do they think you've been kidnapped again?"

Alex laughed and pushed the sleeping tabby off her lap.

"I'm busted. Let me get out of here before somebody spots my car and calls the cops. We're going to Mexico. Start packing."

CHAPTER THIRTY-EIGHT

"I had to get out of the house for a while," Alex told her parents when she got home. They were, for once, in agreement, expressing their mutual displeasure with her for leaving.

She called Detective White to apologize for wasting police time. White didn't waste time either.

"We found Shirley Hodges's charred body in the farmhouse. She didn't die in the fire. She'd been shot in the head."

"It could have been us."

"Exactly. That's why you scared the hell out of us, disappearing like that. Please, let us do our job."

Alex hung up. No way that was going to happen. She was going to Mexico.

The sun was coming up over the roof of the country club when Mike drove into the parking lot three days later. He could tell Alex was on edge. "Sorry, I'm late. I had to find the cat. My neighbor's not around to feed him until tomorrow."

"It's okay. Let's get moving before my parents miss me. I left a note saying I had errands to run, but I don't think that's going to cut it. All hell will break loose."

"That's all you're taking? A gym bag?"

"Someone might notice if I walked out of the house with a suitcase."

Mike slid behind the wheel and hit the accelerator, heading for the interstate.

"Your editor approved the trip, didn't he?"

"Well, not exactly. In fact, not at all. There's no money for international travel, and he thinks I've spent too much time on this already. So this is my vacation. I have a week. I have to be back by the end of it or I may be looking for another job."

They were making good time when a patrol car came up behind them.

"Damn, we were almost out of Dalton."

Mike pulled over and waited. An officer walked toward the driver's side window. "You do know this is a residential area. I clocked you doing forty-five in a twenty-five-mile zone."

Alex got out of the car. She adjusted the strap of her top. "Good morning, Officer Dunham. You're out early."

The officer looked up from Mike's license. "Ms. Harrington?"

Her smile broadened. "My friend and I are heading to the mountains for a few days of cooler weather."

Dunham handed the license back. "Slow down, buddy. You have a good weekend, Ms. Harrington."

Mike pulled away from the curb. "Now we really have a mess. As soon as your parents miss you, they're going to call the cops, and your friendly Officer Dunham will know you're with me in my car. We need new wheels."

A half hour later Alex was standing in Mike's neighbor's backyard, frowning at an old gray car with oxidized paintwork. "You think this thing will make it to Mexico?"

"She may not be pretty, but the old girl's ready to rock."

The Chevy sputtered into a dusty garage in Opelika, Alabama, and died. Mike climbed out and looked over the car with a sinking feeling in the pit of his stomach. The temperature was pushing a hundred, defying the metal floor fan's ability to circulate the stale air.

Alex got out and stood beside him, arms folded. "She's not doing much rocking now."

After what seemed like hours the mechanic pulled his head out of the engine. "A busted hose's what stopped you today, but lots more's just about to go. I can patch it up soon's I can get some parts, but I got to order 'em. Should be here in a day or so. You and the missus want to find yourselves a room for the night. Try the Hide Away Inn, cross the street. Don't look like much, but they keeps it pretty clean."

Mike stole a glance at Alex. Her halter top was wet with sweat. She'd been a pretty good sport so far, but this was pushing it.

Alex thanked the mechanic and took Mike's arm. "Come on. I'd kill for a shower."

The clerk at the Hide Away Inn looked up and grinned. "Got a real nice room for you. Good double bed and all. Parking's round the back."

Alex flinched.

"I promise to behave," Mike said, trying hard not to smile.

Alex raised an eyebrow. "We'll take it."

The clerk winked at Mike.

Minutes later Mike turned the key in the lock, pushed open the door, and looked around the small, dusty room. "Not exactly the Ritz."

"It'll do. I'm starving."

"I'll find us something to eat. Back in a few."

A half hour later he was back. Alex emerged from the bathroom, her wet hair slicked back behind her ears. He stopped short inside the door, the brown paper bag he held containing their dinner completely forgotten. She was wearing a clean, white button down shirt, held together by a middle button.

"That my shirt?" he managed to stammer.

"Um, yes. I forgot to pack anything to sleep in. This was in your bag. You don't mind, do you?" She buttoned the other buttons. "What's in the bag? It smells good."

"That thing never looked as good on me."

She pulled the top of the shirt closer together and smiled.

He sighed. "You like barbecue? I got us some ribs. Alabama-style, with a white sauce. Got some slaw and a six-pack of cold beer."

"You're asking a southern girl if she likes barbecue? I'll take any kind. You didn't use a credit card, did you?"

"Give me a break."

She reached for the beer. "Sorry, I'm a bit edgy. The real problem is tomorrow when we have to pay for the repairs in cash."

"I cleaned out my bank account. I've got enough to last us for a while."

Alex reached in the bag and pulled out the ribs. When they were done eating, she stuffed the containers and wrappers in the bag.

"Would you please dump this stuff outside so the room won't smell of barbecue and beer?"

Feeling human again, Mike grabbed the bag and disappeared out the door.

Alex turned on the portable TV to the local news and flopped down on the bed just as Mike came back in the room, grinning at the sight of Alex's long legs.

"Montgomery. Following a raid, police today arrested two men on charges related to holding women captive as sex slaves for over a year."

"See. I told you this story was big." Mike opened a road map and spread it on the bed. "If we drive straight through we should get to the Mexican border in less than two days. We can cross around noon when the traffic is heaviest. No one's likely to pay attention to a young couple in an old car. We can always write, 'Just married' on the trunk."

Alex ignored him and moved to the bed. "The floor's not very clean. You can take the other side of the bed. I trust you."

"Damn. I hate that."

"When we get to Mexico City, I want to visit the orphanage first. Nobody's willing to talk about it, but I have a feeling it's critical to this whole thing."

"Could be interesting. We can check it out before we meet with Espinosa."

Alex yawned and turned on her side. "I'm absolutely wiped out." Within seconds she was breathing heavily. The shirt rode up on her tanned thighs.

Mike wiped his forehead and settled back in a chair. She might be able to sleep, but he sure wasn't going to be doing much of that himself.

CHAPTER THIRTY-NINE

Vargas answered his phone. He hadn't had any good news in a long time. His beloved Lucky Dan was dead; hundreds of thousands in stud fees gone. The vet bills had been out of sight, and all he had was a dead horse. The Zetas were outbidding him for quarter horses only half as good as Lucky Dan. Alex Harrington's kidnapping had brought the full force of the U.S. government down on his operations. His network in the U.S. was broken. He'd had to pull all but a few men out of Dalton, and he was back in Tenancingo trying to regroup. What if he lost everything and had to go back to life as a small-time thug? He couldn't take orders again. If the competition saw him as weak, they'd take over. Everything he'd worked for would belong to them. He'd have nothing.

He was worried about El Caballero too. He'd brought Billy Williams back with him, but he didn't like the way the man looked at him, and besides, Billy wasn't enough leverage to keep El Caballero from going to the FBI and demanding immunity. El Caballero was a weasel. He needed more.

His phone rang. He answered, listened, and smiled. "They're coming here? That's very good news."

Cuchillo stood beside him, smiling.

Vargas slicked his hair back, feeling better than he had in weeks. "The Harrington woman ran away from home. Her reporter friend is with her. They're coming here. I told you I would get her. She will not escape this time."

"Here? To Mexico?" Cuchillo asked.

Vargas gave a high-pitched laugh. "Of course. The reporter wants a story. She wants revenge. When I'm finished with the two of them, they'll be begging for mercy."

"How you gonna find them?" Diego asked.

"Two beautiful young *gringos* like them? It won't be hard."

He looked at Diego. "Word is the reporter is a friend of Espinosa's, the *La Prensa* reporter who's such a pain in the ass. They're sure to meet up. We can deal with them all at the same time."

CHAPTER FORTY

MEXICO CITY

Alex's lungs were filled with the thick, acrid air of Mexico City. She coughed. It had taken two days to get the car fixed and another two to reach Mexico City. The stucco houses and tile roofs brought back the horrible memories she'd tried hard to suppress. She had vowed never to come back. Now she was here. Her dread and sense of loss were overwhelming.

"You okay?" Mike asked, looking across at her.

She nodded, unable to speak. Her hands clutched the coarse upholstery of the car seat until her knuckles turned white. They were going up against Emilio Vargas in his own country. Vargas was responsible for the deaths of both Cristina and Mariana. There would be more. He wouldn't stop. They didn't have a choice.

Mike stopped the car in front of a sprawling two-story building whose cracked stucco and missing roof tiles showed decades of hard use. A weathered sign hung above the front door, *HERMANAS DE LA CARIDAD*. "The Sisters of Charity Orphanage," she translated aloud in English.

Mike gave her another quizzical look.

She had a feeling she'd been here before, sometime long ago. Her stomach hurt. Her heart beat faster. She tried to smile. She took a deep breath, grasped the door knocker, her knocks tentative at first, then bolder.

Minutes passed before the roughhewn wooden door opened, and

an elderly nun dressed in a white habit squinted at them. *"Buenos días,"* she said, in a voice so soft they could barely hear her.

Alex answered in her best Spanish. "Hello. I am Alex and this is my friend, Mike. We have heard much about your school, and we would like to visit and learn about the work you do here."

"Come in. The day is very hot. You should come in out of the hot sun," the sister answered in English. She motioned for them to follow, her white habit rustling as she walked ahead of them down a long hall.

The hallway triggered some memory. Somehow Alex knew that the nun would turn at the end of the hall and go through a broad archway into a large room with whitewashed walls. Sunshine poured through long recessed windows casting rectangles of light across a worn wooden floor. The aroma of hot, buttery tortillas made her feel at home.

The sister lowered her fragile body onto a straight-backed wooden chair and gestured to a pair of chairs beside her. She smiled at Alex. "I am Sister Milagros. How may I help you?"

Time slowed. Alex perched on a low chair across from the sister and looked around the room as if in a dream. She looked back at Sister Milagros, trying to understand why everything seemed so familiar.

Sister Milagros waited, her hands pressed together, studying Alex. The sister's eyes grew bright. "I know you."

"I don't think so, Sister. We are from a place called Dalton in North Carolina in the United States," Alex said.

The sister nodded. "Dalton? We have a donor from Dalton, a very nice man named Mr. Foley. Do you know him?"

Alex's pulse raced. She tried to hide her excitement. "I do know him, and I understand that he's a big contributor to your orphanage. Does he come here often?"

The sister smiled. "He came here once long ago, but not since then. Every Christmas he sends us five hundred U.S. dollars."

"That's all? Does he send donations from other people in Dalton as well?"

"No, only from him, and we are grateful for what he gives us." The sister smiled at Alex. "A little girl lived here once long ago. She would be about your age now, and I think she lives in Dalton. Excuse me please. I will be right back."

"This doesn't make sense," Alex whispered to Mike. "She can't be talking about the schools project. There should be many donations."

Sister Milagros had disappeared through double doors to what appeared to be the kitchen, returning several minutes later, smiling. "I have something that I want you to see. We keep pictures of people who have lived here in the past. I remember seeing this one in an old album."

Alex took an old, cracked photograph that the sister held out to her.

"This is Angelina. You are very like her, but taller. She is here with her little girl, Nina, who would be about your age now."

Alex took the picture. The woman's oval face, light hair, and olive-shaped eyes were her own. The child in her lap looked much like herself as a girl and there was a curl of white hair mixed in with the chestnut. Blood sang in her ears. She felt faint. She looked up at the sister. "I don't understand."

Mike moved closer and looked at the picture over her shoulder. "You look a lot like the woman in the picture, the little girl too."

She was cold despite the heat of the day. Did she recognize this woman? Was she imagining that she remembered her singing a lullaby? She couldn't be sure.

"This must be a mistake. My mother lives in Dalton, North Carolina, with my father, and she doesn't look anything like this person."

The sister placed a hand on Alex's shoulder. "I think you would like something cool to drink."

"Let me get it," Mike said, leaping up and disappearing through the door that Sister Milagros indicated.

Alex handed the picture back to the sister and crossed her arms, hugging herself. She remembered chance remarks from family friends that had troubled her as a child. "Pity she didn't get Renee's lovely blue eyes," or "she's a dark little thing, isn't she?" or "odd when her parents are so fair."

She continued to look at the picture. The woman's eyes were very like her own.

Mike came back with two glasses of water. "Where are this woman and her child now?"

The sister sipped from her glass. "Let me tell you a story. Sadly, not an unusual one. Angelina was only seventeen years old when she came to us. She was beautiful, with big green eyes very like yours. She was working as a chamber maid in a grand hotel in Mexico City when she met a guest who stayed there often. He bought her pretty things and showed her nice places that she had never seen before. She fell in love. In time, she became pregnant. The man said he was already married. When he found out that she was pregnant, he was very angry. He gave her a little money and left. She had nowhere to go. Our order gives refuge to poor girls like Angelina. Her parish priest brought her to us."

Alex leaned forward and took a deep breath. "Is she still here?"

Tears filled the sister's eyes. "She died many years ago in a traffic accident. Most mothers have their babies and leave. The babies stay with us in the orphanage. Angelina had nowhere to go. She had her baby. Little Nina. After her baby was born, she stayed here, helping with the cooking and cleaning. One day, when Nina was almost three years old, Angelina went to the market to buy food for our dinner. On the way home she was hit by a car. The police never found the driver. Angelina was badly hurt. The doctors could not save her. She is buried here."

"What happened to the little girl?"

Sister Milagros's face clouded. "That is why I am telling you this story. About a month after Angelina died, Mr. Foley came here. He told us that there was a couple in his town who wanted to adopt a little girl. He said they were good people and could give a child everything it could need. We are a poor order. We had many children and barely enough money to feed them. He asked about all of the children and wanted to see all of them, but he was especially interested in finding a little girl your age. He asked how Angelina's child came to be here. When he heard the sad story, he picked her to take back with him. We were sad because we loved Nina so much, but we wanted her to have a nice home."

The sister gave her a sad smile. "I think you are that little girl, now grown and so pretty like Angelina."

Alex tried to speak. Words wouldn't come.

"Do you know the name of the people who adopted Nina?" Mike asked.

"I don't remember exactly. It was something like Harris or Harning."

"Could it be Harrington?"

The sister clapped her hands. "Yes, that was it!"

Mike moved closer and rested a hand on Alex's shoulder.

Her head began to swim. None of this seemed real. She was vaguely aware of voices and of Mike pushing her back into the chair and holding the glass of water to her lips. Slowly, the room came back into focus. Was Angelina her mother? Was her real name Nina? No one in her family had chestnut-colored hair and hazel eyes. Now she knew they came from Angelina.

The sister was beside her, stroking her forehead. "You must rest now. You've had a shock."

Alex sat forward and very slowly got to her feet. "You said that Angelina is here. I would like to see where she's buried."

"Certainly, my dear," Sister Milagros said, grimacing as she pulled her arthritic body from the chair.

With Mike close behind, Alex followed the sister through the kitchen into the play area behind the orphanage where children were playing a game and laughing. A novice held a little girl by the hand. As she walked by, the child's eyes, green like her own, met hers. Alex smiled and waved. The child laughed and waved back. She had been here once, like this little girl. She had lived in this very place with a mother she couldn't remember.

In a pretty garden beyond the playground, Sister Milagros stopped and pointed to a row of small headstones.

Alex stood in silence by the grave. The name on the stone was Angelina Segura. She wanted time to stop so she could make sense of all this. She thought of Cristina and knew that she couldn't. Not now. She had to keep going. She would never know Angelina or how much she had suffered, but she might be able to help other poor women like her. She owed that to them all.

"You are welcome to stay here as long as you like," Sister Milagros said. "It is almost time for lunch. I must help with the children now."

"We have to go, but we'll be back someday soon."

Alex followed Mike to the car and slumped against the seat, trying to collect her thoughts.

"We're due to meet Espinosa at a café in an hour. If you need to be alone, I can drop you back at the hotel," Mike said.

"If Sister Milagros is right, the Harringtons aren't my parents. I'm someone named Nina, and my real mother died in a traffic accident. Why didn't my parents tell me that I was adopted? It was all a lie. They let me think that I was their daughter and brought me up to be a Southern lady. I learned how to curtsy and answer the telephone and to write little thank you notes on vellum stationery. I knew nothing of the life that women like Cristina and Mariana or even my real mother led."

Renee Harrington's life was so much easier that these women's, yet her mother never seemed happy. She remembered her parents fighting one night after she was supposed to be asleep. Her mother was yelling, "Alex, Alex, Alex. She's all you think about. It doesn't matter to you that I've planned this vacation for months. Just because Alex is in a play when we're away, you want to cancel. Why can't you do what I want for a change?"

Mike squeezed her hand. "You were right about one thing. There is a connection between Scott Foley and the orphanage, and also a link to your parents. There may be good reasons why they didn't want you to know."

"I have to know the truth."

"Do you want to go home? I can go on with the story by myself."

"No, I want to stay. I have to, for Cristina and Mariana and for all the others in the warehouse. I'll deal with my parents, I mean the Harringtons, later."

In the car, while Mike battled with Mexico City traffic, she forced herself to concentrate on what they knew so far. There was no schools project and no big contributions to an orphanage of the kind she'd seen in Travis's folder. There had to be a connection between the orphanage and human trafficking. Something the sisters didn't know about.

CHAPTER FORTY-ONE

Espinosa had promised to meet them at noon. Alex crossed to the sidewalk café in the historic city center of Mexico City, barely aware of the passing motorists and tour buses that crowded the busy street.

Mike followed close behind. "I can barely keep up, and I have long legs."

A man looked up from a newspaper and smiled at Alex.

"There. Is that him?"

Mike turned to see where she was pointing. "Could be. He said he has dark brown hair, brown eyes, and would be wearing a short-sleeved tan shirt and slacks, just like that guy."

"Great. That's most of the men in Mexico City."

The man got up, placed a few bills on the table, and walked toward them. When he was within a few feet, he paused.

Mike stepped forward. "*Señor* Espinosa?"

The man shook his head and gave Alex a wistful glance before hurrying off down the street.

"Guess not." She turned back toward the café and scanned the faces of the other customers until she saw a man about the same height as the first, standing in the shadows under an awning. The man walked toward Mike, slipped him a piece of paper and, without a word, disappeared onto the crowded street.

Mike unfolded the paper. "It says to wait here for fifteen minutes and then take a cab to the Zócalo, the main plaza. When we get there, we walk around for a few minutes and take another cab to an address in San Angel near the Plaza San Jacinto."

Mike led her to a table and motioned to a waitress.

"Is all this really necessary?" Alex asked.

"Espinosa knows what he's doing. He told me that over sixty journalists have been murdered in Mexico in the past ten years. We'd better do what he says."

———

Rafael Espinosa was waiting for them inside the door of a small pink stucco building at the end of a narrow cobblestone street in San Angel. Alex judged him to be in his late thirties, his face worn beyond his years with lines that ran from his nose to each side of his mouth.

He smiled and held out his hand. "Thank you for coming," he said in barely accented English. "I apologize for the intrigue, but it is best to be careful. This restaurant belongs to a friend. We are safe here, and the food is very good. Let's eat."

The reporter led the way to the back room of a restaurant decorated with colorful Mexican folk art and filled with the warm, spicy smell of Mexican food, and chose a seat facing the door.

"Is it the drug cartels killing journalists?" Mike asked.

Espinosa lit a Marlboro and inhaled, the creases between his eyes deepening. "Sometimes it's the drug cartels and other criminal groups, but it is too easy to blame them for all of it. Much of it comes from those in power, government officials both local and national who do not want their corruption made public. There's a special prosecutor, but he does not have the budget or people he needs."

A short, plump waitress set bowls of tortilla soup in front of each of them and a steaming platter of chicken empanadas in the center of the table. She giggled at Mike's obvious delight, and turned to Espinosa. "Will there be anything else, *señor*?"

"You spoil me, Marta!" He looked around the restaurant. "Where is everybody today? Where is Jorge?"

"He will be here soon. Mondays are quiet. Not so many people," Marta said.

As soon as Marta went back to the kitchen, Alex asked, "Why do you do it?"

"It is my job. Somebody has to find the truth. We can't live in fear. But enough of this. We have work to do. I've been asking around. My sources confirm that a human trafficking pipeline out of Mexico goes through your city."

A loud crash came from the kitchen. Espinosa ducked under the table, pulling Alex down with him. A second later he stood up with a rueful smile and reached down to help Alex up. "Sorry. I'm a bit on edge."

A short man of about fifty came through the kitchen door, followed by Marta who carried a flan and four plates.

Espinosa got to his feet and threw his arms around the restaurant owner. "Jorge, meet my friends from the United States. Jorge knows much of what goes on here, and his English is very good too."

Jorge beamed and slapped Espinosa on the back, then slipped behind the bar, coming back with a tray of four small glasses filled with a dark brown liquid. He put a glass in front of each of them, then settled his heavyset frame into the empty chair and proposed a toast while Marta bustled around serving the flan.

"Kahlúa, to celebrate new friends."

While they ate the flan and sipped the liqueur, Espinosa turned to Mike. "Tell Jorge and me what you've found so far."

Mike told them everything that had happened in Dalton and their reasons for being in Mexico, ending with the visit to the orphanage.

"I think someone in Dalton is funneling money into Mexico under the guise of charitable contributions, using the orphanage's name," Alex said.

Jorge didn't hide his skepticism. "Are you saying the nuns are trafficking in children?"

She shook her head. "No, but I do think somebody has set up an account using the orphanage name without their knowledge. I just can't prove it yet. We're hoping you can help us."

"We want to know about this end of the business and how it connects with Dalton," Mike said.

Espinosa tensed. "It's terrible. Human traffickers recruit girls from southeastern Mexico where your victims are from and send them to the United States. The traffickers have many ways of bringing money back to Mexico. It is possible that there is some scheme to launder money using the orphanage's name."

"Have you heard of a man named Vargas?" Alex asked.

"Emilio Vargas is one of the biggest operators. He and his gang work out of a place called Tenancingo, about a hundred kilometers southeast of here. Vargas is as brutal as any drug lord, and like the drug cartels, he thrives because of official corruption."

"Vargas runs the human trafficking network that operates in Dalton. He had Alex kidnapped, once here and also in Dalton." Mike said.

Espinosa looked at Alex. "Two times? Why would Emilio Vargas be after you? "

"I don't know why. I only know that a young woman died here and another in Dalton because of him."

"We need to go to Tenancingo," Mike said.

"That is a very dangerous place. You should keep your investigations to Mexico City where your embassy can help you if you get in trouble. There is much for you to discover here. You told me that your contacts in Dalton gave you the names of people. I have more names for you. Start with them. But be careful. Trust no one."

Mike nodded. "I may need help locating them and understanding how they move money around."

Espinosa searched his phone. "I can help. I also know someone who understands the financial side of this, a friend named Ramona Miranda who is a fellow reporter for *La Prensa*. That's her expertise. I'll send her a message now to tell her to expect a call from you."

They watched while Espinosa sent the message, then wrote a phone number on a napkin and handed it to Mike, who handed it to Alex.

Alex tucked the napkin in her purse next to the notebook containing the names that the gang in Dalton had given Mike.

Espinosa held out a thumb drive to Mike. "Here is a summary of what I have found and some background about Vargas. Don't let anyone know you have this until you get back home. Remember, you're going after dangerous people."

Mike nodded and took the drive from Espinosa's outstretched hand. "Thanks. If we can confirm any of this, we can hope that authorities on both sides of the border will have to do something about it."

Espinosa stood up. "We will talk again soon. Wait here a few minutes, then leave. Act like you are a young couple on vacation so no one will suspect why you are here. Everyone loves young lovers."

They watched the reporter walk out of the restaurant and into the lobby.

Alex was reaching for her guidebook when a series of popping sounds came from the street.

She sprang up. "What was that?"

Jorge ran out from behind the bar. "Gunshots."

She raced toward the door, Mike and Jorge behind her. Marta followed, looking very scared.

Half way down the street Espinosa was staggering and clutching at his stomach. He swayed, then pitched forward, and lay still.

Jorge pulled Marta back into the restaurant, yelling to Mike and Alex to get back inside. They ignored him and ran toward Espinosa.

Two men raced away toward a large black car that stood idling at the end of the street.

The one closest to Alex stopped and turned toward her, dark eyes glinting. It was Diego. The other man she recognized from the farm-house. Cuchillo.

Diego raised his gun. Mike pushed Alex to the ground and threw himself on top of her. Bullets cracked above them and buried into the stucco facade of the restaurant.

Police sirens whined in the distance, coming toward them. The two men jumped into the now-moving car. Tires squealed and the car was gone.

Mike rolled off Alex onto his feet and ran toward Espinosa. Alex followed. The reporter wasn't moving. Mike bent down and felt Espinosa's neck for a pulse. "It's very faint, but he's alive."

Espinosa's eyes opened. Blood bubbled from his mouth.

"We need something to stop the bleeding," Alex said.

She got up and raced back to the restaurant entrance where Jorge was cowering with Marta.

"Espinosa needs help. Hurry."

"You can't help him. He needs an ambulance. I called. The police are coming. Stay out of this," Jorge said.

She started to protest when a police car turned into the street and stopped where the black Mercedes had been. Two more police cars and a van converged on the scene from the opposite direction. Police poured onto the street. An ambulance rounded the corner. Medics jumped out, rushed to Espinosa, picked him up, and loaded him onto a gurney. Doors slammed. No more than a minute later the ambulance was gone, its siren receding into the noise of the city.

The police surrounded Mike and forced him into one of the police cars.

"What are they doing? Where are they taking Mike?"

The police cars sped away, tires squealing.

She started to run toward the police cars. Jorge grabbed her and held her back.

"He'll be all right. You can call your embassy for help. If the police see you now, they will take you away too, and you won't be able to help him."

Before Alex could break away, the police cars pulled away, and the street was silent, as if nothing had happened. Only the pool of blood remained.

CHAPTER FORTY-TWO

Alex followed Jorge back inside, and, without thinking, picked up the chair she'd knocked over and sat down. She opened her mouth, but no sound came out.

"*Señor* Espinosa. He is dead?" Marta asked, setting a bottle of water in front of Alex with trembling hands.

"I don't think he is going to make it," Jorge said.

Marta turned and slowly walked toward the kitchen, wiping tears away with her apron.

Jorge's face was purple as he paced back and forth in front of the bar. "We warned him. All of his friends were afraid for him. He has a wife, a small child. What will they do without him?"

"The police didn't even stop to investigate the crime scene. They just took Mike and left. What do they want with him?" Alex asked.

Jorge shrugged. "Probably they want to question him. They will take him to the police station and from there, who knows."

"They can't think he had anything to do with this. He doesn't even have a gun."

"Maybe they think he knows something. They have to do something. The newspapers will scream that the police do not protect journalists in this country. Your friend is an American. They won't do anything to him. They will let him go after they make a big show of investigating."

She rubbed her forehead. "How long will that take? We have to do something. The people we're looking for will find out we're here before we've had time to track the human trafficking network back to Dalton."

"We could try to bribe someone. The police, clerks, judges all have their hands out, but there will be much media attention so, in this case, I don't think that will work. Go back to your hotel. I will call you if I hear anything. I have to call Espinosa's family and his friends."

Alex's heart was pounding. She tried to think. She could hear Jorge in the kitchen, talking into a phone, but she couldn't make out what he was saying. Should she call the embassy, tell them about Mike, get their help in securing his release? How long would that take? If her parents suspected she was in Mexico City, they would be here by now. The ambassador knew who she was from six months ago. Once she called the embassy, the people there would call her parents, and it would be all over. Her notebook lay open on the table with the phone number of Espinosa's reporter friend, Ramona Miranda. She pulled out her cell and dialed.

The phone rang once. A woman answered. "*¿Hola?*" The high-pitched female voice was brittle with tension.

"*Señora* Miranda? *Señor* Espinosa suggested that I call you."

"I don't believe you. Our crime reporter just called. Espinosa is dead. Who are you?"

"I'm Alex Harrington, from the U.S. An American reporter friend and I were meeting with *Señor* Espinosa. We saw two gunmen shoot him, but he was alive when the ambulance took him away from here a few minutes ago. He's dead?"

Ramona Miranda's voice broke. "Word travels fast among journalists. I understand that Espinosa was dead on arrival at the hospital. Would you recognize the men who shot him if you saw them again?"

"Yes. We saw them clearly. My friend and I both saw them. I recognized them. My friend is an American reporter, Mike Murray, who has been working with *Señor* Espinosa on a human trafficking story."

"Did the killers see you?"

"I'm sure they did. They shot at us before taking off."

"That's a problem. You're a witness. You were with an American reporter, you say? Who else saw the shooting?"

"Jorge, the restaurant owner, and a waitress named Marta were there. The police took Mike away. I have to find him. Can you help?"

"We should meet. Stay inside the restaurant. I'll be there as soon as I can. Traffic this time of the day is very bad." Ramona hung up without giving Alex a chance to answer.

Jorge came back in, followed by Marta.

"Ramona Miranda says that *Señor* Espinosa is dead. She heard it from someone at her newspaper."

"I know her. If Ramona says something, it is true," Jorge said, and he stared at the wall without moving for several seconds.

Marta sank down on a chair and covered her face with her apron, sobbing.

"Ramona's going to help me find Mike."

Alex was waiting at the front of the building ten minutes later when a white Hyundai sped up to the front of the restaurant and jerked to a stop. A long-limbed woman reached across the passenger seat to unlock the door. A white silk scarf was pulled tight around her head, obscuring her mouth, and oversized sunglasses hid her eyes.

"I am Ramona Miranda. Get in, hurry," she said. "Lock your door. Pull down the visor so no one can see you."

The car took off, tires grinding into the pavement. From the little Alex could see of her, Ramona Miranda appeared to be about forty, with dark hair peeking out from beneath the scarf, a long face, and no make-up. Eyes fixed on the road, steering around push carts, honking at a cab driver who tried to cut her off, the woman tore through Mexico City traffic. The Hyundai narrowly missed a pedestrian.

Alex forced herself to take a deep breath. This woman was an even crazier driver than she was. "Where are we going?"

"To the offices of *La Prensa*. My editor and other journalist friends of Espinosa's want to meet you. Why did Espinosa give you my name?"

"Mike and I want to find how the human traffickers are moving money back to Mexico. We want to know who is responsible for the death of a young woman in Dalton. Someone in Dalton is working with a man named Emilio Vargas. We want to find out who that person is, and to do that we need to know who sends the money from the trafficking operation in Dalton back here, and where it goes when it gets here. Hispanic gang members in Dalton gave Mike the names of people who may be able to help us."

"Give me the names. I will find them," Ramona said.

———

Fluorescent lights flickered and buzzed overhead. Alex looked around the scarred wooden conference table of the news office. Ramona had removed her scarf and sunglasses and was talking to a gray-haired man of about fifty who introduced himself as the editor-in-chief of *La Prensa*. After several minutes of intense conversation the two stopped and turned to look at Alex.

The editor regarded her for what seemed like a very long time before speaking. "You and your friend have come to Mexico to take up the fight against human trafficking. Tell us what you know."

She filled them in, starting with her first trip to Mexico City, Cristina's and Mariana's deaths, and ending with the visit to the orphanage and her belief that Emilio Vargas was laundering money. She left out only the FBI's ridiculous suspicions of her own father's involvement. She kept her theories about the orphanage as a conduit to herself, sure that the editor would not believe her.

"Who else knows why you're here?" the editor asked.

"Only Jorge and the waitress, Marta. Clearly Espinosa thought we could trust them."

"Go through again what you told me in the car about Espinosa's murder," Ramona said.

When she was done, Ramona and the editor were silent.

Ramona's mouth drew into a tight line. "We Mexicans are accustomed to injustice, official corruption, and rampant crime waves that are ignored by authorities. This time we are not going to let them get away with it."

The editor leaned forward. "Like Espinosa, we believe that Emilio Vargas is running a human trafficking network from here to the U.S.

It would not surprise me if your murders in Dalton were the work of his people. We will help you with that, but first we must get your friend out of jail."

"*Señor* Espinosa said that we shouldn't trust the police, that they don't want to solve the murders of reporters or stop human trafficking," Alex said.

"That may be true. If your friend recognized the shooters, he is not safe. There is much corruption. Your embassy will help us, and then we will put pressure on our government to solve Espinosa's murder."

CHAPTER FORTY-THREE

Mike sat on the narrow metal shelf that served as a bed. A single bulb shone in the hall outside the cell; a filthy toilet bowl stood in the corner. He had read about Mexican jails, but he'd never expected to be in one. The sound of someone retching came from a neighboring cell. The stench was terrible. He leaned against the cinder block wall and closed his eyes. He had no idea how many hours had gone by since the police had brought him in. The sliver of light he could see through the cell window was gone. It must be night. Interrogators—some friendly, others hostile—had pelted him with questions: how much he knew, why he was meeting with Espinosa, who else was there. When he'd demanded to talk to a lawyer or someone from the U.S. Embassy, they'd laughed.

He was worried about Alex. She knew as much as he did. She had seen Espinosa's killers too. She was a pretty resourceful person and a lot tougher than she looked, but she was alone in a strange place. Nobody even knew she was there. He was beginning to think that was a mistake. Would Jorge watch out for her? He hoped so.

"They treating you real nice, boy." The gravelly, and definitely American, voice of his cell mate came from the shelf above him.

He looked up and focused on the grizzled face. The man in the top bunk appeared to be around sixty, though he could have been a hard-rode forty for all Mike could tell.

"Yeah? How you figure that?"

"Ain't got a mark on you. Weird 'cause from what I hear they want to know what you know real bad. I reckon the kid gloves is because you're a reporter and an American."

"How do you know I'm a reporter?"

The man rolled off his bed, shuffled across the cell, stuck his face in Mike's, and curled his upper lip into a grimace, showing rotting yellow teeth.

"I hear things. Word is, you saw what went down today, and you know who gunned down a Mexican reporter."

"Yeah? What else are you hearing?"

"You come here to bust some guys who run whores, is what I hear. You're messin' with some bad dudes. Wonder you ain't dead too."

Mike fought to keep his voice steady. "You're telling me the reporter is dead?"

"That's what they're sayin'."

"Where'd you hear that?"

"Just around."

"Where are you from?"

"Born and bred in Texas. Amarillo. I come here 'bout ten years ago when things got too hot for me up there. Hey, you got any U.S. dollars on you? I can get us pretty much anything we want in here if you got some money. Drugs, booze."

"I need information. Anything you can find out about the shooting."

"Names, if I can get 'em, are gonna cost you plenty."

"You won't get anything out this little piece of shit."

Mike had no idea how long the lead interrogator had been standing outside the cell. A guard and a buttoned-up man with ramrod posture in a gray suit stood beside him. On a nod from the interrogator, the guard unlocked the cell door and pulled Mike out into the hall.

The interrogator looked at him with a smile that was not at all pleasant. "You have important friends who want you out of here, *Señor* Murray. This gentleman is from your embassy. Perhaps we will meet on another occasion."

Cat calls, whistles, and sucking sounds followed them from the cell block, through a metal door and into the station.

"What about my passport and wallet?" Mike said when he reached the station door.

The interrogator nodded to the American in the gray suit. "The man from your embassy has them."

When they were outside, the embassy official handed him his passport and wallet.

"I had a thumb drive too."

"The police didn't give that to me," the official said.

Mike grunted in disgust. "How did you find me? The police wouldn't let me make a call."

"The editor of *La Prensa* told us you were here and insisted that you were in danger. The paper carries a great deal of weight. It wasn't easy. The Mexican police took some persuading before they agreed to release you. They think you know the men who killed the reporter this morning. I'm taking you back to the embassy. The ambassador wants a full briefing."

"I have to call a friend first."

The official walked ahead to a black Lincoln town car where a chauffeur waited to open the back doors.

"If you're talking about Alexandra Harrington, she's with the *La Prensa* staff. She's fine. Get in. You can call her from the car."

———

By the time she reached the hotel, Alex could barely put one foot in front of the other. She'd talked to Mike. He'd be staying at the embassy tonight. She looked around the hushed lobby. A single clerk at the desk acknowledged her entry and handed her a room key along with several messages. She stuffed the messages in her purse and walked to the elevator. As the elevator ascended, she leaned against the back wall watching the floors flash by, happy to be alone. At the eleventh floor the door slid open, and she stepped out, careful to look up and down the carpeted hallway before walking to her room.

Music came from one room, a television and voices from another. A tray stood outside another, its half-eaten hamburger reminding her that hours had passed since she last ate. She knew she should eat something, but what she wanted was sleep.

She reached her room at the end of the corridor and swiped the plastic room card in the lock. A red light flashed. She tried again. Same result. She gripped the card and swiped again. The light turned green. She pushed the door inward and flipped the light switch. Maybe it was the trauma of seeing Espinosa shot or simply exhaustion, but it was a full minute before she could comprehend the scene before her.

Her bag was open on the floor. Clothes were strewn around the room. Dresser drawers stood open. Her guidebook and maps of Mexico lay torn to pieces on the bare mattress. The room had been torn apart with a viciousness that seemed personal.

She stepped over the threshold and took stock, heart pounding, before moving closer to the mess. She took a deep breath and, jaw clenched, began sifting through the pile of debris. Her notebook and computer were gone. She willed her pulse to slow, picked up the room phone, and with shaking hands made two calls, the first to the front desk and the second to Ramona.

Ramona answered on the first ring. "Ransacked? That's bad. We should never have let you go back to the hotel. You're moving to my place immediately. Whoever did this could have been waiting for you too. This has to be connected to your investigation. What was on your computer?"

"All the material I had on the schools project and the orphanage, the contribution information, my notes on the interview with Sister Milagros at the *Hermanas de la Caridad* orphanage. I also had the name of a woman that Mike got from the gang in Dalton. I can remember a lot of it, but I'm afraid of what Vargas will do with the information once he has his hands on it. It's all encrypted. That's the only good thing."

She turned from the phone to see the desk clerk, a manager, and a uniformed hotel security guard standing in the doorway.

"We are so sorry, *señorita*. The police will be here soon Are you okay?" the manager said.

"No, I'm not okay. My computer, papers. All are gone. Don't you have security cameras in the lobby and in the halls?"

"We are looking into getting some."

"Alex." She heard Ramona's voice and turned back to the phone.

"My apartment's near your hotel. Wait in the lobby. I'll be there in a few minutes. Do not talk to the police. For all we know, it's the police who did this."

Alex hung up. She threw her few clothes and toiletries in her bag and walked into the hall.

"Where are you going? The police are on the way. They will want to talk with you," the manager said.

She went into the elevator and pushed the button for the lobby. "Not tonight."

She was climbing into Ramona's car just as three police cars pulled up in front of the hotel. Ramona accelerated away, narrowly avoiding one of them.

"You're staying with me from now on. It's not safe for you anywhere else. These people know who you are."

Alex sank back in the seat and closed her eyes. Her cell buzzed with two new messages: one from her mother demanding that she come home immediately, the other from Keisha White telling her that Agent Silva would arrive in Mexico the next day.

CHAPTER FORTY-FOUR

The official showed Mike to a room in the residence area of the modern concrete building that housed the American embassy. "You'll find a change of clothes on the bed. Give yours to the staff. Better shower, too. The ambassador is staying up especially to meet with you tonight."

Alone, Mike shed his clothes and put them in a bag in the hallway outside as directed, feeling bad that someone would have to handle the filthy laundry. Then he got in the shower and turned the water on as hot as he could stand, letting it pound on him full force for several minutes to wash the jailhouse stench from his body. Getting the smell out of his memory would take longer. The simple act of putting on a clean shirt helped. He opened a window and was inhaling the cool evening air when a knock sounded at the door.

"*Señor*, the ambassador will see you now." A young woman beckoned for him to follow.

Minutes later he was in the ambassador's office. The official, still in his gray suit, stood in front of a carved stone fireplace next to a tall, silver-haired man who Mike assumed was the ambassador. The clock on the mantel read eleven o'clock.

The ambassador crossed the expanse of thick Oriental carpet, hand outstretched. "We have much to discuss. Please have a seat. Can we offer you something to drink?"

Mike was dying for a cold beer, but this wasn't the time or the place. He needed a clear head. He declined and sat down on a leather couch. The ambassador chose a wing chair next to Mike's. The official remained on his feet.

The ambassador's sharp eyes regarded Mike from behind silver-rimmed spectacles for a full minute before he began to speak.

"You and your friend, Ms. Harrington, have attracted a great deal of attention in the short time you have been in Mexico, Mr. Murray. The FBI, the governor of North Carolina, and the Dalton police are all concerned for your welfare, apparently with good reason. Tell us, please, what you are doing here and how you came to be involved in the assassination of a Mexican journalist."

Mike gave a brief account of the assassination, ending with his reasons for the investigation into human trafficking and his connection with Espinosa.

The ambassador leaned forward. "You say that you saw the people who shot the reporter? Why didn't you tell that to the police?"

"Espinosa warned us not to trust anybody."

"Regrettably, Mr. Espinosa may have been right. You and Ms. Harrington are going home tomorrow. Mexico City is not a safe place for you."

"I can't go home. I have people yet to interview. I'm going to find them. Like me, they don't trust the Mexican police, but I'm hoping to be able to persuade them to talk to me."

"You will do nothing of the sort. Your presence here is a source of tension between the U.S. and Mexico. Please leave the criminals to the U.S. and Mexican governments.

"You will stay here tonight. In the morning the car will take you to the hotel where you will pick up Ms. Harrington and will then take you both to the airport. You're on a noon flight to Dallas, changing planes there for Dalton."

The ambassador held up his hand when Mike started to protest. "Good night, Mr. Murray, and thank you. We will appreciate your cooperation."

Back in his room, Mike took off his pants and shirt and tried calling Alex again. Her cell was off. He tried the main number of the hotel, letting the phone ring before someone answered at the main desk. "I am trying to locate Alexandra Harrington, a guest in the hotel," he said to the desk clerk.

"Ms. Harrington has checked out of the hotel," the clerk said.

Alarmed, Mike tried the cell again. Nothing. He lay down on the bed, intending to call again in a few minutes. The next thing he knew, sunlight was streaming through the window. He sat up, wide awake. He had to get out of there and find Alex. He slid off the bed, pulled on the clothes from the night before, and stuffed his wallet and passport in his pocket. He opened the door to the hall.

"Good morning, sir," a porter greeted him when he reached the bottom of the back stairs. "May I get you some coffee?"

"Maybe later, thank you. I'm just going to step outside for some fresh air."

"Yes sir."

As soon as the porter was gone, Mike slipped out the glass door, through the gate and into the street. He dialed Alex's cell one more time.

This time she answered. "Mike, where are you?"

"I'm just leaving the American embassy now, heading your way. Where have you been?"

He listened while Alex filled him in on everything that had happened since his last call.

"I'm at Ramona's now." She gave him the address. "Get here as soon as you can."

"The ambassador wants us on a twelve o'clock flight home. This is the first time I've been on the inside of a story, and no one's going to keep me away from it. Besides, Espinosa was a friend. He didn't walk away and neither will I. I do think it's dangerous for you here though. These people have your computer. They know why you're here. They've already tried to get you twice. You should go home."

"No way. I came here to find the people who killed Cristina and Mariana and save my father's reputation, and I'm going to do it. We have to find proof that Vargas is behind this and make the Mexican government shut him down."

"Let's talk about it when I get to Ramona's."

Mike stepped out onto the road and flagged down a cab.

Minutes later, he was watching the architecture of Mexico City fly by. He knew Alex well enough by now to be sure she meant what she said.

He knew what he had to do. He'd start by interviewing the people Mañuel had told him about. He was feeling confident by the time the cab neared Jorge's restaurant. He wanted to know if Jorge knew anything more about the men who killed Espinosa. He stopped the cab, got out, and paid the driver, then he walked toward the restaurant, carefully avoiding the dark stain in the middle of the street.

"*Señor* Murray." Jorge greeted him like an old friend. "I have been asking everywhere for you. I'm glad that you're okay."

Marta threw her plump arms around him, and then scurried off for pastries and a *café con leche*.

"What will you do now, *señor*?" Jorge asked.

"I owe it to Espinosa to stay on the story, and I could use your help."

Jorge ran his handkerchief over his forehead while he listened to the names. "These are dangerous people, *señor*," Jorge said. "Your ambassador gives you good advice. You should go home."

"I'm not leaving."

Jorge shrugged his shoulders and sighed. "As you wish, *señor*. Espinosa was my friend. I will help you. Maybe we can find some of these people today. Come with me."

Mike followed Jorge through the kitchen to the back door and out into a patch of dirt to Jorge's car. "I need to stop at Ramona's apartment to see Alex. Can we go there first?"

He gave the address to Jorge. "Do you know where this is?"

Jorge smiled and climbed into the driver's seat. "No problem. It's on the way."

Mike turned his interview questions over in his mind. A half hour passed before he noticed they were out of the business district, moving through a residential area.

"Alex said that Ramona lived near our hotel. We should be there by now."

Jorge pulled a semi-automatic weapon from under a bag on the seat between them and set it in his lap. "You should have listened to your ambassador. Mexico is not a good place for you or for *Señorita* Harrington."

CHAPTER FORTY-FIVE

Vargas couldn't keep still. He paced back and forth. His boots pounded the tile floor of his villa. He stopped and looked at the group of men who stood waiting for orders.

"Alex Harrington has gotten away from me twice. She comes here, and right away she is trouble. I should have killed her in Dalton."

Sweat trickled down his back. He stripped off the jacket of his black suit and rolled up the sleeves of his white shirt.

"She cut me in the neck in Dalton. Now she is here. She saw us shoot the woman at the warehouse and also Espinosa. She can identify me. She has to die," Diego said.

"The police do not care about the woman in the warehouse, and Espinosa is not a problem either. We have taken care of that. It's only the newspaper making noise. They will keep it up for a few days. The police will act like they're doing something, and then it will go away. Reporters get killed all the time. Nobody cares," Cuchillo said.

"This is different," Vargas said. "I hear that even the U.S. Embassy is involved in this now."

He began pacing again. His eye twitched. "We have friends in the *policía* and in the *Federales*. The president's office, too. They had better know what's good for them."

He turned to Billy, who was leaning against the wall behind the other men. "You *gringos*, you're nothing but trouble."

His phone vibrated. He pulled it out of his pocket, listened, and smiled. "Jorge is on the way. He's got the reporter. We can use him to get the Harrington *puta*."

CHAPTER FORTY-SIX

Mike was eyeing the gun, trying to work out how to grab it, when Jorge pulled to the side of the road and slammed on brakes. He reached in a side compartment, pulled out handcuffs, and snapped them on Mike's wrists.

"In case you think of doing something stupid."

Mike glared at the restaurant owner. "Espinosa said you were friends from when you were kids. He trusted you. You betrayed him. Why?"

"Money."

"Money? That's it? Just like that?"

"I gamble sometimes. I owe people. I don't do this? They kill me. *Mi familia* too."

The car turned off the main road at the exit for Tenancingo.

LA CAPITAL MUNDIAL DE LAS ROSAS, the Rose Capital of the World, the sign read. "Certain irony there," Mike said aloud. This was all going in his story, if he lived to write it.

The car sped through the city, passing concrete buildings, small shops, and billboards, some adorned with pictures of voluptuous, naked women, others advertising hotel rooms with water beds at hourly rates. A ten-foot-high mannequin of a woman dressed in a yellow bikini was perched on top of a pole a dozen feet above a roof top.

Jorge shook his head. "There is big money to be made here.

Espinosa was an idiot. I told him to back off. I told him they would kill him. He was stupid, like you. Now he is dead."

The car turned onto a side road, throwing up clouds of dust. It sped past rows of corrugated metal warehouses and stopped in front of a one-story building that stood apart from the others.

Jorge leaned on the horn. "You want to meet Emilio Vargas? This is your lucky day. You are going to get your interview with the boss."

A small door next to the loading dock opened, and two men came out. Mike recognized the scar-faced man in front as one of Espinosa's killers. He had to be the one Alex called Diego. Another man, thickly built with a round face, opened the car door, pulled Mike out, and stuck a gun in the small of his back. The two men marched him into a cavernous warehouse and dumped him on the ground. Jorge disappeared into a group of men who stood outside in the yard, watching.

Inside the warehouse a short, slender man with a pock-marked face was waiting. This had to be Vargas. Deep creases on either side of the man's mouth curled in an unpleasant smile. Vargas's eyes stayed fixed on Mike.

"Welcome to my headquarters. We are very glad to see you, *Señor* Murray," Vargas said in English.

Mike brushed dirt from his slacks. "I believe you are Emilio Vargas, *señor*. I'm a newspaper reporter. I'd like to interview you for a news story I'm writing for a U.S. newspaper."

Vargas laughed. "You do not lack for *cojones, señor*. They will do you no good here. We are looking for *Señorita* Harrington, and you are going to help us find her."

"Like hell," Mike said.

Vargas turned to Diego. "Show him."

Diego punched him in the gut. A flash of pain arched across his ribs. He doubled over, retching.

Diego hit him again. He went down. He stayed still a minute, then struggled to his feet.

Diego started toward him when a high-pitched voice called from the doorway.

Mike backed away out of Diego's reach.

A stocky young man, about nineteen, with over-sized, horn-rimmed glasses, walked toward Vargas, carrying a laptop. "*Tío* Emilio, I broke the encryption. I'm in. There's information about money transfers to a Mexican bank account in the name of an orphanage and names of people here too."

"In my office," Vargas said and led the way.

The others followed. Diego brought up the rear, one hand locked on Mike's arm.

Vargas motioned for the boy to put the laptop on a desk. The boy scrolled through what Mike could see were Alex's notes. Vargas ran a sleeve across his forehead. "She found the orphanage. She'll figure out the connection. Shit."

Mike looked around the office in desperation. There was no way out. He was not going to give Vargas what he wanted. He only hoped he could hold out until Alex missed him and called for help. Even then, who would guess where he was?

Vargas came toward him, holding up a cell phone. "You can make this easy or hard. Call her. Tell her to meet you at Jorge's restaurant."

His stomach twisted. He braced himself, ready for what was next.

CHAPTER FORTY-SEVEN

Alex sat on the terrace of Ramona's apartment house under the shade of a scarlet bougainvillea tree, waiting. The sun was directly overhead. Ramona had left the apartment before eight o'clock that morning, determined to use all of the influence *La Prensa* had to force a full government investigation into Espinosa's death. Mike's call had been hours ago. He should have been there by now. Something was wrong. She dialed his cell again. Still no answer.

She tried the restaurant. "He went with Jorge to meet someone. I don't know where they are," Marta said.

She forced herself to focus on the problem. If she was right that the traffickers were funneling money back into Mexico, how were they doing it without the nuns finding out?

Her cell phone rang. She answered, expecting Mike.

"Alex?" Keisha White said. "I've been trying to reach you for days. Why haven't you called back?"

"Sorry, Keisha. We've been kind of busy."

"Clearly. You were in Mexico one day before Murray was in jail. What have you two gotten yourselves into? We've heard from the Mexican police and from the U.S. Embassy in Mexico City. "

Alex gave the detective her own account of Espinosa's murder and the hotel break-in. "Mike's out of jail, but I have no idea where he is. He was supposed to meet me hours ago."

"Silva should be there in a few hours. He has your cell. He should be able to help."

"I sure hope so. What's going on at home?"

"A lot, actually. We found a blue van parked behind Billy Williams's house. The techs are going through it now. Turns out he's Marvin Moore's first cousin."

"So that's what he meant at the farmhouse when he said that helping me was payback for Marvin."

"Williams is missing, and we can't find your father. Have you heard from either of them?"

Alex frowned. "I don't know where Billy is, and my father could be anywhere. He travels a lot on business. If he knows I'm in Mexico City, he'll be on the way here."

Her cell beeped. "Sorry, Keisha. I have a call coming in. It may be Mike."

It was Jorge. "Hello, *Señorita* Alex. Marta said you called."

"Jorge, thank heavens. Is Mike with you? He was supposed to meet me hours ago."

"You know these reporters. He is after a story. Probably just forgot to call. I know where he is. I can take you to him."

A key turned in the front door, and Ramona rushed in.

Alex covered the phone. "Jorge says Mike wants me to join him."

"Tell Jorge you'll meet him and Mike later. There's something else we have to do first."

"Jorge didn't like being put off," Alex said when she hung up.

"He'll get over it. I've been searching for the people you remembered from Mike's list, and I've found a woman who is willing to talk with us. She's some kind of relation to the gang member and a maid for Vargas's banker. This may be the break we need. We have to meet her at the house before the banker gets home."

Minutes later she was back in the passenger seat of Ramona's Hyundai winding through Mexico City traffic. In a tree-shaded street of luxury townhouses, Ramona turned off the ignition and dialed a number.

"Consuelo? We are outside the house now."

A round-faced young woman in a maid's uniform opened a large oak door and stepped onto the paved driveway.

"May we come in, Consuelo? This is very important," Ramona said.

Consuelo nodded and motioned for them to follow her through the door and into the kitchen where she pointed to two chairs at a small wooden table.

The kitchen smelled of cinnamon and chocolate. They sat and waited while Consuelo set pottery mugs in front of them. A rainbow of ceramic plates decorated the walls. Music played softly on the radio. This would be a peaceful, homey place under ordinary circumstances, but Alex could tell from Consuelo's troubled expression that she considered their visit anything but ordinary.

Consuelo's hands shook as she poured steaming hot coffee into the mugs.

"You said over the phone that you know a man named Vargas," Ramona said.

Consuelo twisted her apron into knots. Her face contorted with rage and she began speaking rapidly in Spanish. "That evil man took my friend to the United States and kept her prisoner for five years. He made her have sex with many men every night. One of the men helped her get away. Now she lives in fear that Vargas will kill her and her family."

Ramona patted Consuelo's shoulder. "You can help us stop Vargas from doing that to other women. What is the connection between your boss and Vargas?"

"My boss, the banker, meets with Vargas here in private. I hear them talk about money that comes from the United States. My boss makes sure that the money goes to this Vargas. They say that it goes to the Sisters of Charity, and they laugh."

"We need proof that this money goes through his bank. Does the banker keep records here?" Ramona asked.

"He has papers that he shows to Vargas."

"We need to see them," Alex said.

Consuelo trembled. "The papers are in files in his desk in the library, but if he comes home and finds you, he will tell Vargas, and Vargas will kill us all. That man likes to kill people."

"Please. We will be quick. This is our only chance to stop this man," Ramona said.

Consuelo's hands closed until the knuckles turned white. "Okay, but you must hurry." She led them down a dark hallway, pulled a circle of keys from her apron and let them into a large room. "This is where they meet."

Light streamed from the garden through a French door at the end of the room. Consuelo crossed the plush Oriental carpet to an over-sized mahogany desk and reached under the middle drawer, pulling out a small key.

"The banker keeps his important files in this drawer," she said, fitting the little key in the lock.

Manila legal-size files lay in neat stacks. Alex gathered several for Ramona and kept the rest for herself. "We're looking for anything with the name of the orphanage, *Orfanato de las Hermanas de la Caridad*."

"Hurry, please," Consuelo said, leaving them with the files.

The room was silent except for the rustle of papers. Minutes passed.

"Here it is, a file marked with the name of the orphanage, and it's thick," Ramona said.

A horn sounded from the street outside. Consuelo rushed into the library. "He's here. You must leave. Quick. Through the door to the garden."

A deep male voice called from the hallway. "Consuelo, whose car is in the driveway?"

Consuelo's eyes grew wide with terror.

The file slipped from Ramona's fingers, spilling papers across the floor. She stooped to pick them up.

Alex ran to help.

They heard a gruff voice. "Consuelo, where are you?"

Consuelo ran from the room. They could hear her in the hall, her voice high-pitched.

"I've got most of them," Ramona said.

"Quick, through the French door." Alex jammed the rest of the loose papers into the folder.

Once outside, she stopped. "We can't leave Consuelo with that man. The banker will find that his file is missing. You heard her say Vargas would kill her."

"Not now, Alex," Ramona said, running ahead.

They heard the deep voice at the door. "*¡Alto!* Stop!"

A tall man in a pin-striped suit started running toward them with surprising speed.

Ramona grabbed Alex's arm and propelled her toward the car, then jumped in the driver's side, and gunned the engine.

The Hyundai's tires squealed, leaving the man standing beside the road, red-faced, waving his arms.

"I'm scared for Consuelo," Alex said.

"Stop worrying. Consuelo will tell the banker that we forced our way in and took the files. She'll be fine."

Alex looked back at the house, not at all convinced.

CHAPTER FORTY-EIGHT

Mike woke up on a cold cement floor and looked around what appeared to be a basement. Cockroaches scurried across the floor each time he moved. He was covered in cuts and bruises, and he hurt all over. He'd survived that beating, but it wouldn't be the last. He'd refused to call Alex or tell them where she was, and he was sure they weren't going to stop until they got what they wanted or he was dead.

Everything hurt. Ropes bound his hands and feet, and he'd lost all feeling in both. He had to get out of here fast. He worked at the knots until the skin on his wrists and ankles was raw.

The floor above creaked. His heart beat faster. He waited, holding his breath, but nobody came.

Light came from a small window high on one wall. He worked the rope around his ankles, until at last the knots were loose enough for him to stand. His feet were asleep. He stomped them until the feeling returned and he could shuffle around the basement. He searched until he found an old washboard leaning against a laundry tub. Bracing the washboard with his feet he worked the rope around his wrists back and forth against the metal edge. Sweat rolled down his back. Trucks roared in the distance, coming closer. He rubbed harder, ignoring his cramping arms. Voices sounded from upstairs. The men were back.

He watched the stairs. Still no one came. Heart pounding, he kept at the ropes until at last he broke through. His hands were free. He bent down and freed his feet.

He could hear the men, walking around above, shouting to each other. He ran to the window and felt for a lever. The window was fixed in the wall. It didn't open. He raced for the washboard, then back to the window and swung the washboard in the air above his head, bringing it against the glass with all the strength he had left. The glass shattered, sending shards flying.

Footsteps crossed the floor above.

He pushed the remaining glass out the window, cutting his hands, and pulled himself up and through the window frame, landing on soft dirt outside.

He wiped his bloody hands on his pants and looked around. He was at the back of a large stucco building, some kind of villa surrounded by a wall only twenty yards away. He took a step toward the wall when the back door of the villa opened, and two men came out. A match flamed. Embers glowed and the pungent scent of Mexican tobacco hung in the air.

He ducked back in the shadows.

"If Vargas don't get that American *puta* soon, we're all dead,"

"He's loco."

Someone yelled from inside the villa. "Cuchillo, Diego," and the two men disappeared back inside.

The sky was the color of wet cement and growing darker by the minute. Large drops of rain spattered the ground. Mike raced for the wall and pulled himself up. He dropped to the other side, and landed off-balance on his left leg. Searing pain shot through his ankle.

He was standing beside a large shed. He leaned against the shed wall, waiting for the pain to die down, and was just starting forward again when he heard angry male voices.

Vargas's men poured out into the yard. They'd discovered he was gone. He grasped the handle of the shed door and the door swung open. He dove inside, pulling the door shut behind him. He listened, trying to hear over the thudding of his chest. The men were shouting, their voices closer. They were over the wall.

A burro turned and regarded him, solemn-eyed, from behind a half wall. He squeezed in beside the burro, and crouched down, praying the animal wouldn't start braying and give him away.

Someone was outside the door. He stopped breathing. The door opened, and Cuchillo stood silhouetted in the doorway. A flashlight beam played across the shed floor.

The burro stomped at the floor and snorted. Mike shrank further back in the stall.

The light swung across the walls and up into the rafters.

"Nothin' in here but a dumb donkey."

The shed door closed. Footsteps receded toward the villa. The yard was quiet.

Mike waited for several minutes before sliding out of the stall. He saluted the burro and opened the shed door. He strained to see through the rain. His ankle throbbed. The land beyond the villa was rolling wasteland. It was his only chance. Vargas's men wouldn't be able to see him out there. He needed some kind of a stick to lean on. He searched around the outside of the shed, found one that would do in a pile of brush, and set off in the direction of what he hoped was a town.

CHAPTER FORTY-NINE

Alex could hardly wait to find Mike and tell him what they'd found at the banker's house. She wondered who he'd found to interview. Ramona had dropped her at Jorge's restaurant, promising to call when she had finished analyzing the file.

Alex followed Jorge to his car. "Where are we going?"

"A place south of here. We're meeting *Señor* Murray there. I was able to set up appointments for him with some very important people."

"Why didn't he call me himself?'

Jorge opened the passenger side door for her and made a little bow. "He called me on his phone on the way. It's a few miles from here. Perhaps he didn't have a signal when he got there. It won't take us too long."

Her mind wandered as Jorge merged into fast moving traffic. She was still tense after the escape from the banker's house and worried about Consuelo. She barely noticed the scenery change from tall buildings to an open arid landscape dotted with small houses and sparse vegetation. Jorge turned the car radio up loud so that casual conversation was impossible.

Time passed. Music blared. Heavy clouds gathered in the sky.

"I thought you said this wouldn't take long," she yelled over the music.

"We're almost there."

Minutes later the car turned off the highway. The sign read Tenancingo. Her stomach clutched. They were entering the human trafficking capital of Mexico. Espinosa had warned them about this place. Had Mike found a source here, maybe an insider who would talk to him? She pulled out her cell and tried Mike's number again. It went to voice mail. Damn. Her phone worked out here. Why didn't he pick up?

Lightening cracked, thunder rolled. The rain started, light at first, turning into a downpour as Jorge maneuvered the car through the streets of Tenancingo.

She shifted in her seat. Jorge was Espinosa's friend, and he trusted him.

"You're sure this is the place?"

Jorge nodded. His eyes were fixed on the road ahead. He drove through an area of rickety shacks, past corrugated metal buildings that looked like warehouses and onto a street of luxurious villas. The car stopped at a large wrought iron gate. A man stepped out of a guardhouse, squinted at the windshield and opened the gate. The car stopped in a tiled yard in front of a sprawling villa. Rain was coming down hard, turning the stucco walls of the building to a dark coral.

A line of men filed out of the house and stood waiting, oblivious of the rain.

"Where are we?"

Jorge turned off the engine. "This is the home of *Señor* Vargas."

She was hot, then cold. "Oh dear God. What have you done?"

Jorge wouldn't look at her.

She shrank back against the seat. Espinosa had said to trust no one. Why hadn't she listened? She'd been such a fool.

The line of men parted, and a slight man walked out of the house. This had to be Vargas. A younger, stockier man wearing wire-rimmed glasses walked beside him, holding an umbrella. The two men reached the car, and the younger man opened Alex's door. Vargas leaned into the car. His close-set black eyes glistened. "Good afternoon, *señorita*. Welcome to my *hacienda*."

She pushed back into the seat, refusing to budge.

A face she knew well appeared behind Vargas. Diego leered at her. Another man, also familiar, joined him. Cuchillo.

Cuchillo reached around Vargas for her arm and pulled her out of the car.

She pitched forward, then, found her balance. She went into a crouch and sprung at Cuchillo, hands together, straight out, connecting with his throat.

Cuchillo fell back, choking.

She grabbed the umbrella from the stocky young man and held it as a weapon.

Diego knocked the umbrella to the ground and lunged for her. He wrapped his arms around her in a vice-like grip and picked her up off the ground.

She tried to kick, but her feet only thrashed in the air.

Cuchillo slugged her in the stomach, then nodded to Diego who threw her over his shoulder and carried her, kicking, through the open door and threw her down on a hard tile floor.

She lay on the cold floor, struggling to meet the hostile eyes of Vargas's men as they closed around her.

"Tie her up," Vargas said.

Cuchillo lifted her off the floor, set her in a heavy wooden chair, and wound ropes around her wrists and ankles.

She looked around the vast space. Her own bleak reflection stared back at her from the many gilded mirrors that lined the wall. Pillars at least ten feet in circumference reached to a thirty foot ceiling. This was a room designed to impress, to make all who entered feel small, and its owner feel important. She would not be intimidated. She was outnumbered. She had to use her wits. She'd escaped before. She would do it again. Somehow.

Across the room Jorge was talking with Vargas. She looked around for Mike, careful not to move. The ropes bit into her wrists and ankles. Her body was stiff. Even the smallest movement hurt.

"Where is Mike Murray?"

Vargas's jaw muscles clenched. He lit a cigarette, pulled on it, then threw it down, ground it into the tile, and lit another. He began to pace. "He won't get far. He's a dead man."

So Mike had been here. He'd got away. She shut her eyes and prayed he'd make it.

Vargas's eyes narrowed. "You think your boyfriend will save you? He will not."

Rain drummed on the tile roof. Wind rattled the windows. Inside the villa no one spoke. A fly buzzed on a windowsill. Vargas picked up a magazine from a side table and brought it down on the fly, over and over.

The roar of motors came from the back. The front door flew open, and a dozen men rushed in.

Vargas faced them. "You got him?"

The men stood before Vargas, water dripping from their hair and clothes. "It's black out there, rain blowing sideways. We can't see more than a few feet ahead of the Rovers. The arroyos are raging. No way he's gonna make it."

"You stopped for rain? Get back out there. Take everyone. Find him."

The men exchanged looks.

"Damn it, move. Cuchillo, Diego, you too."

The men ran out. Motors revved outside.

She was alone with Vargas.

CHAPTER FIFTY

Nightfall gave Mike cover, but progress was slow. He'd only gone about a mile when he heard the sound of engines and saw headlights coming toward him. The rain wasn't stopping them. He dove into an arroyo and pulled what little loose brush he could find over his head.

Two Land Rovers, each with half a dozen men hanging over the side, raced by and separated several yards beyond, one moving north, the other south. The sound of the engines faded in the distance.

He waited, soaked to the skin. A flash of lightening lit up a ragged line of trees up ahead. The rain came down harder. A thin sheet of water rushed over the sandy soil. The water was up over his ankles and rising fast. He splashed through the shallow current, holding onto the brush on the side of the arroyo. The water was up to his knees.

Lightning struck close by, illuminating the vast landscape. There was no shelter in sight. Thunder cracked. The ground trembled. He reached for a branch, hoisted himself onto the bank, and lay there, panting. Rain pounded his back while the water rushed below.

Half an hour passed. His shirt was stuck to his back. He heard the Rovers returning. They were almost on him when he dove into a stand of brush and lay flat. The Rovers stopped, their headlights directed on the bushes above him. The men got out, talking, arms waving, yelling at each other.

A large rat ran across his foot. He hated rats. He jumped, and the brush moved.

The men stopped talking and looked around.

The rat dashed in their direction.

A shot rang out. The rat flipped in the air, and the men laughed. "The *gringo* will die like that rat."

Lightning snaked across the sky, silhouetting the group.

"We won't find him tonight in this weather."

The men climbed back into the Land Rovers. Taillights disappeared in the direction of the villa. They'd be back at daybreak. Mike's ankle throbbed. He still had the stick. He clutched it and set off in search of some kind of cover.

The pain in his ankle was worse. His clothes were soaked. He moved on in the dark, leaning on the stick, limping forward over the uneven ground. His spirits sank with each agonizing step. He was close to giving up when the rain stopped at last, and the clouds parted to let the moon shine through. In the distance he could make out the dark shape of a building. He picked up the pace and was almost there when he heard the dogs.

Three huge mongrels raced toward him, snarling. He turned his body sideways, hoping to deflect them. It didn't work. The dogs came closer, circling, baring their teeth. He tried not to show fear, not so easy considering he was surrounded by several hundred pounds of snarling animals. The lead dog bared its fangs and lunged. Mike jammed the stick in its mouth. The other dogs leaped at him, one sinking its teeth into his thigh, the other tearing his arm. Pain ripped through him. He fell back under the sheer force of the dogs' bodies and went down.

"Ciro, Rico, Sato."

The dogs hit the dirt, whimpering. A large man carrying a shotgun in hands the size of small watermelons, face creased from years in the sun, walked toward him. "Who are you?"

Mike used his childhood Spanish, introducing himself as a reporter who was writing a story about Tenancingo for his paper in the states.

The man frowned. "What kind of a story?"

"He's bleeding." A woman's voice came from the shadows. "Bring him inside."

The man turned to a small, dark-skinned woman. "It's because of him that Vargas's men were here tonight. We are simple farmers. Vargas's men have guns. This reporter will only bring us trouble."

"Vargas." The woman spat the name and turned toward the house.

The farmer held the shotgun in one hand and gripped Mike's arm with the other, marching him into the house.

The farmhouse was a small adobe structure with a red tiled roof. Inside, colorful pieces of cloth decorated rustic pine furniture. A fire warmed the room. The woman pointed to a chair. "You need to change. Get out of those wet clothes."

She brought a bowl of hot water and began wiping blood and dirt from the teeth marks on his arm, then rolled up his torn pant leg and dabbed at a deep gash. The farmer went into a back room and came back with some dry clothes.

"You didn't get those bruises on your face from the dogs," the man said. "Why is Vargas after you?"

"I saw Vargas's men murder a friend of mine, a Mexican reporter. He hates reporters, me especially."

"He is a pig," the woman said.

"He's going after a friend of mine. I have to warn her. Do you have a telephone?"

"The nearest telephone is in town. It would be very dangerous for you to call from there. Vargas has people everywhere. Tomorrow I am taking vegetables to the market in Mexico City. Wait until then. You can ride in the truck under the vegetables."

Mike looked in the direction of Vargas's villa. The man was right. He'd call Alex in the morning. She was with Ramona and safe, at least for now.

CHAPTER FIFTY-ONE

Alex leaned forward, working her hands behind her back. The ropes were getting looser. She kept her eyes on Vargas.

Vargas answered his cell. "*¿Hola?*" His voice echoed in the cavernous room. As he listened a purple flush spread across his face. His free hand balled into a fist. He cut his eyes toward her.

"They took the file? You are sure it was a woman reporter and a *gringo* girl? Stay where you are. I am sending someone to take care of it now. Make sure that your maid doesn't get away."

Alex caught her breath, praying that Consuelo was all right, knowing she wasn't.

Vargas closed the phone and turned toward her. "Two times you got away from me. You cost me good men. Now I hear you have files that are important to me. Where are they?"

She met his gaze. She would not show fear, no matter how her stomach churned.

Vargas pushed his face in hers. His cigarette-breath turned her stomach. "Where is the file?"

She twisted away just as the phone rang in the pocket of her jeans.

Vargas slid his hand into her pocket, pulled it out, and glowered at the display. "How did we miss this? Your friends are looking for you. It will be too late when they find you."

He threw the phone on the tile floor and ground it to pieces with the heel of his shoe, then gave a near-hysterical laugh that was more disturbing than anything he could say.

She twisted her wrists. Maybe she could win him over, at least until she could free her hands.

She fought back a wave of nausea and forced herself to look at Vargas. "That's probably my friend, Ramona, from *La Prensa*. She says you are a big man in human trafficking. The most important of all."

Vargas came toward her, eyes glittering. "I kill reporters who say bad things about me."

"Ramona isn't like that. She wants to write about who you are. Who you really are, as a real person."

Vargas paused, frowning. The deep flush in his cheeks began to fade.

"Ramona says that you come from a very poor family. You are a self-made man. She says it would be a good story."

He cocked his head to the side and gave her a quizzical look. "She really said that? She's right. Nobody gave me anything. I made it on my own."

The ropes were slippery with sweat. Her wrists moved more easily.

"How did you do it?"

Vargas smiled and sat down beside her on the sofa. "I was the youngest of twelve. My mama had to clean rich people's houses. We went to bed hungry many nights."

She inched away.

"The kids where mama worked had lots of money. They were buying eighty-dollar shoes. I wanted them too. I met a man who told me that all I had to do was drive a truck across the border."

"How old were you then? Weren't you scared?"

"I was sixteen and afraid of nothing. I did what he said, and for the first time I had money. I could buy all the shoes I wanted."

"How did you get from driving a truck to being a boss?"

Vargas reached a hand toward her and touched the white streak in her hair. "Such a pretty lady."

Her skin crawled. She swallowed her disgust.

"I went to the police academy, and I learned how to find people and capture them. After I graduated I became a policeman and a kidnapper for the narco-traffickers at the same time."

She nodded, trying to look encouraging, to keep him talking. "How did you get from doing that to where you are now?"

He gave a low mirthless laugh. "One day I realized that the narcos owned me. I made a lot of money, but they made much more. I knew I couldn't compete with them so I changed from drugs to humans. Now I give my former bosses a cut, and they leave me alone."

Heavy-lidded reptilian eyes raked her body. "I have a wife, but many men like me have more than one wife, some as many as forty. You could be my wife, live in my villa, and have anything you wanted." He ran a hand down the front of her blouse.

Bile welled up in her throat, and she spat it at him.

Vargas shrank back and wiped his face on his shirt sleeve, then slapped her across the face. "*Puta*, you will pay for that. I will sell you to the Asians. You will bring a high price."

All of the rage building inside her since Cristina's death exploded. She tore her hands free from the ropes, screamed, and lunged at Vargas, clawing at his eyes.

Vargas punched her hard in the stomach, again and again until she doubled over. He threw her down on the sofa and pushed her face into the pillows.

She couldn't breathe, and her temples were pulsing, her eyes blurring.

He turned her over, and hit her again. His diamond ring carved a gash on her forehead.

She brought her hand up to her face and wiped away the blood, bracing herself for more blows when the back door opened and Vargas's men trooped in. Mike wasn't with them.

Vargas walked toward them. "Where is he?"

"It's too dark out there. We couldn't find him, but the arroyos are full. We'll find his body in the morning."

"He better be dead or you will pay tomorrow. Right now I have more important business to take care of. I have a job for Paco."

Vargas looked at Alex. "Diego, you take her into the office. Tie her up good."

Diego walked toward the couch, leering, and grasped her wrists.

"You don't look so pretty now, *puta*."

She kicked him as hard as she could with her bound feet, connecting with his groin.

Diego howled. "You gonna die, *puta*."

"She will die, but not here. I have plans for her," Vargas said.

On a nod from Vargas, Cuchillo helped Diego carry Alex to a small room off the main hall. They tied her hands and feet to a chair and wedged the chair between the wall and a chest so that she couldn't move.

Vargas followed. "Not so brave now, are you, *señorita*?"

An intercom on the desk buzzed. Vargas punched a button on the wall.

A voice said, "He's here."

Vargas's narrow face broke into a smile. "Ha. Bring him in."

Vargas turned and went back into the great hall, followed by Cuchillo.

She strained to hear and could just make out Vargas's voice. "We've been expecting you."

"I have what you want. I brought the money in U.S. dollars. Where is my daughter? I want to see her, now."

She knew that voice. It was her father. Thank God. She was going to get out of here.

Vargas gave another high-pitched laugh. "Why so impatient, Caballero?"

CHAPTER FIFTY-TWO

MEXICO CITY

Mike jumped down from the vegetable wagon as soon as the farmer reached the market on the outskirts of Mexico City. The farmer and his wife had risked their lives to help a stranger. He struggled to find words in Spanish to thank them.

"If you can stop these people that will be thanks enough," the farmer said.

He began searching for a public phone, finding one outside a small bodega. His first call was to Alex. Her cell went directly to voice mail. Frustrated, he tried Ramona. No answer there either. His uneasiness grew. He dialed the main phone number for *La Prensa*.

Ramona picked up.

Mike told her about Vargas and his escape.

"You say you were at Vargas's villa? How did you get there?"

"It was a trap. Jorge is one of them. He's working for Vargas. He took me to Tenancingo so that Vargas could use me to get to Alex. He's obsessed with her."

"Wait. Alex didn't come back to my apartment last night. I thought she was with you. Jorge was taking her to find you."

"Oh God, Vargas has her."

"You're at the farmers' market? Stay there. I'm coming to get you."

Mike was frantic, waiting for Ramona. When at last she pulled up to the vegetable stand, he jerked the car door open.

"He's going to kill her. We've got to get to Tenancingo now."

The horn of a four-wheeler blasted when Ramona shot out in front of it. "You've seen Vargas's fire-power. We need the *Federales*. We need help to get past the layers of corruption that protect Vargas if we want to see Alex again. *La Prensa* was able to get a meeting with the president of Mexico in his office in an hour."

"Will the president help us?"

"He will have to. Your ambassador will be at the meeting and some-one from your FBI. Vargas is holding an American citizen hostage. Alex and I found proof that Vargas is engaging in human trafficking and laundering money from the U.S. to Mexico with the help of a prominent banker. Today the banker is dead, along with his maid."

"All this happened yesterday? How did you find this banker?"

Ramona's voice cracked. "Through the woman whose name you got from the gang in Dalton. She was the banker's maid. Her name was Consuelo. She helped us, and when the banker came home, we left. I was so excited about what we found that I didn't listen when Alex said Consuelo was in danger. I honestly didn't think the bank-er would hurt her. The worst I thought would happen would be for Consuelo to lose her job, and I knew that my paper could help her get a new one. We think Vargas found out and killed them both."

"Vargas got to them that fast?"

Ramona nodded. "Emilio Vargas is far more vicious and efficient than I realized. At first he seems like a ridiculous little man, always trying to prove how important he is. He wears fancy clothes and surrounds himself with beautiful models. It's easy to underestimate him. I did that, and it cost Consuelo her life."

Mike's stomach lurched. Ramona was the best chance he had of getting Alex out alive. He had to pull himself together and follow the reporter's lead. This was her country. She was right. Hot-dogging it out to Vargas's villa and taking on the whole gang was only going to get Alex killed.

Ramona glanced at Mike's worn shirt and faded jeans.

"Ordinarily, there's no way I could take you into the president's office looking like that. I'll have to convince the president's people that this is an emergency. A life is at stake."

The president's press secretary was waiting for them in the lobby. Mike and Ramona followed her into a palatial, brightly lit conference room already populated with official-looking people in expensive suits, including the Secretary of the Interior and the head of the Mexican Federal Police, better known as the *Federales*. At the far side of the room, Agent Silva stood ramrod straight next to the American ambassador and the editor of *La Prensa*.

After an official round of introductions the room was quiet. The ambassador flinched at Mike's clothes, and then looked away. Only the buzz of a fluorescent light overhead broke the silence. Minutes dragged by.

Mike leaned toward Ramona. "We're wasting time."

Ramona motioned to him to keep quiet just as two large doors opened at the end of the room, and the president entered, flanked by a large barrel-chested man with a neck as thick as his head. The president acknowledged the American ambassador and walked to the head of the table and sat down. Everyone else took a seat in rank order.

"You requested this meeting on behalf of *La Prensa*," the ambassador said, focusing on the editor. "Please proceed."

The editor's expression was grim. "Emilio Vargas, one of the most notorious criminals in Mexico, is holding an American woman, Alexandra Harrington, captive. He is also responsible for the death of a prominent banker and his maid last night, and for the assassination of a *La Prensa* reporter. We ask that you rescue *Señorita* Harrington and apprehend this criminal."

"I'm sure that the police are working on these matters," the president said.

"The police have many crimes to investigate," Ramona said. "Men like Vargas have much influence with the police. If we don't find Alex Harrington soon, she will be dead too. We need you to make this a priority."

The president looked from face to face around the room, stopping at the American ambassador.

The ambassador cleared his throat. "Mr. President, the United States Government is very concerned about the safety of Ms. Harrington."

"I assure you that we will do everything within the power of the government of Mexico to find this young woman," the president said.

"What about the three murders? Espinosa and the other two. What about all the other reporters who have died?" Ramona asked.

"I will personally guarantee that these matters are given the full attention of the Mexican government. Too many people have died. The secretary will deal with it all."

The president rose. Everyone in the room stood and waited while he left the room.

The Secretary of the Interior raised his arm. "We will adjourn now to headquarters for a full review of what we know about the disappearance of Alex Harrington, the murder of Rafael Espinosa and the others."

Mike stood. "We don't have time for that. We have to get to Tenancingo now."

The secretary glared at him. "We are as eager as you to save the American woman, but we want her alive, do we not? These things take time."

CHAPTER FIFTY-THREE

"Here is your beautiful daughter, Caballero. We are enjoying her company, as you can see."

Sandy Harrington looked at Alex, then back at Vargas. "You bastard."

Vargas laughed. "First, the money."

On command from Vargas, Cuchillo shoved a gun into Sandy's back and propelled him toward the door.

Alex watched Cuchillo take her father away. Vargas had called her father El Caballero. The two men obviously knew each other. She didn't like this at all.

Minutes passed. Sandy came back into the office, carrying a large box that he placed on the desk. Cuchillo was behind him with another box.

"Count it. It's all there. My daughter and I are going home now."

"Because of you and your precious daughter, my operation is broken. I have to rebuild my distribution system. Even the Mexican police are turning on us."

She felt rather than saw a change in her father. Confidence seemed to drain out of him.

"*Señor*, you have all the money that I could get together, from savings, my business, from friends. I mortgaged the house. The business will be running again soon. There will be more money."

A chill seized her. They were talking about human trafficking. Her father was involved in human trafficking. She opened her mouth and closed it, unable to speak or even to think.

She looked from Vargas to her father, catching her breath.

Vargas threw his head back and laughed. "Your money does not begin to make up for your incompetence. Your daughter is part of what you owe. She will bring us a pretty penny in Asia."

Vargas's cell rang. He answered, listened and scowled.

He beckoned to Diego to come closer. "The police are done now."

He turned to one of his men. "Paco, take these two down to the basement. Make sure they don't get away."

Sandy Harrington reached inside his box, pulled out a gun, and pointed it at Vargas.

Vargas laughed. "You don't have the guts."

Paco lunged for the gun. The shot went wild. Cuchillo sprang from the other side and wrested the gun out of his grip while Paco wrenched his empty hand behind him and pushed him toward the basement.

Sandy tried to break away.

Cuchillo caught him around the neck and slammed his head into a wall, over and over again until he slumped to the floor.

"Get them out of here," Vargas said.

Alex watched as the men carried her father down the stairs.

Cuchillo came back for her, untied her, and then picked her up, threw her over his shoulder as if she were weightless, carried her down the stairs, and dumped her next to her father on the cement floor.

Paco pulled a chair from under the window and sat down, his eyes glued on them. "Come on. Try to get away. Give me a reason to shoot you."

Alex lay on the floor, her unconscious father beside her. She had never felt so alone.

CHAPTER FIFTY-FOUR

Alex had no idea how long she had been in the dank basement. She could just make out her father's face in the dark.

Sandy Harrington was awake, ashen and grimacing from pain. She looked away. She tried to get away from him, but the ropes around her wrists and ankles wouldn't let her. She flinched from the pain. "I believed in you. How could you put women and children through living hell?"

"You have to understand, sweetheart. I had no choice. Vargas is an evil man. I had to protect you and Renee. He would have killed you if I refused to do as he said."

"What are you saying? You're a human trafficker because of us? How dare you!"

"At first, it was just a business opportunity. A group of Mexican businessmen wanted to rent property and make connections in return for good money. They introduced me to high level officials in Mexico who could ease business transactions for me there. They offered me an opportunity to invest and promised a twelve-percent guaranteed return. How could I pass that up? When I brought in other investors, I got a finder's fee too. I told the potential investors that only an invited few would be allowed to participate. When they saw the amount of money they'd make, people begged to be part of the fund. The Binghams, the Foleys, even the governor. Everyone made at least a twenty percent return."

"It was all about the money. You don't give a damn about human suffering."

"I didn't know what they were doing."

"You didn't want to know."

"When I understood what was going on, I wanted out. That's when Vargas tried to teach me a lesson by kidnapping you the first time."

"Why didn't you tell the FBI, or at least me?"

He looked away. "How could I tell you that I was the one who put you in danger? You would have blamed me. The FBI would have arrested me. I would have gone to jail."

He met her gaze. "Vargas didn't know that you'd put up a fight. I was proud of you, but I was afraid for you too. Nobody gets away from Emilio Vargas. He vowed to get you again and punish you unless I did whatever he said. I had no choice. We brought you home. I thought we could protect you there. I thought that, with our influence, Vargas wouldn't dare go after you."

"Why did he kidnap me twice?"

"After Carmela brought Mariana to the center and the police started looking into her death, we had to stop the Dalton operations. Vargas blamed me and demanded huge amounts of money to compensate for lost business. I didn't have it. He didn't believe me. I threatened to go to the police. He took you to keep me quiet and to force me to raise money for him. I got more from the investors, but it wasn't enough. Then you got away again. It wasn't all about me anymore. He hates you. He blames you for his problems. He's crazy. That's why I tried to get you out of the country, to Europe, where I hoped you would be safe, but you wouldn't go."

"I had to show my passport at the border. That must be how he found out I was here."

"He has people everywhere. He got you here, and called me, gloating. I knew he would kill you. I did what he said. I mortgaged everything I had and came here. You're more important than anything I have. Can you at least try to see?"

Her heart pounded. She jerked at the ropes around her hands and feet, numb to the pain. "What I see is Cristina and Mariana. I see Teresa's terror and grief, the squalor in the house on York Street. I'm only glad that you're not my real father."

"What are you saying?"

"I've been to the orphanage. I know who my real mother was. I know that I'm adopted. My name is Nina."

"You know about Angelina?"

Footsteps sounded on the stairs. Vargas appeared out of the darkness, Cuchillo and Diego with him.

"Take El Caballero outside and kill him."

Alex screamed.

"Knock her out. I'm sick of her."

Diego jammed a cloth over her face. A pungent, sweet smell filled her nostrils. She tried to fight. Diego pushed harder. She held her breath until her lungs screamed.

———

She woke up, still in the basement of the villa, with no idea how much time had passed. Her head ached. She groped around with bound hands, touching her father's inert body beside her.

Someone struck a match. She smelled sulfur and saw Billy's face. One eye was completely closed, his nose was broken, and his right hand was wrapped in a bandage.

"Billy, is that you? What happened?"

"After the reporter got away, Vargas went crazy. He made his men beat me and cut off my thumb. They would've killed me if Diego hadn't stopped 'em."

"Why Diego?"

Billy almost smiled. "I took care of him at the farmhouse. Guess he liked me after that."

"Where is Vargas? We've got to get out of here."

"Vargas and the rest are at the warehouse. Some local police paid them a surprise visit. Soon as they're done paying off the police, they're gonna come back here and finish with you."

Billy worked at the ropes around her wrists with his left hand until the ropes fell away. The feeling began to return to her ankles.

Billy moved on to her father. "You okay, boss?"

Sandy stirred. His voice cracked when he tried to talk. "Ah, Billy. I knew I could count on you. I'm alive. Can you get us out of here?"

"Tryin'."

Billy used his good hand to help Sandy Harrington to his feet, then turned to Alex. "There's a Land Rover out back. If you can take your father's other side, we can get him up the stairs before they get back."

She held her father's arm, and they started an agonizingly slow climb up the stairs.

Billy was breathing hard. "If we can get to the Rover, we can head out across open land."

They were almost to the top of the stairs when the basement lights blazed.

Diego stood in the doorway at the top of the stairs, his gun trained on them. "Only one thing wrong with your plan, *amigos*. You will not live to carry it out." He looked at Billy. "You piece of shit. I should've killed you before."

Sandy flattened himself against the wall along the stairs and pulled Alex to him.

Billy fired at Diego.

Diego gripped his stomach, swayed against the door frame, then straightened, and fired back.

Billy pitched forward onto the steps, and was still.

Diego stood for another second in the doorway and then slid to the floor.

Everything was silent. Smoke hung in the room. Alex struggled to her feet. As she bent to help her father to his feet, she heard footsteps and voices in the hall above.

Cuchillo was standing on the top step, his gun pointed at Alex and her father, staring at the bodies. Paco was behind him.

"*Jesús, María.* Diego and Billy are dead. Paco, take them to the warehouse and don't let them out of your sight. I'm gonna make them suffer."

CHAPTER FIFTY-FIVE

Mike rode in the back seat of a military vehicle beside Silva. Their driver, a *Federales* soldier, didn't say a word as they followed the *Federales* commander's Humvee along the same road out of Mexico City that he and Jorge had taken only two days before.

Silva had been sounding off since they left the president's mansion. "If you and Alex had just let law enforcement handle this, none of this would have happened."

"Yeah, but you would never have been able to pin this on Vargas without us," Mike said when the agent drew a breath. "There's no way you could have got hold of the documents in the banker's house without Ramona and Alex."

"And the banker and his maid might still be alive if they'd let us handle it."

Mike tuned him out and focused on the road ahead. Why weren't they moving faster?

At last the procession of trucks and Humvees passed through Tenancingo, with people lining the streets to watch. He started to sweat. There was no way Vargas wouldn't know they were coming.

They reached the gate of Vargas's villa. Military trucks rolled into the yard and stopped. *Federales,* heavily armed and clad in blue and black fatigues, spilled onto the courtyard, four heading for the back, another ten taking positions in the front.

When their car reached the villa, Mike was out and past the

Federales' vehicles, reaching the commander at the head of the line in seconds.

"Commander, this is where Vargas kept me. Alex Harrington's got to be inside."

Silva caught up to him, breathing hard. "Murray, we're here as observers only."

"I am in command here. Wait in the car," the commander said, and left to join his men.

"You can't butt in here, Murray. You're going to get yourself killed. Stay in the car. The Mexican government let us come along to show that they're doing everything possible to save Alex. We have to go back to the car."

"Jesus. Alex's life is at stake. These guys don't care about her or us."

The commander answered his cell and listened, his eyes shifting from his men to the Americans and back.

Mike frowned. "Who is he talking to?"

The commander shut his phone and waited. Minutes passed. Nobody moved.

"What's he doing? Vargas has to see us out here. He'll kill Alex."

Ten more minutes passed. They waited. Nothing happened.

"I'm going to go nuts. What's this guy doing? Is he on the take? He's giving Vargas time to get away."

The commander answered his phone again, listened, nodded, and then checked his watch.

Ten more minutes passed before he raised his arm and brought it down. *"A la carga!"*

The *Federales* advanced toward the villa, crashed through the front door and disappeared inside. No shots came from the villa, only the soldiers' shouting. A young officer appeared at the front door and motioned to the commander, who went toward him and disappeared inside.

Silva gripped Mike's arm and held on. "Do not even think about going in there until the commander says you can."

Mike strained to hear. Time slowed. He couldn't make out what they were yelling. His heart pounded. Seconds turned to minutes until he couldn't stand it. He was going out of his mind. Sweat poured down his forehead, stinging his eyes.

An eternity later the commander came out with the young officer and walked toward Silva, ignoring Mike.

"There was a fight here at some point, but Vargas is not here. There are two bodies behind the villa, both shot," the young officer said. "You can see for yourselves."

"Where's Alex? Is she in there?"

Mike didn't wait for an answer. He turned and ran toward the villa, through the splintered front door into the great hall. He stopped and looked around, stunned by the smashed furniture. Bloody drag marks led out the back door. He followed them onto the yard.

Silva yelled at him to wait, catching up outside in back of the villa where soldiers were covering bodies with a tarp.

Mike stumbled forward shaking almost uncontrollably and silently repeated the prayers he remembered from Sunday school.

The young officer was beside them. "One of them is Diego Rivas, one of Vargas's men. We don't know the other one. We didn't find the American woman." He nodded to the soldiers to pull back the tarp.

"The other one is Billy Williams. He's from Dalton," Mike said.

"How long have they been dead?" Silva asked.

"Not long. Maybe an hour or two by the state of the bodies."

The commander reached them. "This is a crime scene. The local police will handle it now. Our job here is finished."

Motioning to the young officer to follow, the commander walked back into the villa.

"Can you believe that? The bastard is going to let Vargas get away. He doesn't care what happens to Alex. We have to call the ambassador, the president. We've got to do something."

"Wait and see what happens before we jump to conclusions. He didn't say that he was done looking for Alex," Silva said.

Mike blew out his breath and followed Silva, shoulders hunched.

The commander was issuing orders for roadblocks and a search of the countryside. Turning to Silva, he gave a forced smile. "I do not forget the American girl. See, you will tell your government that we are doing all that we can here, please."

Silva looked at Mike. "You have to be patient. The commander is still looking for Alex. This is his operation, not ours."

"You heard the guy say it's been an hour or two. Roadblocks are too little, too late, and that bastard knows it. He's in Vargas's pocket."

The *Federales'* trucks pulled out toward the main road. Armored Humvees drove off across the barren land behind the villa. The young officer and several soldiers stood beside their vehicles, waiting for orders.

"What about Vargas's warehouse? It's here in Tenancingo. That's the first place they took me," Mike said, his voice rising.

The commander looked at Mike, his disdain obvious. "This is Mexican government business, not of the Yankees. You will leave now."

"What if Alex is in the warehouse?"

Silva stepped in front of Mike, pushing him out of the way. "I apologize, commander. Mr. Murray is concerned about his friend. We understand that you are in command here."

Mike's chest was heaving. "If he's not going to check out the warehouse, I will." He pushed Silva out of his way and ran to the commander's armored Humvee, which sat empty, still idling, and jumped in.

Silva ran after him. "What the hell are you doing?"

Mike leaned over and pushed open the passenger door. "Get in."

Silva colored, hesitating. "Damn it. You're going to create an international incident."

"You want Alex's death on you?"

Silva threw up his hands and jumped into the Humvee.

Mike mashed his foot on the gas. The Humvee leapt forward, leaving the commander in a cloud of dust.

In the rear view mirror Mike could see the young officer race for the military vehicle that he and Silva had ridden in.

"Murray, you crazy son-of-a-bitch. Stop."

"We got to check out the warehouse. That bastard's not going to do it. I know I'm right. Alex is there."

"You got a plan?"

"The commander's behind us. He has to go in after her once we show him Alex is there."

A round of bullets bounced off the back of the Humvee. Silva wiped his forehead. "The *Federales* are shooting at us. Better rethink that plan."

Mike gave Silva a crooked grin. "Forget 'em. Look at this monster. It's heavy as hell, must be armored to the hilt."

Silva focused on the Humvee, the commander momentarily forgotten.

"I haven't seen anything like this since Iraq. Look at the MK19 on the roof top hatch. That's a forty millimeter grenade launcher, deadly to fifty yards. You don't even need to aim this thing."

"Think we can take Vargas ourselves with this baby?" Mike asked.

"Do we have a choice? What the hell does the commander need with something like this?"

Mike looked behind him. The commander was catching up with the rest of the *Federales*' vehicles behind him.

Silva swiveled around to look. "Only question is, who's gonna get us first, the *Federales* or Vargas?"

CHAPTER FIFTY-SIX

Voices exploded, bouncing off the warehouse walls. At least a dozen of Vargas's men raced around the cavernous space, piling guns and ammunition near the front and back doors.

Alex lay on the floor in a back corner where the men had dumped her and her father after the move from the villa. Tape bound her hands and feet. She watched the pandemonium, men racing from front to back. Her skin was raw from floor burns and splinters. Sandy Harrington was beside her, moaning in pain. In the mayhem, no one had thought to tie him up.

She heard one of Vargas's men say something about needing the hostages, the reason they were still alive, no doubt. Another glanced in their direction. Vargas stood at the front of the warehouse, barking orders, pacing. He stopped to light a cigarette, drew on it, threw it down, and ground it with his boot, lit another.

Beside him Cuchillo answered his cell and listened. "The *Federales* are here," he yelled.

The men raced to take positions by the doors. She saw Vargas walk toward his office, stop, and look around the warehouse before entering. The door closed behind him.

No one was looking at her. She rolled into a crouch and looked for a way to escape. Her best chance was a side door some ten yards away. It was her only chance.

Her father shifted beside her. He was awake now. He reached out to her. "Alex. Don't. They'll kill you."

"I'm going to die if I stay here. Help me get this damn tape off."

Gritting his teeth, Sandy reached out and began working at the tape. When her hands were free, she reached down and pulled off the remaining tape. She got to her feet, forcing herself to move slowly, watching Cuchillo. She reached the side door, took hold of the handle and pulled. The door stuck. She pulled again. No luck. Frantic, she worked the handle back and forth.

Behind her Cuchillo yelled. She gave the door another yank and it gave way. The cold night air hit her face. Headlights shone from the front of the warehouse. She ran toward them.

Cuchillo burst through the door after her.

She ran toward the front of the building, caught her heel on the edge of an oil drum, and went down.

"Alex."

She heard Mike's voice, saw him silhouetted against the lights. He was running toward her, calling to her.

Cuchillo was on her, lifting her off the ground, slinging her over his shoulder. She kicked at the air, raging and helpless. She heard Mike yell again before the warehouse door shut behind her.

CHAPTER FIFTY-SEVEN

Mike was sure it had been Alex. He had seen the white streak in her hair clearly in the light from the warehouse door. He raced toward her and reached the side door just as it slammed shut. Alex was back inside. He tried to pull the door open. Shots came through the door. He jumped back. If only he'd moved faster, he could have helped her. Gunfire continued from inside the warehouse. He ran back to the Humvee, shaking with rage. They had to go in now.

Two of the *Federales*' vehicles were in front of the warehouse, back from the roadblocks, next to the Humvee. Two *Federales* were holding Silva.

The commander strode toward Mike, his face purple with rage. "You stole government property. You disobeyed my orders. You're under arrest."

"Alex is inside. I just saw her. Vargas's men are holding her. We have to save her."

"I don't see a woman. There is nothing to do here."

The commander turned to his men. "Arrest him and the FBI agent and get back to the roadblocks."

A soldier grabbed Mike, threw him down, and began dragging him, kicking and yelling, toward the vehicles where Silva was standing with the young officer.

A voice boomed through a bull horn from inside the warehouse. "We have two Americans. Leave or we'll kill them."

The soldiers let Mike go and rushed to join their commander in front of the warehouse.

"What is he talking about? Who's the other American? It can't be Billy. He's dead," Mike said to Silva when he reached the Humvee.

"Other than Alex I don't know," Silva said.

A bullet cracked past Silva's head. Mike grabbed his jacket and pulled him behind the Humvee. The young officer dove for cover beside them as machine-gun fire strafed the ground in front of them.

The commander stood still for a second, transfixed, mouth gaping, his eyes on the warehouse.

The barrage of gunfire continued.

The commander retreated toward the vehicles and, once behind the Humvee, took out his phone and punched in a series of numbers.

Mike strained to hear what the commander was saying. "*Alto el fuego*, ceasefire. Vargas knows me."

Vargas's men kept firing.

The commander backed further behind the Humvee, shaking his head and grumbling to himself, "Don't they know who I am?"

The shooting continued.

Mike moved back beside Silva. "The commander is clearly on Vargas's payroll, so why are they still shooting at us?"

"Beats me."

The commander stepped from behind the Humvee, waving his arms and yelling.

"Is he off his head? What the hell is he doing?" Mike said.

More shots came from the warehouse. The commander spun around and fell face forward, blood soaking into the dirt.

Two *Federales* ran forward and dragged the commander back behind the trucks.

Grenades blasted from the warehouse, exploding around them. Two soldiers fell. The remaining *Federales* dove for cover.

Mike crouched beside Silva. "Why shoot their own guy?"

"Maybe because he screwed up. Either that or Vargas isn't in there. We can keep them busy, but that's it. They have an arsenal in there. We're outnumbered. We have to wait for backup," the *Federale* officer said.

A barrage of bullets hit a pile of oil drums beside the warehouse, setting off sparks against metal. Oil spilled onto the dirt. The drums began to explode as flames leapt from drum to drum. Dense, black smoke billowed from the burning oil. More drums exploded, blast after deafening blast filling the air. Blinding soot showered from the burning drums as the fire reached the warehouse walls.

"Alex could get hit in the crossfire if we go in," Silva yelled.

Mike choked on the acrid air and wiped his eyes. "She'll die in there, if we don't." He covered his ears, ran to the commander's Humvee, and jumped into the driver's seat. Silva raced after him.

The Humvee leaped forward, picking up speed, and smashed through the front entrance of the warehouse. Bullets bounced off the armored panels.

"Cover your ears," Silva yelled and fired one round from the M60, then launched the grenade, aiming high, setting off a series of intensely loud bangs.

Vargas's men fell back from the door, hands over their ears. Some dropped their weapons, others collapsed.

Once inside the warehouse, the Humvee continued to move forward. Silva aimed and fired. The warehouse walls shook with the sound of gunfire and exploding grenades. Vargas's men were cut to half strength in seconds.

The *Federales* followed the Humvee through the front door, firing at the remnants of Vargas's force.

Shots sputtered to a few exchanges, then died. Only a few of Vargas's men were still alive. They threw down their weapons and held up their hands.

Smoke billowed through the warehouse. Mike could barely make out the shapes of bodies on the ground. He jumped from the Humvee and ran from one body to the next, frantically calling Alex's name.

CHAPTER FIFTY-EIGHT

The noise was deafening. Alex held her hands over her ears. Acrid smoke filled her lungs.

Her father dragged himself toward Alex, and, with surprising strength, threw himself on top of her. She knew he was trying to protect her, but she could no longer move. Her father had made them both an easy target. She struggled under his weight, unable to push him off.

An agonized cry erupted near them. One of Vargas's men flipped in the air, screaming, and came down on the floor a few yards away. His gun flew out of his hand and skidded toward her.

She stretched out her arm to get it and couldn't reach.

More shots rang out. Cement chips sprayed off a nearby post. Sandy Harrington groaned. Blood was seeping from a wound in his neck.

She tightened her stomach muscles and rolled him off her as gently as she could, and then rolled onto her knees and crouched beside her father and reached for his hand.

From the corner of her eye Alex saw someone running toward them. She turned her head to see Cuchillo, coming toward them fast.

She dove for the gun, rolled on her side, and fired.

Cuchillo pitched forward and lay still.

She crawled back to her father's side and pressed her hand against his neck. Blood seeped through her fingers.

His eyelids fluttered. His face was gray, but his lips were still moving.

She leaned closer, trying to hear.

Men screamed. Gunshots drowned out her father's words.

Saliva ran from the corner of his mouth. His eyes were glassy. She thought he was dead until he raised a hand and whispered something.

She could make out only one word. "Angelina."

Her father shuddered, his hand falling to his side, and then he was still.

Mike knelt down beside her, his voice low. "It's all over, Alex. We can go home now."

She looked around the warehouse, tears streaming down her cheeks. The shooting had stopped.

"You're hurt," Mike said, helping her to her feet, using his shirt to wipe the blood from her cheek.

"I'm okay. Did they get Vargas?"

"Not yet. The soldiers are looking for him."

Silva ran toward them from across the warehouse, shaking his head.

"There's a trap door in his office floor and steps to a tunnel underneath that leads out back. He was ready for this. He's at least twenty minutes ahead of us. The *Federales* are organizing a search of the countryside and setting up roadblocks, but Vargas is a clever bastard. It won't be easy to find him."

"Was all this was for nothing?" Alex said.

"At least we got rid of a corrupt commander and broke up a whole human trafficking operation. Vargas will have a hard time starting over. The bastard has more enemies than friends. If we don't get him, maybe one of them will," Silva said.

Alex looked back at the carnage. She was light-headed and very tired. She swayed.

Mike caught her. "Let's get out of here."

The young *Federales* officer and two soldiers rushed up to Mike.

"Not so fast. I have orders from headquarters to detain you and the FBI agent for stealing and damaging government property and for impeding a military operation. I am to demand your passports and take you directly to the Federal Police Building in Mexico City."

Mike stared at him, open-mouthed.

"We just saved this woman's life and helped you break up a major human trafficking organization," Silva said.

The officer motioned to the soldiers. One of the soldiers put handcuffs on Mike, and the other did the same to Silva.

"Go to the orphanage," Mike called as the officer led him and Silva away. "I'll find you there."

————

"We didn't think we would see you again so soon," Sister Milagros said.

It didn't seem soon to Alex. It felt more like months since she and Mike had parked in front of the orphanage. In the days since then, the world as she knew it had changed completely. She was still trying to come to terms with all that had happened. Silva was right. They had made some progress even if Vargas was still on the loose. The men who killed Cristina were dead. Mariana's killer was dead too.

She thought about growing up in Dalton. Maybe it was the memory of her own mother, buried somewhere in her heart all those years, that had made her so different from her classmates. She'd never been able to fit into the life of a well-bred Southern girl that her parents had wanted for her, as hard as she'd tried.

It would be a long time before she'd be able to sort out her feelings about her father. He had done unspeakable things and caused great suffering. Still, he was the only father she had ever known, and, angry as she was with him, she knew that some part of her would always love him. He had tried to redeem himself at the end and had probably saved her life. The sisters would urge forgiveness. It would be a long time before she'd be able to manage that.

Mike came straight from jail to the orphanage. It had taken days of negotiations and all the persuasive powers the U.S. Ambassador had to convince the Mexican government not to prosecute him. He was in the clear. His job with the *Dalton Herald* was another story. Roush had given him a week off for the trip to Mexico, and he'd been gone for three already. He sent a text, saying he'd be back soon, and concentrated on writing a series of articles on human trafficking and his time in Mexico. Roush's only response so far had been a curt, "See me when you get back." He wasn't looking forward to that reunion.

Agent Silva stopped by the orphanage to say goodbye. Silva was free to go too, but relations between the Mexican president's office and the U.S. Department of State would be strained for a while. The FBI agent still had a job. He was on the way back to the U.S. to take part in a series of raids that would close down a number of human trafficking operations across the U.S.

The *Federales* had seized the most visible of Vargas's other assets, including his prized horses. The Mexican government promised that the money from the sale of the assets would go to the families of the journalists who died and to victims of trafficking. *La Prensa* would do its best to hold the government to its word, but Ramona said she'd believe it when it happened. Jorge was in jail, and Alex took some comfort knowing that he would be there a long time.

She made the nuns very happy when she showed them how to access the bank account in their name. She rationalized that the sisters didn't need to know where the money came from. At least it would do somebody some good. It would pay for much-needed repairs to the orphanage building and fund operations for a long time. The sisters intended to use any money that was left over to shelter and support victims of human trafficking.

———

Alex ignored Renee's entreaty that she fly home immediately and instead set off with Mike for a leisurely trip home. With Ramona's help they'd found the old Chevy in a police compound, and after a week in the repair shop, a kindly old Mexican mechanic assured them that the car might make it back to Dalton if they didn't push it too hard.

"I know a great little place to stay in Opelika," Mike said, when they crossed the border into Alabama. "There's a good barbecue restaurant nearby too. I've got a sentimental attachment to the place."

The manager recognized them, welcoming them like regular customers, and gave them their old room back.

"We aren't the same people we were when we stayed here before," Alex said, happy to be out of Mexico and she had to admit, after all they'd been through, even happy to be alone with Mike.

She was coming out of the bathroom when Mike knocked on the motel room door. She wrapped a bath towel around her and had the door open before he could get his key in the lock.

The crooked grin she'd grown to like spread across his face. "Love your outfit."

She took the bag of take-out barbecue from him and put it on the table, then put the six-pack beside it.

"I'm not ready to eat just yet," she said. She let the towel slide to the floor and put her arms around his neck. "At least I won't have to borrow your shirt this time."

CHAPTER FIFTY-NINE

Vargas had never thought he would be back in Los Perdidos. The town still did not have paved roads. Rain dug rivulets into the dirt, and women carried buckets of water from a town pump every morning to tamp down their mud-caked walkways. There was no electricity. Only a month ago, he had been an important person, with wealth beyond the dreams of the people who remembered him as a child. Now he was back where he had once picked corn with his mother and sister to make masa for the tortillas they would use to mop up their beans and rice.

Cuchillo and Diego were both gone. The rest of his men were dead or in prison. Only his nephew was with him now, always eager but better with computers than guns. He spent hours trying to train the kid to shoot, and maybe soon he would succeed.

The *Federales* had seized his mansions and his warehouses. They took his beautiful quarter horses. His eyes filled with tears when he thought of their grace and speed, the races they had won, and all the crowds cheering them on. Even the trophies were gone.

The coals burned low in the grate. A night hawk screeched. Through the open door he watched bats dart through the trees to catch mosquitoes. The air was heavy with the smell of burning charcoal. His wife had left him, but at least his mother was happy that he was home. He lived in the beautiful house he had built for her as soon

as he had some money. He could still buy the loyalty of the local officials and the few people who lived here. He was safe as long as he kept
to himself, but he would not be important any more. He would not
wear elegant clothes or dine in luxurious restaurants. There would
be no lovely women to smile when he approached, and he would never
again stand in the winners' circle.

Worst of all, his enemies would win. The politicians who betrayed
him would continue to get rich from others, and filthy swine would
take over the remnants of his network. Alexandra Harrington and
her reporter friend would not be punished for what they had done to
him. No, he would not let that happen. He would rebuild. He would
get his revenge.

CHAPTER SIXTY

Happy memories of the trip home faded once Alex was back in Dalton and was forced to deal with the woman she had believed for so many years to be her mother. She tried to be supportive. Renee Harrington was an unwitting victim of her husband's schemes after all, but Alex lost patience when Renee refused to answer her questions about the adoption or talk about her father. Renee Harrington was more interested in planning an elaborate funeral and telling all her friends that her brave husband had died a heroic death in Mexico, than in talking to Alex.

No one believed any of it after Mike's articles on human trafficking appeared on the front page of the *Dalton Herald*. The articles included a detailed account of Sandy Harrington's role as head of the operations in Dalton. Newspapers across the country reprinted what he wrote. Mike was invited to appear on numerous TV talk shows, and there was talk of a Pulitzer.

She wasn't mad at Mike. She'd spent every night with him since coming back to Dalton. He was the only one who fully understood what she'd been through. "I understand now that it's your job to write about what happened and to tell people about women like Mariana and Teresa," she said. Sill it did hurt to read his articles.

She rode beside her mother to the church, dreading the ceremony. She had to admire the woman's determination. The funeral was going forward and to hell with public opinion. Renee walked through the double doors of the church and looked around, stopping and taking a step backward when she saw the near-empty pews, stifling a gasp. None of the Harringtons' friends were there. Even the Foleys and Peaches and Travis Bingham had stayed away. Renee squeezed her eyes shut and rubbed her forehead, then straightened and walked down the aisle to the family section in the front row and sat down.

Alex followed. Organ music resonated through the church. The over-ripe scent of lilies made Alex dizzy. She walked to the front of the church and placed her hand on her father's coffin. How she longed to be away in a quiet place, somewhere in the mountains, inhaling the clean, sweet smell of laurel and pine, where she could put the last weeks behind her and think about the future.

Gladys sat a few pews behind Alex in the church, her shoulders squared, head high. Since Alex's return, Gladys had been her greatest supporter, never once condemning her father to her face despite the deep disappointment Alex was sure Gladys must feel. Alex knew that Gladys more than anyone understood the turmoil that raged within Alex because of her father's actions. It was Gladys who was keeping the center going, giving Alex time to put her life together and figure out where she was going. Alex was grateful.

At last the service was over. Professional pall bearers lifted the coffin and carried it down the aisle toward the back of the church. Renee Harrington walked behind it, her head high, her mouth set in a grim line. Alex followed the little procession to the back of the church.

Mike stood alone in the last pew. He raised a hand and smiled. She waved back.

Keisha White was waiting for her outside the church. "You all right?"

She flinched. "Is it that obvious? There's a lot more I want to know, and mother won't answer any of my questions. Any word about Vargas?"

"We're still on the case. Meantime, you be careful. Vargas is still out there, and he's not going to forget about you."

Renee Harrington's high-pitched voice commanded attention. "Alexandra, are you coming? We're leaving for the cemetery."

Alex closed the front door of her mother's house. The funeral had been rough. She was on edge. She had tried once more to talk to Renee and got only a curt, "Not tonight." The woman she had thought of as her mother climbed the stairs to bed without another word.

The house fell silent. Alex fixed a cup of herb tea and wandered around, her heels clicking across the hardwood floor to Oriental carpets that muffled her steps. When she had walked off some of her nervous energy, she went into the library.

Sandy Harrington's portrait looked down from above the fireplace. His patrician face was a model of respectability. How could this man have profited from human trafficking? A silver-framed picture of herself as a toddler sat on the desktop in front of her. She set her tea mug down and reached across the expanse of mahogany for the picture.

Her elbow hit the mug, spilling the tea. She picked up the frame, pulled tissue from a brass box, and wiped up the mess. When she set the frame back down on the desk, a piece of paper slid from behind the picture and floated to the floor. She stooped to pick up it up and froze, staring at the picture of a pretty young woman, her birth mother, Angelina. Now there was no doubt in her mind that Sandy Harrington was her father. He had kept the picture all these years, hidden from those around him. He had said her name as he lay dying.

She collapsed into the desk chair, and tried to make sense of it all. She'd known since childhood that relations between her parents were strained. She'd heard them arguing many times long into the night, but she had never known why.

She didn't hear the footsteps approaching until a floorboard creaked beside her. She looked up at Renee, standing next to her.

"Give me that."

"It's a picture of my mother."

Renee snatched the photo from Alex and ripped it apart, letting the pieces float to the floor.

"How dare you?"

"She was a whore."

Alex exploded. "All these years you knew. You pretended to be the loving wife and mother, and it was all a fraud. You never cared about us."

Renee flushed red with rage. "I couldn't allow Sandy to humiliate me. He was a disgrace to my heritage. My family is one of the oldest in the state. We go back before the American Revolution. I come from senators and governors. They may have fathered bastards too, but never in public. All of them were respected community leaders. They had a position to maintain. He would have thrown all that away. I wouldn't have it."

Alex stooped to pick up the pieces of the picture and stood, fitting them back together on the desk. "When my father was dying, he said the name Angelina. It was the last thing he said. I didn't understand until tonight what he was trying to tell me. He loved my mother, and he loved me."

Renee's laugh was brittle. "He loved my family's money more."

"If you felt that way, why did you adopt me?"

"He always wanted children. I couldn't have them. After your mother died, he didn't give me a choice. He insisted that we take you in. We even moved here from Virginia and told everyone that you were our child. My parents knew, but they didn't want our name disgraced either."

She stopped and looked off into space. "I did care about him once. As a young bride, like everyone else I thought he was wonderful. I was stupid enough to think that adopting you would make things better. It didn't. Every time he looked at you, he saw her."

Alex was seized by a chill that penetrated to her bones. She thought of all the times her father had played with her while Renee Harrington stood back, watching.

"He was a good father and a good person. How come he got involved in human trafficking?"

"Good person. What a joke. After that bitch died, he stopped paying attention to the business and lost all our money. The credit ran out. My father discovered that he was embezzling from the charitable foundation that my family had established."

"Why did you stay together?"

"My family didn't want anyone to know that their daughter was married to a crook. They gave us money, but it was never enough. I was so ashamed."

"I remember your fights. You screamed at each other. I used to cover my head with a pillow."

"You made it worse. We had to pay for your private school and debutante balls. The debts kept piling up. We were going to have to sell the house, resign from the club. Sandy even started reading job ads. He told me I was going to have to go to work too. Me, go to work. Can you see me as a typist?"

"There's nothing wrong with having a job."

"Maybe not for you. I couldn't face my friends. He went to loan sharks, and that made it worse. Then one of the money lenders told him about a Mexican businessman who needed help expanding into this country. That's when he met Emilio Vargas. At first he was stupid enough to think it was a legitimate business deal. All he had to do was make some introductions. Before he knew it he was in over his head."

"Why didn't he go to the police?"

"He was afraid of going to jail. When he told Vargas that he wanted to get out, Vargas went after you in Mexico City to teach him a lesson. Sandy did whatever Vargas said after that, but Vargas never trusted Sandy again."

"So you knew about it all along."

Renee Harrington looked at Alex. "You needn't be so self-righteous. How do you think we paid for your college? We even bought you a condo. You work in the center I started. What would you be without our money? You're nothing without me, just like your father."

————

Renee's words stung. Alex watched as the woman she had called mother for so many years pounded up the stairs and slammed the door to the master bedroom. She felt as if her throat were closing.

Even though they'd never gotten along, she'd thought it was just the usual tensions between mother and daughter and never had any idea that the woman resented her very existence.

She was sure now that Renee knew about the human trafficking network and may even have been a part of it. The hall clock chimed twelve, too late to call anybody tonight, and what did she have other than her word against Renee's. She wanted to know for sure. She set to work, with blind, cold, shaking fury, rifling through papers in the desk and paging through all the books on the shelves until her head spun with exhaustion. Just as she was about to give up for the night, she remembered the safe behind her father's portrait. She dragged a chair to the fireplace, took down the picture, and tried the only combination she remembered. It didn't work. At least she knew where to begin in the morning.

She started toward the hall when she remembered Keisha's warning and turned back to the library for her father's gun. She found it fully loaded in the bottom desk drawer.

She left the library, armed the security system in the hall, and climbed the stairs, each step harder than the one before until finally she made it to the top.

The hall clock chimed once. She passed the master suite directly across from the stairs. She could hear heavy breathing coming from the master bedroom. How could the woman sleep?

When she reached her bedroom at the far end of the hall, she couldn't be bothered undressing. She put the gun on the bedside table, threw herself on the bed, and wrapped the bedspread around her.

She woke from a fitful sleep as the clock was striking four. Moonlight streamed through her window, glinting off the gun on the bedside table. She sat up, wondering why she was awake. The house was silent. Surely the alarm would sound if anyone broke in?

Then she heard the stairs creak. She reached for the gun. It could be nothing more than the settling of an old house, but she didn't think so. She got up, crept to the bedroom door, and opened it, peering into the hall, and waited.

The silence was heavy. A door hinge squeaked, followed by a

piercing scream. She heard a shot, then a scream, followed by a man's voice, yelling.

Her heart in her throat, she gripped the gun and raced toward the master suite.

A man came out of the master bedroom, crashing into her. She went down, rolled, and got to her feet. Her hand shot out, connecting with the man's nose.

The man screamed and dropped his gun. It slid across the floor, hitting the wall. She still had hers.

The man was on his feet, reaching for his gun.

She fired, hitting him in the shoulder.

He went down, face forward, landing on his gun. Twisting, he took hold of the weapon, and pulled the trigger. The shot was wild, hitting into the wall three feet above her head.

She gripped her gun with both hands and fired again.

The man grunted and clutched his stomach. Blood seeped into the carpet. He lay still.

Alex scrambled to her feet, coughing from the smell of burnt gunpowder, and ran into the bedroom, still holding the gun.

Renee was on the floor, emitting low, guttural noises. Blood soaked the front of her nightgown. A nail file, wet with blood, lay beside her.

Alex raced to the bathroom, coming back with every towel she could find. She pressed the towels against the wound in Renee's chest with one hand, and reached for the bedside phone with the other.

CHAPTER SIXTY-ONE

Mike was frantic. The police scanner said two people had been shot at the Harringtons' address. He stepped on the gas. An ambulance was parked in front of the house. He jumped from his car and raced up the drive. The paramedics were maneuvering a stretcher down the front steps and into the ambulance.

Alex came out of the house, her mouth set in a thin line, and climbed in beside the stretcher. Doors slammed and the ambulance sped off in the direction of the hospital, lights flashing, siren screaming.

He reached the front steps just as Keisha White came out the front door.

"What happened? That was Alex getting into the ambulance."

"She's okay. It's her mother. Come in the house. I need you to look at a body. Remember, same deal as always. Nothing in print until we say so."

A second ambulance turned in the drive.

"Who is it?"

"I'm hoping you can tell me. A man, maybe Mexican, broke into the house, and shot Renee Harrington. Renee got him in the neck with a nail file, and then Alex shot him. He's dead. You do not want to mess with these Harrington women."

"Was he one of Vargas's?"

Two members of the M.E.'s staff got out of the vehicle and went through the front door, carrying a stretcher and a body bag.

"Top of the stairs," White said. "Alex thinks she saw the guy in Tenancingo. Come on and take a look before the M.E. takes him away."

Mike followed Keisha into the house and up the stairs. The body lay in a pool of blood.

"You know him?"

Mike looked at the face.

"Yeah, I know him. He's Vargas's nephew. How did he get in the house? This place is wired for security."

"The nephew must have been good. He disarmed a pretty sophisticated security system. He shot Renee Harrington, but he could have been looking for Alex."

"It had to be Alex. Why would Vargas want to kill Alex's mother?"

"The guy went directly to the master bedroom and shot Renee Harrington at close range. You'd think he would know it wasn't Alex."

"It was dark, and as I recall he wore thick glasses. He probably couldn't see too well."

White moved away from the body to a table at the far side of the room and motioned for Mike to follow.

"Before she ran out of here, Alex told me that Renee was involved in human trafficking along with her father. Maybe the woman knew too much, and the guy was sent to kill them both. I have her laptop. The answer could be in the laptop, but it's password protected," White said.

"Let me try. You got a birth date?"

"I've got the driver's license from Renee's purse."

Mike typed in the date, and a screen opened showing two file folders. He clicked on each of them. "Damn, they're encrypted."

White's cell phone rang. She answered and listened, then turned to Mike. "It's Alex. Renee's dead. The hospital pronounced her dead on arrival."

"Can I talk to Alex?"

White handed him the phone. "Sorry about your mother," he said. "I'm working on her computer. You got any idea how we can get into her encrypted files?"

"She wasn't my mother. Try her family name, Sterling. She always used that."

He typed "Sterling," and the file opened.

White hung over his shoulder. "Those look like financial records."

"I think these are copies of the files that Alex and Ramona found in the banker's house in Mexico City."

"Silva was never convinced that Sandy Harrington could run the Dalton operation on his own. It makes sense that his wife would be part of this. Renee Harrington was not some shrinking violet who would sit back while her husband ran the show. Open the second file," White said.

Mike typed in "Sterling" again, and the second file opened. Page after page scrolled by with dates, transfer routes, and the names of women and children trafficked from Mexico to Dalton, along with the names of Dalton citizens who had invested in the operation.

"This clinches it," he said and pointed to the names "Mariana" and "Teresa."

CHAPTER SIXTY-TWO

The flight attendants moved through the cabin, closing overhead compartments and reminding the passengers to fasten their seatbelts. Alex was in the first seat in coach. She sat back and looked out the window. She felt hollow and very much alone.

She was eager to get out of Dalton. People tried to be polite. Some old friends called, but awkward silences followed the initial pleasantries. She'd run into Kelly at the grocery store. "I feel so sorry for you, Alex. I always thought you had it all, money, a good job, any guy you wanted. How awful to find out that your parents were criminals." She didn't need pity from Kelly or anybody else. She needed a new life.

Disclosures about the Dalton network covered the front pages of the *Dalton Herald* for weeks, all under Mike's byline. The files in Renee's computer told the story of the human trafficking network and of the Harringtons' part in it. The FBI had pieced together evidence of money transfers across the state. When the FBI opened the safe in the library, they found a detailed list of Vargas's activities in the U.S. with names and locations in other cities.

Her father's accountant had asked for immunity. Forensic accounting uncovered payments to Officer Craven from both Vargas and her father over a period of years. A nationwide FBI crackdown had uncovered trafficking operations and corruption from Texas to Atlanta and the Northeast, and others in Nevada and California. A nationwide sting operation led to more arrests.

"Scott Foley tried to hide behind attorney-client privilege, but it didn't work," Keisha told Alex. "He was the mastermind behind a complicated money laundering scheme, working with the banker in Mexico City. The FBI's sure there's more money both in Mexico and offshore, but so far Foley isn't talking."

Many of Dalton's prominent citizens had invested money in the operations, probably unwittingly, although that remained an open question. Peaches Bingham hadn't left her house once in the weeks since the news broke. Travis was out of a job with the closing of Foley and Forebush and was looking for a new job any place but Dalton. Even the governor had money invested with the JoVille Group, much to the delight of his political opponents. Alex was sure that North Carolina would have a new governor after the next election.

Through a friend of Gladys's she'd found a room to rent in a Manhattan apartment on the Upper West Side, and heard about a relief organization that was looking for someone who spoke Spanish.

The Center for Child and Family Health was struggling to survive. She was sad to be leaving, but knew that the last thing the center needed was the involvement of anyone named Harrington. Even if she changed her name to Segura after her birth-mother's family, she'd always be a Harrington in Dalton. If anyone could keep the center going, it was Gladys, and the center would continue to help women and children in need. Elena would be there and Carmela too, who, because of her cooperation with the investigation, was likely to receive a suspended sentence for her activity with the human trafficking network.

She thought of Mike Murray. She'd miss his crooked grin and the way he had of showing up when she least expected it. She smiled, thinking of the hours they'd spent trying to make sense of all that had happened. There was always email, texts, and the telephone, but they both knew it wouldn't be the same.

She pulled the airline magazine from the pouch on the back of the seat in front of her and began flipping pages when she heard a commotion in the front of the plane.

"Another minute and you would have been out of luck," a flight attendant said. Alex looked up to see Mike pushing aside the curtain that separated first class from coach. He threw his duffel bag up into the overhead compartment and folded his tall frame into the empty seat beside her.

"May I join you?

She felt herself flush. "You already have."

The plane pulled away from the gate. The pilot's voice came over the speaker announcing arrival time in New York in an hour and a half.

Mike leaned over and kissed her. "I've had it with the *Dalton Herald*. I can't go back to writing about the town council after what we've been through. I think I'll try freelancing for a while. It'll suit me better anyway, and New York's as good a place as any."

Alex started to answer when the magazine slipped off her lap and fell open to a picture of an Atlanta restaurant.

Mike reached for the magazine and stopped. "You see what I see?"

She looked at the picture. Two men sat at a table in the back of the crowded restaurant, engrossed in conversation. One of them looked an awful lot like Emilio Vargas.

ACKNOWLEDGMENTS

Many people have helped in the writing of *Brutal Silence*. Profound thanks go to Nicki Leone for her always insightful comments and encouragement. Also to Steve Yount for his steady guidance and to the members of my writing group: Sylvia Adcock, Sharon Addison, Radhi Bombard, Richard Domann, Ramona DuBose, and Amber Forbus for their creative investment in this project.

I am very grateful to William Berndardt for providing sage advice and the benefit of his illustrious career as a thriller writer and to Rick Amme for adding his journalistic perspective. Rick Williams provided inspiration and encouragement throughout. Maria Scanga read *Brutal Silence* and provided editorial suggestions and help with all things Spanish. Many thanks too to Marschall Runge and Karen McCall for reading and offering their thoughts. Special thanks to my editor, Alison Williams for greatly improving the final book, to SP for jumping in to save the interior design, and Charles Fiore for guiding me through the publication process.

Louise and Steve Coggins have contributed their extensive knowledge and profound commitment to combatting human trafficking and have connected me with the increasing number of dedicated people who work tirelessly to help its victims every day. Many thanks to them and to Jackie Resnick and Linnea Smith who worked with the University of North Carolina at Chapel Hill to hold the two ground-breaking conferences on human trafficking that inspired me to write this book.

Finally, my heartfelt appreciation goes to my husband, Tommie Smith, for his patience and encouragement throughout this project.

CPSIA information can be obtained
at www.ICGtesting.com
Printed in the USA
LVHW01s2222120218
566243LV00003B/698/P

9 780692 851043